Sign up for our newsletter to hear
about new and upcoming releases.

www.ylva-publishing.com

OTHER BOOKS IN THE DESTINY AND DARKNESS SERIES

DAUGHTER OF FIRE

THE DARKNESS RISING

KAREN FROST

DEDICATION

For Kim, Lellie, and Anita
For encouraging me to write, write, write

CHAPTER 1

"When hope is lost, it takes a character of great courage to find it again."

— Author unknown

"There are no innocents. Only victims."

— Vardan Ironwill, Captain of the King's Regiment

IF YOU'RE NOT CAREFUL, THE hungry ghosts of your past will eat you alive. As the less-than-noble knight Sir Idras once told me, a drowned man always wants companions. The dead may be lonely, but only a fish can survive underwater.

Just a few months ago, I'd been a daughter of the Ice Crown, the land of snow and ice. I had parents from whom I'd never spent a night apart and brothers for whom I'd have walked the length of our kingdom Ilirya and back again. Everything I had, everything I was existed in a tiny world of its own, a single snowflake in a snowstorm. And then, like a candle blown out by careless lips, all of it had been extinguished in an instant. I had neither a home nor a family anymore. I was adrift—with only my ghosts to keep me company.

I'd have given all that I had and more to change the past, to save my family from the enemy raid that killed them, but there is no magic that can turn back time and undo what has been done; time only runs in one direction. And Death doesn't give back what he takes. With my once happy life shattered, all that remained was survival. Putting one foot in front of the other, taking my days by the hour, I had traveled to Windhall University, where I started training as a war mage. What else could I do? With my old life in ashes, I had to build a new one, however I could. As a war mage, it would one day be my fate to be the sword that cut down Ilirya's enemies, then be cut down myself in the unending circle of violence that had engulfed the kingdom's southern border for four decades. Miraculously saved from slaughter at the hands of the villainous Northmen, I was expected to die in the south for a kingdom I barely knew. Then there would be no one left to avenge the destruction of my village.

It was at this intersection of past and future, family and expectations, duty and destiny, that I found myself as I lay on the floor of Windhall's infirmary. By coincidence or fate, I had been snatched from the jaws of death by the healer Timo right before the one event I never expected could happen. The ambassador of the Northmen, those murderers of my people, had appeared in the infirmary. As weak as I was from my brush with death, this was likely the only chance I would ever get to take revenge for everything that had been taken from me. I had drawn every ounce of magic that I possessed with the goal of obliterating her from the earth, but then I'd been tackled to the ground. With every second I remained pinned to the floor by the healer-student Lyse, the chance to avenge my family was slipping away.

"Your family lives." She whispered the words into my ear, low and urgent. Her breath tickled my skin, and I could almost feel her lips as they moved. If I'd thought about those lips so near to me, it had always been in a different context, not like this. But the words made no sense. They might as well have been in another language. They had no meaning. I had to get up. I had to avenge my family.

Everything was spinning, blurring, falling as my head reeled. My body burned with my magic, which, frustrated by Lyse's tackle and the presence in the infirmary of Draks, a mage bane able to extinguish the magic of other mages, seethed angrily in my veins, looking for release. I had told Lyse a dozen times what had happened to my family. She had sat and held me while I cried for them. So why was she stopping me from doing what she herself would surely have done under similar circumstances? I gritted my teeth and tried to shimmy free.

Of all the people in my new life at Windhall, it was Lyse for whom I cared most of all. Lyse had been the first friendly face I'd seen, the guide to my new life. In time, she had become the most important part of my newfound family. More than that: She was my lodestar. Even so, my emotions for her were subsumed in that moment by the hatred I felt for the Northmen and the overwhelming desire to attack the ambassador. Hate, after all, is a hungry beast that only becomes more ravenous the more it's fed. I didn't have time to think about what she was trying to tell me. Whatever it was, we could discuss it after I'd avenged my family.

No matter how hard I tried to wriggle out from under from her, my body refused to obey. What was happening? From the corners of my eyes, I saw the glow of white magic around me: It was Timo's magic, which Lyse was able to channel through their shared magical bond. Using it, she was pulling energy out of me, enough to keep me still and helpless on the ground, away from the ambassador. No! My head began to feel light and fuzzy. If I didn't shake her off soon, my opportunity would be lost.

Chancellor Vandys, the head of Windhall University and the ambassador's escort to the infirmary, stared down at me. Disgust and horror mixed with surprise writhed across her face. She hadn't expected a student to attack her guest. The Northman woman, however, seemed unconcerned. Her casual indifference infuriated me. Could she not tell from my pale skin and thin frame that I was an Ice Crowner, a victim of her people? She should at least have had the decency to look worried when I charged her. Was I really so inconsequential in her eyes? Chancellor Vandys took her elbow and whispered something in her ear, glancing at me as she did so. "Whatever the meaning of this, I will address it later," she snapped to Lyse and Timo.

"Chancellor, please don't be upset!" Lyse's voice was strained. "Aeryn isn't herself. We almost lost her just now in a training accident in Raelan's class. I'm sure this is a lingering effect of her near-death experience. She may think she's still in the training salle. She'll be fine in a few minutes."

I didn't need Lyse to protect me. I needed her to release me. The Chancellor huffed, glaring at me through narrowed eyes, but said nothing in response. My eyes burned back at her. She murmured to the Northman woman just loud enough that I could hear, "Very well, we'll tour the academic building. Please come with me. I apologize for this."

The two headed for the door, the Chancellor looking over her shoulder at me reprovingly. No! I ground my teeth, fury turning to anguish as I tried desperately to shake Lyse off and follow them, but I couldn't. The infirmary door closing behind them sealed forever my only opportunity to avenge my family. All the life and energy went out of me at once, like a sugar cube thrown into water. Misery swept over me in a heavy, oppressive wave.

Lyse's hands started stroking my hair. "They're alive, Aeryn. They're alive. It's okay. You don't have to fight. Let her go."

I couldn't hear her words; they were too much for me. Far too much. All the bitterness, the sadness, the loss, and the grief that I'd experienced over the last few months came rushing in to take the place of the mindless rage that had filled me upon seeing the ambassador. Not an hour before, I had almost died when my fellow war mage Faegan had sent a knife hurtling into my chest. I had been so close to going home, to reuniting with my family. Now I was once again left with ashes. The taste was bitter on my tongue.

Lyse didn't have to hold me down anymore; I lay with tears pouring down my face, sobbing for everything I had lost and would never recover. "My family is dead, Lyse." My voice was like the wail of a young child: small, pitiful and lost. "You know they're dead. How could you let her get away? How could you take from me my one chance to avenge my family?"

"Your family may not be dead," she said. "Listen to me, Aeryn, please."

She moved off me, and I slowly got to my knees. I was too weak to stand, so I sat cross-legged on the floor instead. My chest heaved as I tried to recover my breath. It was as though I'd been running for hours. It had likely been dangerous to try and use so much of my magic so soon after almost dying. I was lucky I hadn't passed out from the effort. I rubbed the spot on my chest where Faegan's knife had penetrated. Why did everything seem to happen all at once here at Windhall?

Lyse took up a spot on the floor across from me, our knees almost touching. Her soft brown eyes were intense and full of concern as they stared into mine. Of all her qualities, it was her deep empathy that always stood out most to me. When she reached out and wiped the tears from my cheeks, her hands were gentle and caring. They lingered on my face without her realizing it, and I resisted the desire to lean into them and rub against them the way a cat does the hands that stroke it. I was no longer angry at her. Nothing that had happened in my life was her fault. All she'd ever tried to do was make my life better. I was barely aware of wishing she would hold me.

4

Her voice was low and urgent when she spoke, too low for Timo and Draks to hear. "Aeryn, I've made some enquiries. No one has heard of the Northmen raiding into Ilirya."

I shook my head as though it would clarify the meaning of her words, but it didn't. "I don't understand. What are you saying?"

"Do you think that Chancellor Vandys would be walking around Windhall with a Northman if we had resumed war with the Northmen? The ambassador is the only Northman allowed in the entire country, and she would have been kicked out of Ilirya at the first report of resumed fighting."

"Maybe the chancellor hasn't heard yet," I said, confused. "In the Ice Crown, news travels slowly. And who would notice if some Ice Crown villages were snuffed out?"

"But Aeryn, think about it: *You're* here. Everyone you've met, from the members of the King's Regiment who found you, to the knight who brought you here, to even the university administrators would have known about what happened to Thamir, all because of you. Moreover, the ambassador surely would have known if her own people had resumed war against us. So why is the chancellor talking to a Northman ambassador? Because there was no raid." Her eyes bore into mine, lit by an intense glow.

"No, that's—no—that doesn't make sense," I protested, unable to believe what I was hearing. "Jale told me that I told him about the raid; about how all the houses were burned and everyone killed. It—happened. Of course it happened."

"You were told a lie. Aeryn. Have you remembered *anything* about the attack since coming to Windhall?"

"No." I hung my head. It was my greatest shame: After all these months, I still couldn't remember a single thing that had happened on the worst day of my life. All I remembered was waking up in a rest house in Ithaka, far away from Thamir.

"Because it didn't happen," Lyse insisted, shaking her head.

"Lyse, that's crazy!" My head was swimming. I closed my eyes and dug the heels of my palms into my eyes to steady myself.

Lyse put her hands on my knees. Her voice was hushed and tight. "The kingdom needs more war mages, Aeryn. We're hemorrhaging at the front, badly. Would you have left your family willingly to come to King's City if soldiers from the capital had come and asked you? What if they'd told you that you would probably never see your family again?"

I frowned. In my wildest dreams, I had wanted to come to King's City and attend a mage university to learn to be a powerful mage. But in reality, I had been nervous even at the thought of going to the provincial capital Namoreth, which was only a few days away from my home in Thamir. I wouldn't have been able to bear being as far away from the Ice Crown as King's City, and I certainly wouldn't have left Thamir if I'd been told I could never return.

"You were kidnapped, Aeryn," Lyse said. Her eyes were soft with sympathy.

"But—How could I forget something like that?" I objected half-heartedly, feeling as if I was sinking into deep snow. How could Lyse be right? It all seemed so conspiratorial. These things didn't happen, did they? "Jale and Gamiel are members of the King's Regiment! They wouldn't lie."

"Wouldn't they?" Lyse raised her eyebrows. "Their duty is to the king, not to regular citizens like us."

I shook my head, which by now was throbbing. I was a wobbling top spinning out of control. I didn't know what to believe anymore. Lyse's arguments seemed impossible—and yet at the same time, they made sense. The thought made me sick. I desperately wanted my memory back. If only I hadn't fallen from that horse on my journey with Gamiel and Jale, I would know the answers to all these questions.

"If I was kidnapped, how did Jale and Gamiel think they would get away with it? If I hadn't lost my memory, I would have told someone. I would have escaped!"

Lyse's eyes flickered over my shoulder. "Timo can erase memories a little to ease his patients' pain. Do you know what Jale's affinity is?"

A memory struck me like lightening. I saw, as from a distance, me and Gamiel standing outside in the morning light, minutes before we parted ways. She and Jale had been sparring. Because they hadn't used magic in their fight, I had asked her what Jale's affinity was. "I call it the mind spike," Gamiel had replied. "With enough force, I would not even have remembered my own name."

I stifled a moan as a wave of cold ran down my spine, making me shiver. The hairs on my arm all stood on end and without my realizing it, my hand rose to cover my mouth. Jale had used his affinity on me. He had destroyed my memories and lied to me about how I left Thamir. Lyse was right. She had to be. It was the only thing that made sense.

Lyse continued, "There have been other students here at Windhall whose stories didn't quite seem to add up. Students who, like you, had affinities that Ilirya desperately needed. I ignored them at the time. I thought I was being silly. I'm sorry I didn't tell you about this sooner, Aeryn, but I had to be sure. When the ambassador walked in, everything clicked into place. I knew what they'd done."

The room was spinning too fast. My fingers curled against the floor, trying to hold on. If Jale had lied to me, then what did that mean for my family? Could Lyse possibly be right that they were still alive? That there had been no Northman attack? Seeing my face, Lyse jumped to her feet. "Let's get you back to the dorm. You look ill. I shouldn't have told you this now. You almost died and you need to rest."

"Lyse…could my family really be alive?" My voice was barely a whisper. The thought was like a patina of ice: If I spoke too loudly, it would shatter into a million pieces.

Lyse nodded. I climbed to my feet shakily, feeling like a sapling. A mild wind would have felled me, leaving my roots exposed to the air. As shocking and terrible as the discovery that I had been tricked by Jale and Gamiel was, the feeling of betrayal was eclipsed by a growing hope. My family was alive! I could see them again!

Lyse took hold of my arm. "Come on," she said gently.

As we walked back to the dorm, I thought I'd become so light I might lift off the ground and fly away, back to Thamir. I wanted to wrap my arms around Lyse, bury my face in her shoulder, and tell her over and over again that my family was *alive*, that the ghosts that haunted me could finally find peace. They weren't ghosts after all.

"Lyse, my family… I can't believe it!" I exclaimed as we sat on her bed in her room. "I have to go back! I have to know for sure. I have to see them again. I have to touch them."

My hands fluttered like agitated birds until Lyse grasped me gently by the shoulders, bringing me back down to earth. Her expression was pained, full of sorrow. Where her palms touched me, my skin burned slightly, even through the fabric of my tunic. Her soft brown eyes were deep pools of regret. "You can't, Aeryn," she said, quietly but firmly.

"I may not have money, but I can figure out how to get back to the Ice Crown as I go," I replied, shaking off her concern. My mind was already halfway to Thamir, calculating what it would take to get there. "I can leave tomorrow. It will take time, yes, but—"

"No," Lyse said, shaking her head as she cut me off. "Think about it: The soldiers who took you wanted you badly enough to kidnap you and erase your memory. There haven't been many war mages at Windhall in the last few years. You're worth too much to the kingdom to be allowed to leave."

"What…what are you saying?" A knot formed in my stomach. All the lightness that I'd felt walking back to the dorm rushed out of my body, leaving me as cold as an Ice Crown winter.

Misery was etched across Lyse's face. "You can't leave Windhall right now, no matter how much you want to go back home. Once you're discovered missing, the King's Scryer will seek you out immediately. You won't make it a full day outside the city before you're found and dragged back. You'll never be able to leave Windhall after that, not even to go into the city for the day. What's more, they'll know you found out that your family is alive and erase your memory again. Everything will have been for nothing."

"So I'm supposed to forget my family?" My voice rose. "Is that it? Stay here and never see them again? I just found out that my family is still alive, Lyse. How can you ask me not to go see them?"

"No, that's not what I'm saying!" Lyse's eyes begged me to understand her, and I did, but not necessarily in the way that she wanted. I was a guard dog of the kingdom, and as such, my life was not mine. Lyse, on the other hand, was free to do whatever she liked. She wore neither collar nor leash. She could go home to see her family at any time. I rubbed my face with my hand in frustration and stood.

"It's just for now. It won't always be like this, Aeryn. One day you'll be able to go back, when you're not being watched so closely. Until then, write a letter instead," she begged. "I'll have it sent myself. That way no one will know that you know your family is alive. It may be slow, but you'll have an answer as certainly as if you went home yourself."

"A letter, Lyse?" I scoffed. "No one in Thamir can read, much less write back. You know that."

Lyse winced. In that moment, I remembered how very different she and I were. She came from a House and had grown up with servants and tutors. She had never hunted for food or trapped for skins with which to make clothing. She had never carried a bow or tanned a hide. She had never known the howling winds of the north, and no ghosts had ever haunted her dreams. But she was still the Lyse whom I adored, the one for whom I'd have done anything. I relented. "A soldier at the garrison may be able to read it for them."

"Aeryn..." Lyse reached out to take my hand, but I pulled away. I needed to be alone, and I needed time to think. So much had happened in the last hour that I had to process it or my head would explode. Too many emotions experienced too close together had turned my insides to knots.

"I'll talk to you tomorrow," I said, striding to the door before she could catch me.

I didn't feel like going back to my room, so I walked to the training field behind the dorm, stopping briefly by the armory to collect a bow and a quiver of arrows. Round archery targets were set up at the far side of the field, and I stomped over to them. This, at least, was something I knew and understood; something that reminded me of home. I notched an arrow, pulling the string back to rest against my cheek. After a breath, I let the arrow fly. It hit dead in the center of the target. I notched another arrow, pulled back, and released. It split the first arrow in two. I notched a third arrow, pulled back, and now the three arrows were all exactly in the center of the target, the last two each splitting the arrow that came before it.

In the Ice Crown, this ability to aim true would have kept me alive by always keeping me fed, but here in King's City, it was a curse that was keeping me from seeing my family again. Moreover, it was one of the reasons I'd been taken from them in the first place. The thought made me want to burn Windhall and everything around it to the ground. I should have been elated that my family was still alive—and I was—but finding out that I wouldn't be able to return to them and hold them in my arms again left a taste more bitter than an unripe berry in my mouth. How dare anyone—from the King's Regiment to the king himself—keep me from them? Why did they get to choose my life for me? How could the King's

Regiment, which was supposed to defend the kingdom, turn out to be nothing more than a band of child thieves?

"You are looking angry," said a voice unexpectedly at my side.

"Pavo!" I exclaimed.

Pavo came from the last of the nomadic hunting tribes in the far southwest of the kingdom. His long, strong limbs attested to a lifetime of walking desert and savannah plains. He was colorful, exuberant, and good-natured. He was also a weather mage, a desperately needed affinity in some parts of the kingdom, including his own home. Although Pavo couldn't have been more different from me, we were similar in our alienation from the world in which we found ourselves at Windhall University: two fish out of water.

"Well? What is making Aeryn unhappy today?"

"I want to go home, but I can't because I'm a war mage. I'm trapped here." There was no use explaining everything. It wouldn't change anything, and besides, I was tired. Exhausted, in fact. The physical effects of my near death earlier that day were starting to set in, and I felt sluggish.

Pavo nodded understandingly. He reached into the leather satchel he wore slung at his side, rummaging around until he drew something out. It was a book. My eyes widened in surprise. Based on our classes with Professor Kalmath, I was sure he couldn't possibly read it. He drew out a quill, too, which still had some residual ink on it. He flipped open the cover of the book and, to my amazement, wrote something on the inside cover. Then he closed the book, tucked the quill back into the satchel, and handed the book to me. He said, "I am hoping you are seeing your family soon, Aeryn."

"You can write?" I sputtered.

Pavo grinned, then winked. "I am liking Professor Kalmath's class. We are doing *so* well at learning, no?"

Before I could think of a response, he sauntered away. Curious and astounded, I opened the book. On the inside, in beautiful, looping script that was nothing like how he wrote in Professor Kalmath's class, Pavo had written: *Not all caged birds are tamed.* I looked at Pavo's retreating figure and shook my head. In the course of one day, I had survived near death and found out that my family was still alive and Thamir safe. Why shouldn't it also turn out that Pavo had been faking in class just for his own amusement?

I walked to the targets and pulled out the three arrows. The first two were ruined, but the third I placed back in the quiver. Then I walked back to the armory and began to make new arrows to replace the ones I'd broken. In the quiet, I could almost pretend I was back in Thamir fletching arrows. It was the closest I would come to home for the foreseeable future.

That night, as I lay sleepless in bed, I made the constellations over Thamir dance on my ceiling. The Monkey, the Twin Sisters, the Horse, the Water Jug, the Beetle, and the Fox sparkled blue above me, as vivid as they were high in the sky over the Ice Crown. Here in King's City I couldn't see the Sisters or the Beetle, but I knew exactly how they looked. My mind was full of thoughts and emotions. How could Gamiel and Jale have made me believe that all I loved had been destroyed? How could they have lied so brazenly and without conscience? What sort of a King would allow a girl to be kidnapped from her family and forced into being a war mage?

My rage alternated with joy. For all my suffering, for all my anguish, my family was still alive. Far from where I lay in my bed in Windhall, my brother Kyan might be turning in for the night after working the forge at the garrison all day. My brother Kem and his wife Danver might be leaning over the crib of my new niece or nephew. And my parents might be sitting before the village fire, fletching arrows of their own and sharpening knives. I might not be able to leave today to return to them, but they were *alive*, and I *would* find a way to get home to them. I would start by having Lyse help me write them a letter, and then I would plan how to get home. I was caged, but not tamed.

The next day, neither Faegan nor Raelan turned up for our mage skills class, so Cayleth—who had become one of my closest friends in the short time I'd been at Windhall—and I went apple picking in one of the orchards next to the university instead. We brought with us a small hand-pulled cart in which we planned to gather the dusty red apples. Cayleth had worked out an agreement with the cooks by which we would pick the apples and in return they would make apple tarts for dinner. There were so many apples that we'd filled the cart after only an hour, so we climbed a tree and sat on its branches watching traffic far in the distance file toward the western gate of the city. After everything that had happened the day before, picking apples with Cayleth felt surreal. How could we be doing something so banal when the day before I'd almost died, then found out that the family I thought was dead was in fact still alive?

"When you almost died yesterday, did you see the Eternal Realms?" Cayleth asked.

She took a bite of an apple. It crunched crisply beneath her teeth. My hand unconsciously felt the small pink scar on my chest where the knife had lodged. It was almost in the center but slightly to the right. Had it been to the left, it would have hit my heart, and then even Timo couldn't have saved me. I shook my head. "No, only blackness."

"Huh." I could hear her shrug, her red tunic rubbing against the rough bark of the tree. A moment later, she said, "Faegan shouldn't have thrown that knife. It was a dishonest move. You could have died. The only reason you didn't is because of Timo and Lyse. They should expel him, but they won't because he's the Baron of Ardeth."

"We both know Faegan hates that he's not as strong a pyromancer as I am, and he *really* hates losing. I should have been watching for him to try something."

"That's no excuse. And the Baron of Ardeth should be especially careful. What kind of leader is underhanded like that?"

Now it was my turn to shrug. After everything that had happened yesterday, I didn't have the strength to care. I had more important things to think about, like how to return to my family and how long it would take.

"We should go back." I shaded my eyes and looked at the angle of the sun in the sky, which was sinking lower in the sky. "The cooks will need the apples to start the tarts and we need to get to combatives class."

"Let's stay a little longer. Maerys won't mind if we're late," Cayleth said, referencing our archery instructor. "After all, it's not like you need any archery practice. You're better than she is and you both know it. And of course, she'll have heard about how you almost died yesterday. She can spare you an afternoon to lounge in the orchards."

I gazed up at the sky, unexpectedly happy to have an excuse to avoid going back to the campus. After a minute, I hazarded a question that had been bothering me. "Cayleth, what would you do if you found out that your older brothers were alive and that you'd been kidnapped from home in order to get you to Windhall?" There was no easing into the question; I had to be blunt.

Cayleth's older brothers, Bron and Baylen, had been killed fighting on the southern front while serving in the army. When we'd met, Cayleth told me that she had enrolled at Windhall to become a war mage as a way to protect her last brother, Baran, who was now also in the army. Her affinity, illusion, could be used as war magic, but unlike pyromancy, could also be used for other purposes. This meant that while I had no choice but to be a war mage, she did. She *wanted* to be here.

She sighed. "That's a hard question." She shifted on her branch, moving closer to me. "Lyse told me about your family and what happened. I'm sorry." Her voice was soft.

"She told you?" My eyebrows shot up. It wasn't Lyse's secret to tell. I stifled a stab of resentment and hurt; Cayleth needed to know, even if I hadn't been the one to tell her. She needed to know for whom she was fighting. Did she really want to fight for a kingdom that kidnapped its own people?

"Lyse thought it would be good for me to talk to you since we're both war mages. She's worried about you, Aeryn. A lot happened yesterday. You almost died, for one thing. And then you tried to charge a Northman? In front of the Chancellor? It must be a lot to take in. I can't imagine what you must be feeling."

"What am I supposed to do, Cayleth?" My mouth quirked into an unhappy line. The bitterness from last night was back, and with it an overwhelming sense of being both tricked and ensnared. I hated nothing more than feeling trapped. In the wild, an animal will chew a limb off rather than remain trapped. What was the price of escape here? "How can I trust anyone here in King's City?"

"I know," Cayleth said, shaking her head, her black hair whipping into her eyes. "What happened to you was wrong. There's no excuse for it. In your shoes... I can't imagine how angry I would be. I understand if you hate everything about Windhall right now. Know that I'm here for you, whatever you need. And I support whatever you choose to do."

We lapsed into comfortable silence for several minutes more. The cool fall air and the warmth of the sun on my face were nice, even if they were temporary. I couldn't hide from Windhall forever. Finally, Cayleth swung down from the tree and took hold of the handle of the heavy cart. I took up a position behind, and together we trundled back down the orchard's rutted grass toward Windhall. The cooks wouldn't be able to complain that we didn't bring enough apples.

Lyse was waiting for us at the gate. A glow of happiness filled me, and I smiled. The anger I had felt at her yesterday for stopping my attack on the ambassador and for delivering the bad news that I would have to wait to see my family was long gone, replaced by the usual pull I experienced whenever I was near her. She didn't return my smile, however. "There's been another person reported missing in the city," she said, her expression serious. "This time, it's a noble."

My stomach dropped. With everything that had happened, I had forgotten that I wasn't the only person who had been kidnapped. King's City had been eating its children for years, and I was the only one who'd cared enough to notice. Now, it had swallowed another person.

CHAPTER 2

"Bravery cannot be taught."

– Knight Commander Bronwen Lionheart

*"Policing a city is hard, not to mention it's made harder
by the fact that the City Guard is often no more lawful
than the criminals it is their duty to apprehend."*

– Pergam, Lord Marshal of King's City

ALTHOUGH THE DISAPPEARANCE OF THE noble could have been a coincidence, there was no question I had to find out more. So far, Lyse and I had discovered five people missing from the city in the last year, and those were just the ones we knew about. How many more were unknown to us? Lyse had dismissed my suggestion that it could be Dark mages kidnapping the northwest quarter's denizens for their own nefarious purposes, but if not that, then it still had to be something coordinated. These hadn't been the types of people to disappear on their families. Now that I knew that I, too, had been kidnapped, I felt more of a kinship with the missing than ever. I didn't deserve to be snatched from my home, and nor did they. If no one else would look for them, I would.

We had to wait until the seventh day of the week, our free day, to venture into the city, and in the meantime, the week dragged on endlessly. I was impatient and distracted in all my classes. With Lyse's help, I had carefully drafted a letter to my family, taking care to stress that I was fine and I would be home as soon as I could. I needed it to look as innocuous and unremarkable as possible, just an anonymous citizen writing home.

Even though Lyse had told me it would take weeks for the letter to reach Thamir, it was hard to stem my impatience. This was my first link to my family in months. I wished I could snap my fingers and the letter would be there instantly. How would I survive the agonizing wait until a response might come? Could my family get a soldier at the garrison to write a letter to send back? How long would that take? At least while I waited for news, I could use the investigation of the noble's kidnapping to distract myself.

On the seventh day, Lyse met me in the dining hall as I finished breakfast. My heart thrilled to see her, and even my magic surged in my veins a little. Her eyes, too, sparkled when they found me. "Are you ready?"

Her delight at seeing me was entirely dissimilar to how Cayleth or Kaylara reacted around me. It was…something more. After the events in the infirmary, it was impossible to deny that she had some sort of feelings for me. I had seen the fear in her eyes when she thought I might die and heard the terror in her voice. Even so, that knowledge didn't change anything between us. She was with Timo, and there didn't seem a way to bring up this unspoken aspect of our relationship after she had avoided addressing it the last time. Still, I knew the issue would come to a head eventually, whether she wanted it to or not. It was just a matter of time.

"Ready," I replied, smiling back at her.

"Let's go then," she said, linking her arm in mine. "We'll have a long walk since we'll be headed to the eastern side of the city today."

As we strolled across the green toward the road to the city's western gate, I asked, "What do you know about this missing noble?"

"His name is Theratos. He comes from one of King's City's Houses, albeit one of the lesser ones. He teaches music."

"When did he go missing?"

"Two weeks ago. Timo heard about his disappearance from a patient in the city whose daughter took lessons from him. By now, the city guard will surely have started to investigate."

"Could he have left King's City and gone somewhere else?" I asked, echoing the argument that Timo had once made about the disappearances in the northwest quarter.

"He could have," Lyse agreed, shrugging. "Or perhaps he'll have already been found with his face in a tankard of ale in the northwest quarter or lying dead in an alley somewhere in the city."

"You don't think that's the case or else we wouldn't be going to investigate."

"Something feels wrong about it, but I can't say why," Lyse said, unlinking our arms and rubbing her hands together unconsciously. I had noticed she only did it when agitated or anxious. Theratos's disappearance unnerved her. Still, I immediately missed the contact and wished she would reach out again.

"Are you starting to believe me yet about Dark mages?" I arched an eyebrow at her.

"You and your theory of a grand conspiracy of the Dark mages!" Lyse exclaimed with feigned exasperation. She tossed her long dark hair and looked at me with a playful smile curving on her lips. My heart doubled its time in my chest. The pull between us was as overpowering as it had ever been. Maybe even stronger, if that was possible.

I had to remember not to lose my head in the heady feeling of being near her, so to remind myself that she was promised to someone else I asked, "How's Timo?"

I hadn't spoken to him since the day in the infirmary. Although I had caught sight of his shockingly silver hair across the green or leaving the dining hall a few times, we seemed to exist in two separate worlds. In truth, I didn't mind. Even though he had saved my life, seeing Lyse with him made my stomach churn, and I had found myself quickly making excuses to leave whenever they were together. It was unfair to resent him for his relationship with Lyse.

Lyse fidgeted with a lock of hair, looking away from me and into the distance toward King's City. "He's been busy. There's been an outbreak of plague in Port Bluewater, probably carried in by the sailors. He left Windhall a few days ago."

"Will he be back soon?"

"As soon as he can. It's hard to know in advance with these sorts of things."

"I'm sure you miss him."

"Of course!"

She didn't look at me as she said it, and I knew she was thinking about more than just him. I couldn't stop myself. The subtle signs of conflict on her face were too tempting an invitation to press her. I smiled playfully. "Would you miss me, too, if I was gone?"

Her smile flickered, the way a candle does in strong wind. Lyse knew what I was asking. She looked at the ground, and for a long time, I thought she wouldn't answer. Then she said in a voice barely above a whisper, "Of course I would miss you very much."

Without my anticipating or planning it, we'd hit the very inflection point I knew had been pending. The wall that Lyse had built to cordon off her emotions was showing signs of crumbling, and I had to know what lay on the other side. I had to know how strongly she felt the pull between us…even if that meant I was asking her to choose between me and Timo. I pushed forward. "More than you miss him?"

Fear and panic filled her eyes. Tension pulled her body taut like the string of a bow. "You can't ask me that." Her voice was a hoarse whisper, her eyes pleading.

"I know you feel it, too." With my words and with my eyes, I was trying to urge her to be honest with herself and with me. To admit that she felt that same electric connection between us that I did.

She shook her head. "No. I don't know what you're talking about."

"Yes, you do! Every time you're near to me… I know you feel it."

"Timo… I'm bonded to *Timo*. We're a *pair*. I…hardly know you," Lyse protested. She wasn't protesting against me, however, but against her own feelings, and we both knew it. She stopped walking. Her eyes were wild now, dark with fear.

I raised my hands, palms facing her in half-supplication. I wanted her to know that it was okay to have feelings for someone other than Timo. She wasn't betraying him by having them. Her heart belonged to her alone. "Some things happen without anyone planning it. It's okay to feel—"

"Do you know what you're asking me?" Lyse hissed, looking around as though someone might overhear us. "Timo is a Great Mage! My family will benefit from the pairing. We'll be able to overcome some of the cloud left by my great uncle Nagyar's Dark Magic when Timo is the King's personal healer."

My stomach lurched. Acting as I was on impulse, I hadn't thought through what I was asking of her if she chose me, and it hurt like a kick from Sir Idras's horse Snowflake to hear it from her so plainly. How could I have been so stupid? Of course a pairing with an Ice Crowner was undesirable for someone from a House. The Ice Crown was so poor and rustic that it didn't even have Houses. Nor, as a war mage, would I ever become either wealthy or important. Everything I couldn't change about myself was exactly what made Timo a good match for her.

My shoulders slumped, and my body tried to make itself as small as possible. What had I been thinking? That she would confess her feelings for me and give up everything that she could have with Timo to be with me instead? What could I offer her in return for all that? My stomach started to hurt. Why hadn't I kept quiet?

I considered whether we should abandon our trip into King's City. What use was it to go now when the morning was ruined? When Lyse met my eyes, however, the expression of quiet longing and doubt on her face said all the things that she refused to. Just because Timo was a good marriage match didn't mean I was wrong about her feelings for me. Without thinking, I reached out and ran my thumb along her cheek. She quivered at my touch, but she didn't pull away. In a voice quiet as the wind through the trees, she whispered, "Yes, I feel it, too."

What might have been tears glimmered in her eyes. Then she took my hand and set it back at my side. "I'm with Timo, Aeryn." That was it. She spun on her heel and began marching toward King's City, leaving me standing alone in the middle of the road. The conversation was over. She had made her choice, and I was to understand that it wasn't and couldn't be me.

Theratos lived in a multi-story rectangular house, whose tall windows overlooked the cobble stone street. The houses in this neighborhood were pressed tightly together and had triangular roofs, giving them the appearance of jagged and broken teeth in a giant creature's mouth. This part of the northeast quarter was mostly quiet but for pedestrians and occasional carts passing through, carrying fish from the wharves to the King's castle and other noble houses. I could faintly smell salt in the air, which Lyse told me came from the sea half a mile to the east. It was the type of neighborhood from which I imagined people generally didn't go missing.

Lyse knocked on the door of Theratos's house, and it swung open slowly to reveal a small man with a narrow face, a crooked nose, and owlish eyes. He scowled at us, his face sour. "What do you want?" he asked suspiciously, looking around us as though we'd been accompanied by a small army.

"We're looking for Theratos," Lyse said.

"He's not here."

"We know that. We mean we'd like to help find him. What do you know about his disappearance?" I asked.

The door started to close in our faces, but Lyse stopped it, catching it with her left hand while reaching into the satchel at her waist with her right. The servant saw the flash of coins that materialized in her hand. He licked his lips, calculating their value against talking to us further, and then his hand flicked out and the coins disappeared into a fold in his robes. "What do you know?" Lyse's expression was stern.

"Master Theratos left to teach a lesson in the southeast quarter in the morning and never returned. When he didn't come back by nightfall, I walked to the merchant's house and asked after him. The servants there said he had left hours before. That was all I ever learned."

"Is there any place else he might have gone? Had he ever disappeared before?" I questioned.

"No. He was a quiet man. Spent all his time at home with his nose in a book when he wasn't teaching."

"Did he have any enemies?"

"A flute teacher? Hardly," the servant scoffed.

"Could he have left the city? Did he have family he might have gone to visit unexpectedly?"

The servant looked disapprovingly at me. "Would Master Theratos have left the city without having packed a single thing or informing me of his travel? No."

"Then could he have owed someone money and left to avoid them?"

The servant didn't bother answering. It was clear he was becoming impatient with my questions. Lyse's coins—and therefore our time—were running out. "Is there *anything* else you know? Something that stands out to you as being unusual? Perhaps something that Theratos did or said before his disappearance? Perhaps you saw someone watching the house or following him?"

The servant shook his head. "The Master has disappeared into thin air, it would seem. It is a mystery."

He shut the door, and Lyse and I were left standing on the street, no wiser than when we'd left Windhall. I tried to push away my dismay. There was no use dwelling on our failure. I asked Lyse, "What do we do now?"

"I don't know." She shook her head.

Since there was nothing more to be learned about Theratos's disappearance, I had another idea. "Can we go to the Boar's Tusk Tavern?" When he'd dropped me at Windhall, Sir Idras told me that if I ever needed to get in touch with him, I could pass word to him there. It was a long shot, but perhaps if he was in the city, he might even be there now. I missed the giant, rambunctious knight. He had been the closest thing to family after I had been taken from Thamir. Lyse nodded. I could tell she was still avoiding meeting my eyes, and it hurt.

It took us half an hour to reach the old, ramshackle tavern in the southwest quarter of the city. The Boar's Tusk Tavern was small and unassuming, identifiable by a peeling wooden sign painted only with the head of a black boar. Two tiny, dirty windows looked out over the street, which was narrow and had an intangible air of disrepute. Inside, several men and women were eating lunch at the handful of small, square tables. I could tell immediately, however, that none of the tavern's patrons were the unmistakable Sir Idras. I swallowed my disappointment. I had wanted to tell him about my kidnapping. Together, we could have plotted my return to Thamir. Deep down, he was an honorable man; he wouldn't let this injustice stand. He would help me.

Lyse walked to the bar, where the tavern owner stood rinsing mugs using a bucket of water and a rag. She wordlessly held up two fingers, and he nodded and filled two mugs with ale, which he handed to her. Lyse passed him some coins and sat down on a stool in front of him, motioning for me to join her.

"Has Sir Idras been here lately?" I asked the tavern owner, taking a seat.

He scratched the rough black stubble on his cheek. "No, he's been gone a while. A few weeks, maybe? He'll be back. He always is, that one."

More disappointment. This day was turning into one letdown after another. We might as well go home now.

"When you see him again, will you tell him Aeryn came looking for him? Tell him I'm from Windhall. He'll remember me."

"I'll do it," a young woman's voice said from behind us.

I turned at the sound and saw a female knight approaching us, a mug in her hand. She was only lightly armored, with a combination of scale and chain armor on her torso over a light purple tunic. Light-brown leather bracers ran from her wrist to her upper arms, and solid metal greaves reached from her ankles to her knees. A sword in a royal-blue scabbard hung from her leather belt. Her long brown hair flowed down her back freely but was kept out of her face by two thin braids. She smiled and sat down on the free stool next to me. Her face was open and friendly.

"Hi, I'm Asher," she said, extending a hand to me in greeting.

I shook it. "I'm Aeryn, and this is Lyse." I gestured to Lyse, who waved.

"Why are you looking for Idras?" Asher asked.

"He's a friend. I'd like to see him again. It's been a few months."

"I squired for Idras several years ago. He's a...very unique knight."

"That he is," I agreed, smiling as I thought of our adventure to steal back Snowflake after he'd lost her while gambling.

"Once I watched him wrestle an actual bear as part of a bet," Asher said.

"Who won?"

"Depends who you ask. Idras is the victor in all his stories, haven't you noticed?" She chuckled, her eyes sparkling. "I don't blame him; we should all be the hero of our story. Are you from the city?"

"No, we're from Windhall. We're visiting for the day."

"Mages! There's a surprise. I can show you the city, if you like. I know all the best sights." She winked. I blinked in surprise, taken aback by her brazen flirting. No one had ever been so forward with me. We'd just met! I wasn't sure how to react. Although my heart still longed for Lyse, she had been clear in her rejection of me that morning. And Asher was undeniably attractive. I blushed. Beside me, Lyse stiffened.

"Actually, we're on a bit of a mission," I said.

"Oh?" Asher arched her thin eyebrows. "Tell me more." She put her chin on her fists and leaned forward, her eyes shining.

"It's nothing," Lyse said, elbowing me hard in the ribs. Whispering so only I could hear, she said, "She'll think we're ridiculous if you tell her."

I whispered back, "No, she won't! Maybe she can help! She's a knight; maybe she knows something." Returning to face Asher, I said, "A noble has gone missing in the city. Have you heard?"

"No," Asher replied, cocking her head. "Is this person important to you?"

"No, not exactly. Many people have gone missing in the city, particularly in the northwest quarter, and we're trying to find out why."

Asher's eyebrows knit together in puzzlement. "Isn't that the job of the city guard?"

"Well, yes, but they're clearly not doing a good job if it keeps happening."

She nodded. "Fair point. What have you found out?"

"Nothing. The man vanished into thin air."

"A real mystery," Asher said, looking interested. "What did the city guard say?"

I dropped my gaze. "We haven't gone to them. Why would they tell us anything?"

"Nonsense!" Asher exclaimed. "If there's news of your missing persons to be had, the city guard will have it. Would you like me to take you to them?"

"Yes!" Hope bubbled in my chest. Could this be what we needed to finally start uncovering who was behind the kidnappings? Maybe our trip into the city wasn't a waste of time after all. The city guard might have ignored two students from Windhall University, but they wouldn't ignore a knight.

As we walked north through the city on the way to the city guard's northwest garrison, Asher regaled us with tales of training to become a knight. She'd become a page at the age of seven, then she'd become a squire at fourteen and was assigned to serve Sir Idras. Sir Idras, being known in the knighthood for his less-than-noble reputation, was most commonly not given a squire, but since the knighthood was thinly stretched by the war, she had been assigned to him for a year until a more appropriate knight could be identified. She'd then spent the next three years serving Lady Avrill of Qarys before she was knighted.

"Idras gave me my first warhorse—we call them destriers—after I was knighted, but don't ask me how he got Stormcloud because I don't want to know." She smiled and winked.

I laughed. Asher's good humor was infectious. "Will Sir Idras be back soon?"

"Yes. He's out riding the circuit, which means traveling through the countryside to maintain law and order. With so many soldiers pushed to the southern front, brigands, thieves, and lawbreakers of all kinds are taking advantage to wreak havoc. We try to send knights out to keep some of the lawlessness tamped down, but it's hard. We've even had some knights killed in the last few years."

I thought back to the band of brigands that Jale, Gamiel, and I had encountered on our travel toward King's City. "It sounds dangerous," I said.

"It is!" Asher grinned. "But no one becomes a knight who's afraid of riding into danger head on."

The second she said it, her face froze for a moment, then fell. Her eyes misted over with a profound sadness and her mouth twitched as she tried and failed to regain the smile that had been there. She ran her hand over her hair, and I could see that her hand was trembling slightly. Had someone close to her paid for their bravery with their life?

"You must be *very* brave," Lyse said. Her condescending tone, which I hoped that only I could hear, was so out of character that I gaped at her for a moment. Why was she being rude? It wasn't like her at all. Asher didn't hear the comment, however, lost as she was in whatever thoughts she was thinking, and I was glad. We needed all the help we could get to find who was kidnapping people from the city. It wouldn't do to alienate our new ally. I wondered if she might know a way to escape Windhall without being caught. Maybe I wouldn't have to wait for Sir Idras.

A few minutes later, we arrived at the garrison. It was a long, low stone building with dark and ominous windows and the city guard's wooden heraldic shield hanging above the door. Inside was a single room with several desks at the front and a large cell with thick bars at the back. A few prisoners milled around behind the bars, looking bored. One slept on a pallet bolted to the wall, a hand over his face. The desks in the room were unoccupied but for two. Neither of the green uniformed guardsmen sitting at them seemed to have noticed or cared about our entrance.

Asher walked up to the closest desk, whose occupant sat with his feet propped up on it and a hat slouched over his face. She rapped on it sharply.

He had been sleeping and awoke with a twitch. "Excuse me," she said, "we're here to inquire about some missing people."

The guardsman looked from her to me to Lyse and back to her. His lip curled. "What's this?" he asked. "Is it children's hour?"

"Do you have a list of the people who have gone missing from this quarter and what the investigations turned up?" Asher asked, crossing her arms.

"Oh aye, I'll get that for you, will I?" the guardsman answered in a surly tone.

"Thank you," Asher replied as though his question hadn't been rhetorical.

The guardsman gaped at her. "Go on, jog on. I've got better things to do, runts."

Asher sighed. I wondered whether we shouldn't leave now, before he became even more abusive toward us. Clearly there would be no winning him over with charm. "You know," Asher remarked with studied casualness, "when my father Ivar, the late Lord Chancellor, requested that Lady Marshal Heika reform the city guard, he intended that it become an open and friendly service, to rebuild the trust of the people after years of corruption under the previous Lord Marshal. I'm sure that this is exactly the sort of thing he would have pointed to as a positive example of helpful behavior."

The guardsman jumped to attention, his feet slipping off the table and his hat almost sliding off his head. His eyes wide, he breathed, "You're the daughter of Lord Chancellor Ivar?"

"I am," Asher said. "Not that it should matter to the performance of your duties. Now, Aeryn, please tell him what we need."

I fumbled for words for a moment before I managed to squeak out, "We'd like the names, locations, and dates of any unusual disappearances in the northwest quarter."

The guardsman looked at us with an inscrutable expression on his face that I thought might be disbelief, then walked over to another desk in the room. Sitting upon it was a large, leather-bound book, which he carried back to us and dropped with a thud on his own desk before us. He pointed to it.

Asher's eyebrows knit together. "The list is in there?"

"That *is* the list," he answered.

"It's massive!" she exclaimed. "How many years does it go back? Twenty? Thirty?"

"This one? Eh." He picked it up and weighed it in his hand. "Five years, give or take."

CHAPTER 3

"Empty the prisons and send the inhabitants to me, if you must.
We need more fighters if we're to survive the winter."

— *Private Letter from General Oran, commander*
of the King's Army, to King Hap

"All animals leave a trail, Aeryn. All you have to do is look for it."

— *Jax*

LYSE GASPED. HER HAND FLEW to the base of her throat. "Only five years? How can that be?"

The guardsman shrugged, his eyes dull and uninterested by the subject. His uniform had a dark stain on the front, and his hat looked like Snowflake had walked back and forth over it several times. I thought of Jale and Gamiel's perfectly clean and polished armor. Even Sir Idras had taken care to always keep his armor presentable. If this was the type of person who was supposed to find the quarter's missing denizens, I could see why they hadn't been found.

Asher flipped to the first page of the book. A name was written on it in an untidy black scrawl and below it, I assumed, the details of their disappearance. Asher rubbed a hand over her face. "All right, Aeryn, what do we need to know about these missing people of yours?"

"I—I don't know," I stammered, slightly dazed. "I didn't think there would be so many." I thought for a moment. What might be recorded in that book that would help us? We were looking for tracks in the snow to see what animal left them and where they went. What would my father have said? I chewed my lip. "We're searching for clues; some sort of pattern:

From *where* are people disappearing? *When* did they disappear? Did anyone see anything unusual?"

Asher nodded. "We're going to have to take notes to keep track of it all."

She walked around to the other side of the guardsman's desk and sat in his chair. She asked him, "Do you have a quill and parchment we could use?"

It took a moment, but he furnished the requested items to Asher, who dipped the quill into the inkwell at the desk, then poised it above the parchment. "Aeryn, will you please read the first page for me?"

I blushed. "I'd better not. I don't read very well."

"That's all right," Asher replied, smiling at me. "Will you, please, Lyse?"

Lyse leaned over the book and began to read: "Waran, age thirty-eight, cobbler. Missing near the Hogshead Market on the fourth day of the eighth month, mid-morning. Last seen wearing brown trousers and a shirt. Missing the small finger on his right hand, one tooth. No family outside city. No witnesses." She added, wrinkling her nose, "That's not very helpful."

"Too soon to tell. Try the next one," Asher said.

Lyse continued. "Olun, thirty-one, wheelwright. Missing near the western gate on the twenty-third day of the sixth month, noontime. Last seen wearing a blue tunic and gray trousers. Brown hair and eyes, average height. Wife suspects disappearance could be related to gambling debts."

After reading a dozen or so reports, with Asher dutifully copying down their details in a small, cramped script on the borrowed parchment, Lyse paused. Each of the disappearances so far seemed different from all the ones that had come before. Men, women, children, bakers, laborers, and grandmothers had all gone missing, each in a different location on a different day.

"I don't see any pattern at all," Lyse said, crossing her arms.

"Keep reading. There has to be some sort of clue," I replied. I closed my eyes, trying hard to find the pattern. It had to be there somewhere. Even if not all the disappearances were kidnappings, some had to be. What was the thread that linked them all together?

Lyse turned to the next page. "Zana, age twelve. Missing near the King Hadriel III fountain on the twenty-first day of the sixth month, morning. Last seen wearing a blue dress with small white flowers. Blonde hair, brown eyes, approximately five feet tall. Abducted in crowd during the summer solstice celebration. Parents believe culprit was wearing brown cloak with hood, approximately six feet tall. No further witnesses."

"Now we're getting somewhere!" Asher wrote the information with a flourish.

"A man in a cloak is hardly a good clue," Lyse argued, rolling her eyes.

"Who wears a cloak in the summer?" Asher challenged.

"We need a map," I said. "We need to see where people are going missing."

"That's a good idea," Asher agreed. To the guardsman, she said, "Do you have a map of the northwest quarter that we could use?"

Pages of Asher's neat, precise notetaking later, we had gone through most of the book, and the map of the northwest quarter that the guardsman had given us was full of dots marking the locations of each disappearance. Asher set the quill down, rubbed her eyes, and massaged the muscle of her palm below her thumb. "I hope you see more than I do, Aeryn," she said. "There are a few places, such as the western gate and the Beggar's Market, where the disappearances seem to be a bit more common, but otherwise they're scattered all over the quarter. They happen everywhere, in every month. I don't see any patterns. Are you certain there's a band of kidnappers running around King's City? There are all sorts of reasons people disappear."

I shook my head. Doubt was creeping in. Was I imagining things? Was Lyse right that I was seeing a conspiracy where none existed? Had I projected my own misfortune onto people who, in reality, had suffered their own unrelated tragedies? But no, my instinct told me it wasn't all coincidence. "No, I'm not certain," I replied. "But don't you find it odd that so many people have disappeared in the last few years? Doesn't it seem strange to you?"

"I don't know. I'll ask around and see what more I can find out. Maybe someone has heard something. If you're right, maybe your kidnappers tried to take someone who fought back and escaped." Asher stood and adjusted her sword belt. Then she folded the map up and handed it to me. "Will you return to Windhall now?"

"Yes," Lyse replied quickly before I could say anything. "It's getting late."

"If you'd like to stay in the city longer," Asher said, addressing me, "I'm happy to escort you back whenever you like."

"She's coming with *me*," Lyse snapped. I blushed, embarrassed by her rudeness. Why was Lyse behaving like Asher was an enemy? Asher had been nothing but helpful.

Asher shrugged. "I'll let you know if I find out anything."

"Thank you," I replied.

The three of us walked out the garrison and back into the afternoon sun. Lyse wrapped her arm in mine and smiled at Asher. "It was nice to meet you, Lady Asher. Thank you for assisting us today. I'm sure you must be very busy. We can see ourselves home now."

Her smile was a little too stiff, and her words were all wrong. They were too formal, as though we'd just met Asher and not spent the day investigating disappearances together. I blinked at her. What had gotten into her?

Asher nodded, then said to me, "If you need me, I'm at the knight's garrison next to the castle. Anyone there can direct you to me." She flashed a flirty smile. "Have a good evening."

She turned and headed east, a slight swagger to her step, and Lyse dragged me south toward the western gate. She was walking too quickly, and I almost had to jog to keep up with her. After several strides of this pace, coupled with a heavy and oppressive silence between us, I planted my heels and dragged us to a halt.

"What's wrong with you?"

"Nothing!" Lyse replied, her face flushed.

"You were very rude to Asher! She was being very helpful."

"We don't need her help. We can do it ourselves."

I put my hands on my hips. "No, we can't! We never would have gotten that information without her. Why don't you like her?"

Lyse squirmed uncomfortably. "I don't dislike her."

I threw up my hands. There was no use arguing. "Good," I grunted, "because we need her help. Whoever is abducting people is obviously very clever."

Throughout the next week, I seemed to see Lyse everywhere. She watched from a distance during combatives practice. She helped me write my lines for Professor Kalmath's class and brought me my favorite tart as a special snack before bed. She appeared by my side as if by magic during every meal and walked me every day to Raelan's class. I was torn by this intense interest. On the one hand, I selfishly treasured every glance and every touch from her, but on the other, her attention cut like a knife. She had been clear about her choice, and it hadn't been me. Why reject me only to toy with me? What did she expect? That we could fall back into being the closest of friends but never anything more?

So long as that pull existed between us, the knowledge that we would only ever be friends hurt me far worse than Faegan's knife had. How could I pretend to not have the feelings that I did? How could I be expected to smile and act as though nothing was wrong when it was, to me, all wrong? But I had no choice: I could suffer in silence or I could cut her out of my life entirely, and that was no choice at all. I chose to suffer.

A few days after our trip into the city, Kaylara found me after dinner to tell me that there was a lady knight asking for me. Had Asher discovered something? I jogged quickly to the front entrance, where Asher stood holding the reins of a tall bay horse.

She beamed brightly when she saw me. "Aeryn!"

"Do you have news?" Without realizing it, I held my breath.

Asher grinned proudly. "I have something better: a witness. Can you come now to meet him?"

There was no prohibition against leaving Windhall after classes were over for the day, so I nodded. Asher mounted the bay, who I assumed was the famous Stormcloud given to her by Sir Idras, then reached down to help me up. I landed behind the saddle's high cantle and wrapped my arms around her waist. She was warm and smelled of sandalwood soap. I felt a small shiver of...excitement? It was hard to ignore how close together our bodies were. Only a little farther apart than when Lyse had tackled me in the infirmary. Before I could think about it further, however, she said, "Hold on! Cloud is the fastest horse in the knighthood!"

She clucked once, and he took off like lightning. I clung to Asher for dear life as Cloud's powerful haunches drove forward beneath us. We streaked toward the city, the wind blowing through my hair and snatching at my clothes. Asher laughed with reckless abandon, and her joy was infectious. I laughed, too, letting my arms relax slightly.

When we reached the western gate, Asher reined Cloud in, and we entered the city alongside other pedestrians and carts. We walked north into the northwest quarter, down shabby, meandering streets until we arrived at a particularly rundown area that I estimated must be near the northern edge of the city. Asher pulled Cloud to a halt, and I slid off clumsily, with Asher landing easily next to me a moment later. She left Cloud's reins over his neck, confident he would stay for as long as she needed him to, then walked up to a house and knocked on its rough, unpainted door.

It was opened by a broad-shouldered man with thin, long gray hair that reached to his shoulders. Day-old white whiskers sprouted from his cheeks, and his blue eyes were rheumy. His round nose was round and red. Wordlessly, without even seeming to acknowledge us, he turned and walked back inside the house, leaving the door open. Asher motioned me to follow her. We stepped past the threshold and found the man had taken a seat in a rocking chair in front of a fire in the hearth. He stared into the fire so intently that I wondered if he'd forgotten we were there. Was he ill? Why had Asher brought me here? She hadn't explained on the ride, preferring, I surmised, to surprise me.

"Yorel, will you please tell Aeryn about your daughter Emira, as you told me?" Asher said gently, kneeling and taking his hand in hers. "I've brought her here to listen. She's trying to find people like Emira."

Yorel looked up at me with eyes made hollow by deep loss. His cheeks were soft and sunken. I wondered how old he was. By how many years had his grief aged him? He said quietly, as though talking to himself and not to us, "My Emira was taken from me two years, three months, and a handful of days ago." He looked back at the fire. "She was so much like her mother: so full of life and fire. My shining star."

Asher squeezed his hand, encouraging him to go on when he paused. He coughed, then continued. "It was late and we were almost home. She had been helping me carry bricks from the brickworks. She didn't want me to do it; said I was too old to be doing this work, that I should stop before it ruined me. But of course I couldn't. We needed the money. We both knew that.

"Bad things happen in this neighbhorhood all the time after the sun's set. I knew it was dangerous, but..." A tear ran down his cheek. "I should have been more careful. I shouldn't have let her come. I should have made her stay home. Two men came out of the darkness. They must have been waiting there. For her, for me, for anyone who happened to come past them that night, I don't know. They knocked me over and grabbed her. One of them threw her over his shoulder and began to run.

They must have knocked her out or else she would have fought. Oh, she would have fought! The other man, he did something to me. He magicked me, I know he did. It felt like I was covered in thick black tar. I couldn't move, couldn't fight to get her back. I kept trying to yell, to tell them to let her go, but I couldn't. And then they were gone."

Tears began to run down his cheeks freely, and my heart ached for him. Had my parents, too, watched me be taken, helpless to stop it? I knew Jale's story had been a lie, but I didn't know the truth. What had happened in Thamir that day?

Yorel continued, "When I could move again, I ran after them. I ran all up and down the streets calling for her, but it was like they were ghosts. No one saw or heard a thing. They were gone forever, and my Emira with them. For a year, I looked for her. I spent every copper I had trying to find her. Every day, I went to the city guard and demanded answers, but there were none to be had. She had disappeared."

He fell silent. Asher looked to me, waiting for me to ask a question. I hadn't expected this. This was everything I'd been looking for: proof that there was at least one mage involved in a kidnapping. My triumph was cut short by a small detail that nagged at me: How did the mage or mages evade the city's magic wards? The city guard should have arrived within minutes of unsanctioned magic being used in the city. They would have turned the city inside out trying to root out the mage that had set the wards off. Where were they in Yorel's story?

"After Emira was taken, did the city guard come?" I asked.

"No." Yorel sighed. "But the kidnappers would have been long gone by then anyway. It wouldn't have mattered."

How had the mage done it? Was Yorel mistaken about the magic? Or worse yet, lying about the whole thing? I dismissed the idea immediately. There was no way to feign such deep sorrow.

I ran through possibilities in my mind. Could someone have figured out a way to subvert the wards? Could there be gaps in them, like holes in cheese, and the mage had found them? Lyse had shown such faith in the wards when she told me about them that I had believed they were impossible to trick, but why should they be? Perhaps the mage who had originally set them had inadvertently left a gap that the kidnappers knew how to exploit. Or perhaps they were old and crumbling...or even long gone. Could that be why Lyse had been able to use Timo's magic without triggering them? I also had to admit the possibility that the wards had worked as intended but the city guard simply hadn't bothered to respond. There was no way for me to know the truth.

The mystery of the wards aside, we had our first clue, which was that whoever the kidnappers were, one was a mage who could create a temporary tar-like substance. "Yorel, what color was the mage's magic? Was it red? Blue? Yellow?"

"Color?" Yorel looked confused. "There was nothing. Only black."

"Black magic," I repeated. "You're sure?"

Yorel nodded. A shiver ran up my arms, making all the hairs stand on end. Black magic could only mean one thing: a mage who practiced Dark Magic. I leaned against the wall to steady myself. Even though I had suspected it for a long time, the confirmation was still breathtaking in its ramification: evil had returned to King's City. And no one else seemed to know.

"I'm so sorry about your daughter," I told Yorel. "But I'm going to make sure whoever did this can't take anyone else."

Although I had no way of keeping my promise, I intended to try. No parents deserved to have their children taken from them. I nodded to Asher, and she nodded back. Between us, we could find a way. I just knew it. Asher thanked Yorel for his time and we left him, creeping back outside on tiptoe as though we were leaving a funeral.

"How did you find him?" I asked Asher, laying my hand on Cloud's reddish-brown neck.

Asher grinned and waggled her eyebrows, pleased with herself. "I have my ways. I might even be able to find you more like him. It will be hard, but after hearing his story, I don't doubt that there are others." Then, peering into my eyes, she said, "You looked like you saw a ghost in there.

What's really going on here? Who's taking these people and why? You can trust me."

I bit my lower lip. Lyse wouldn't like me telling anyone else about Dark Magic since no one was supposed to know, but now that I was certain at least one Dark mage was active in the city, it was only fair to tell Asher. After all, we had to start sounding the alarm. The citizens of King's City needed to know. It was bad enough to be kidnapped by members of the King's Regiment, but it was far worse to be kidnapped by Dark Mages. I had been taken to Windhall; Emira, I was sure, was now in the Eternal Realms.

I looked around us. We were alone on the street. Dropping my voice, I said, "She was taken by a mage who uses something called Dark Magic, or Blood Magic. Dark mages use pain to become more powerful."

"I've never heard of it." Asher's light voice showed she didn't fully understand the gravity of what I was telling her. "You're sure it was a Dark mage?"

"Yorel said the mage's magic was black. No other mages have black magic. The only way to have it is to have practiced Dark Magic." I thought of Raelan and his black eyes. My stomach twisted into a knot. Was he involved in this? Or did he know who was?

Asher looked thoughtful, but not scared. "Would the Mages' Council know who this Dark mage is?"

"I don't know. I don't think so. If they did, wouldn't they stop him?"

Asher tapped the pommel of her sword with the pad of her thumb, thinking. "So this Dark mage spends years kidnapping people...and no one has ever noticed him? How has he gotten away with it for so long?"

"I don't think anyone knows to look. Dark Magic was banned in Ilirya a long time ago and all reference of it was scrubbed from the records. Probably there are only a handful of people in the entire city who have even heard of it. Certainly not enough to see the signs and know what they mean."

Asher blew out a puff of air from her cheeks and ran her hand over the top of her head. "Well, since *we* know what it means, we can tell the city guard and they'll find the bad mage and stop it." She looked at me with a half-smile. "You've solved the mystery of the disappearances in the northwest quarter, Aeryn! You did it!"

I blushed and dropped my gaze, but Asher's confidence was contagious. It was so simple: We had all the proof that we needed; the city guard would have to act. They could even get the Mages' Council to help find the Dark mage or mages. I balled my fists. Despite my friends' doubts, I had been vindicated. No one else would be kidnapped by Dark mages now. Their reign of terror was over, starting now. Exuberance made me feel light as air.

At this time of the evening, the city guard's northwest quarter garrison buzzed like a giant beehive, full of guardsmen and women and tough, grizzled criminals packed into the large cell in the back. The garrison looked nothing like it had when we'd last been there. Asher strode into the middle of the open room, head high, and demanded to speak to the garrison's lieutenant from the first guardswoman she encountered. The short, muscular guardswoman, who wore an eyepatch and a crossbow strapped to her back, jerked her thumb at a tall, thin man with dark-brown skin and wavy black hair who stood in a corner of the room next to the cell. "That'd be Lieutenant Bogdan Hookhand o'er there," she grunted. "G'luck with 'im. He's in a right mood tonight."

Asher marched with unflagging assurance to the lieutenant, me in tow. I wasn't sure that now was the best time to approach him. Bogdan was arguing with another guardsman, their faces close together and red, their expressions strained, and their bodies tense. Asher was undaunted. Since the two men appeared to be on the verge of coming to blows, she wasted no time. After clearing her throat to get the lieutenant's attention, she announced formally, "Lieutenant Bogdan, I am Lady Asher. I have a matter that needs your attention."

Bogdan, who did, in fact, have a hook for a right hand, stopped arguing with his subordinate and glanced at Asher. His eyes traveled from her face down to her feet and back to her face again, then he spat on the floor. "Well? What is it?"

"We're here to report that we've found the perpetrators of a kidnapping. And also, the use of something called Dark Magic in the city. The Mages' Council needs to be warned about this, as well as the Lady Marshal, so that swift action can be taken to stop it."

"Is that right?" Bogdan replied coolly.

"*Immediately*," Asher stressed, her brow furrowing at Bogdan's reception of her information.

Bogdan looped his thumbs through his sword belt and rocked back on his heels, sucking on his front teeth as he squinted at Asher. My heart sank. He wasn't going to help us. After a moment, he said, "You know, the thing is, I don't know you from the Queen Consort. For all I know, you could be anyone, coming in here talking about whatever this Dark Magic nonsense is."

Asher's jaw flexed as she ground her teeth together. "Lieutenant Bogdan, I am clearly a knight of the realm! My destrier is standing outside the garrison right now and my name is listed in the codex of the knighthood. What further evidence do you need?"

Bogdan sniffed loudly, then spat again. I wondered how much of the floor that we were standing on was covered with his spit. He challenged, "So why don't you go tell them yourself, Lady Knight?"

"The Dark Magic is in your quarter!" Asher snapped, her face turning a pale crimson. "It is your responsibility as lieutenant of the northwest quarter garrison to—"

Bogdan cut her off, holding his left hand up. "That's right, *I'm* the Lieutenant, not you. You've made your report to me, so I will handle it. Now good day to you both."

Asher looked like she was about to say a good many things that were likely to get us in a heap of trouble, so I grabbed her arm and began to drag her out of the garrison. With her plate armor on, she was harder to move than I had anticipated. It didn't help that she was struggling against me, trying to fight her way back to Bogdan, but I held firm. Bogdan obviously wasn't going to help us, and we were no good to anyone sitting in that cell at the back of the garrison. "Let it go," I hissed to her. "We'll tell someone else."

"How dare he!" Asher fumed. "I knew the city guard in this quarter was renowned for its laziness, but this is unacceptable! He is sworn to protect the citizens of this quarter! What an insolent, lazy, good-for-nothing…"

"We'll find another way," I soothed. "It's getting late; I need to get back to Windhall."

Based on the dying twilight, it would be full dark soon. I put my hand on Asher's shoulder to settle her, and her attention turned to me. She smiled, momentarily forgetting her anger at Bogdan. I smiled back but felt a pang of sadness. I wished it had been Lyse who had made this discovery with me. It should have been the two of us, not me and Asher. I dropped my hand.

Once we were out of the city, Cloud swiftly covered the ground between King's City and Windhall with his long, even strides. The road before us was illuminated by the bright light of the full moon, like a shining white path. When the city was behind us and Windhall only a dark outline on the horizon, it felt as if we were flying. Only the sound of Cloud's feet pounding rhythmically against the ground reminded me that the earth was still below us. Although I clung tightly to Asher, I couldn't shake my residual sadness. Even though Lyse was with Timo, I nevertheless wished it was Lyse whom I held. No matter how good Asher smelled.

When we reached Windhall, Asher pulled Cloud to a halt. The campus was quiet and still. Candles—some lit by mage fire, others by flint—burned in many of the dorm windows as the students studied before bed. I slid off Cloud's tall back and stood next to him while Asher dismounted as well.

"I'll tell the Knight Commander, Lady Bronwen, about what we've learned tomorrow," Asher said. Her voice was full of certainty and conviction. "She'll see that it's handled. She'll tell Marshal Heika and the Mages' Council, and then knock some sense into that stupid Bogdan Hookhand."

She cocked her head, grinning impishly. "I'm glad we met. Who knew that such dark and devious things were happening right under our noses in the city? I grew up here and I still had no idea!"

A wave of melancholy swept over me. "I wish the kidnappers had been discovered earlier. I hate to think of Yorel all alone in his house, missing his daughter. Maybe Emira could have been saved, if only someone had realized what was happening back then."

I wondered what my parents were doing at that moment. I had been gone for months. Were they as hollow and despondent as Yorel? Did they think me dead, or did they have hope that I was still alive? Had they done anything to try to find me? White-hot anger flashed through me. Jale and Gamiel weren't so different from the Dark mages. They deserved to be stopped just as much as the Dark mages, if only I could find a way.

Asher hadn't noticed my shifting moods. She said, "At least we'll stop them now. Thanks to you, we know what we're up against." She shook her head. "I'd like to round up those kidnappers myself."

"Will it really be that easy to catch them?" I asked.

"Absolutely! The city guard may be useless, but the knighthood never fails. Oh! You have a moth in your hair."

She leaned in close to me in order to see better in the dark, then reached behind my ear to pick off a small, light-colored moth. It must have caught in my hair as we were riding. She flicked it away, and it landed somewhere on the grass.

"I should head back to the city," she said, casting a glance over her shoulder at the hulking outline of King's City. "Good night, Aeryn. I hope to see you again soon. I'll send word if I hear anything more."

She took my hand and raised it to her lips, kissing the first knuckle the way I imagined ladies had their hands kissed at the king's court. The action was simultaneously intimate and chivalrous. My body unexpectedly thrilled with excitement in response. Could there be a little space in my heart left for Asher? She winked, then mounted and wheeled Cloud around, dashing off into the night. Within moments, the two were swallowed up by the darkness.

I listened to the sound of Cloud's hooves striking the ground until I could hear it no more, then I turned to go back to the dorm. It was only then that I noticed Lyse standing several dozen paces away with a lantern. I hadn't seen her before because my back had been to her. Although the light of the lantern lit her face poorly, it was impossible to miss the devastation on her face. I raised my hand in greeting and opened my mouth to ask what was wrong, but before I could speak, she spun on her heel and fled toward the dorm. I realized then that from her angle, it must have looked as though Asher had kissed me.

CHAPTER 4

"In theory, it would be possible for a mage with an affinity for spellcasting to create a Gate using a spell, thereby bypassing the need for a Gate mage. However, this has never been tested in practice, given how much power would be required for the spell."

— *A Kingdom and its People, 4th edition*

"Enemies come in pairs. If you only see the first, you'll never see the second."

— *Raelan Bloodmoon, War Mage*

ACCORDING TO THE LEGENDS OF my people, the Salyar, after the first god Bahadil retreated into the shadows, he left the world he'd made to his children. Imitating him, these gods began to create their own children, the demi-gods. The first of Bahadil's children, Death, fashioned three black-winged servants to carry the souls of the wicked to the Eternal Realms: Antar, whose fangs were long as a viper's; Elendir, whose talons were sharp as an eagle's; and Lymon, whose claws were thick as a bear's. Those who had done evil in life would be met at their death by one of the three and dragged screaming to the darkest places in the Eternal Realms. On the other hand, those who were good in life were met by a fourth servant, who had the face of a beautiful woman with hair as white as a stoat. She had no wings, and her name was Zakariya.

That night, after Asher and I had discovered proof of Dark Magic in King's City, I dreamed of Antar, Elendir, and Lymon. The three servants of Death walked together along the streets of King's City, their black wings spread behind them and their faces hidden in shadow. Everywhere they went, they called the souls of the people to them like wind draws the gray smoke from a fire. Their sister Zakariya, however, was nowhere to be seen. Horrified, I cried out, "No! This isn't right! They can't all be wicked!"

Hearing my words, Elendir turned to me and held a curved talon to his beak as though quieting me, but Lymon said in a deep, rough voice, "Where there is Darkness, the wicked and good are judged alike and share their misery until such time as the good can be ransomed by the living."

What did *that* mean? Before I could find out, I awoke with a start and found that I had missed the breakfast bell. If I didn't hurry, I would be late for Father Merek's class. I threw on clothing I'd left strewn on the floor and ran out the door.

Maiara, Pavo, and Kaylara were already seated, so I squeezed onto the bench next to my two friends, leaving Maiara, whose temperament had yet to improve in the time I'd spent at Windhall, to sit alone. Draks arrived a moment later and reluctantly sat next to Maiara, casting a baleful look at us over his shoulder. My stomach rumbled, and I regretted missing breakfast. There was nothing to be done about it; I'd just have to go hungry until after Professor Kalmath's class. Then hopefully I could find Lyse and talk to her about last night.

"Who's your new friend?" Kaylara asked, nodding to me with a self-satisfied smirk.

"Who?" I asked, wrinkling my forehead in confusion.

"The knight? I saw when she dropped you off."

Had half of Windhall been awake and watching? "That's Asher. Lady Asher, I guess. We..." I trailed off. I could hardly explain that we had discovered the existence of one or more Dark mages kidnapping people from King's City to torture or kill. I would tell her later, but with class about to start, now was not the time. "We...were doing something in the city."

Kaylara gave me a suggestive look that said she knew exactly what we'd been up to. Even though she was wrong, of course, I blushed and dropped her gaze, looking around for Father Merek, who appeared to be running late. The bell rang and he hastened in, carrying several books under his arm. He was preoccupied, muttering under his breath. Kaylara poked me, then subtly gestured toward him with an expression of surprise and concern. Father Merek's bald head was sweating profusely, and I could see rings of damp sweat under his arms. I'd never seen him so out of sorts.

41

"Is something wrong, Father?" Maiara asked.

"No!" He smiled weakly, but his smile quickly melted away. "It's—it's nothing."

Kaylara's eyes met mine, and she looked puzzled. I shrugged. It wasn't our business to know whatever was upsetting him.

"Well, it's just...you see...I'm missing a particular tome out of my library," he blurted out. "A very...*valuable* book. I must have misplaced it, although I could have sworn I haven't touched it in years."

"What's it about, Father?" Maiara cocked her head. Perhaps I should have set Maiara to investigating the kidnappings. She was nosy and never knew when to leave things alone.

"Nothing!" Father Merek exclaimed too quickly. He loosed a burst of high-pitched, uncontrollable nervous laughter. "No matter. I'm sure it will turn up. Now, where were we? The history of maritime trade in Gent, was it?"

As Father Merek pawed through his books to find the lesson he intended to teach, Kaylara caught my eye. She whispered, "What do you suppose *that's* all about?"

I shook my head. There was no telling, nor did I particularly care. I had too many of my own things to think about after last night. How had the Dark mage or mages gotten away with kidnapping for so long without being caught? I had an idea. No one knew more about the history and laws of King's City than Father Merek. Maybe he could help. I raised my hand.

Father Merek squinted at me. "Yes, Aeryn?"

"Father, would it be possible for someone not on the Imperial Codex to practice magic in King's City?"

Father Merek froze, his face turning white as the first snowfall in Thamir. His hands began to shake so much that he stuck them in the sleeves of his robe and grasped his elbows to steady them. He licked his lips, looking around the room as though someone might materialize out of thin air. "No. No, that would be utterly impossible, of course. Impossible."

My blood ran cold at the same time that my body began to buzz with a flush of energy. He was lying. Unconvincingly, at that. Did he know that someone had figured out a way to bypass the wards? Was it Raelan? Had Father Merek found Raelan out, and now he was keeping Raelan's secret out of fear? My mind raced with possibilities. I needed to talk to Lyse. She needed to know what I knew. Together we could figure out what to do.

The rest of the class went poorly. Rattled, Father Merek kept forgetting his train of thought, apologizing profusely, and then repeating what he'd already said. Given that maritime trade was already an arcane and soporific subject, Draks's head was on the desk and he was snoring midway through the lesson, while Kaylara and Pavo played a writing game on a piece of parchment.

When Father Merek dismissed the class, I dashed out to scout the academic building's halls, hoping to find Lyse before my next class, but she was nowhere to be found. Nor did I see her after Professor Kalmath's class, at lunch, or any time during the rest of the day. When I didn't see her at all the next day, I started to worry. Was she sick? When I finally tracked her down on the third day after my trip to King's City, she looked exhausted and pale, as though she hadn't slept for days. Still, I was relieved to see her.

"Lyse! I've been looking for you!" I jogged over to where she was hanging wet sheets outside the infirmary to dry, her sleeves rolled up to her elbows and her hair wild. "Where have you been? Have you been sick? Is something wrong?"

She pulled a cloth out of a basket and pinned it to the line, not meeting my eyes. "I've been busy." Her voice was flat and emotionless.

I took a step back in surprise. Her answer was a lie, and we both knew it. Lyse had never been too busy for me since the day I'd arrived at Windhall. If she hadn't been sick, that meant she had been avoiding me. I wasn't sure what to do. Her curt answer seemed to discourage further conversation, but there were things I needed to tell her. Things she needed to know.

Lyse closed her eyes and sighed. "I'm sorry, I'm tired. How have you been? How are your classes? Are Professor Kalmath and Pavo still sparring?"

Her eyes, normally a light brown, were dark as storm clouds, or maybe it an optical illusion caused by the purple bags under her eyes. I didn't know what to make of this uncomfortable new distance between us or how to bridge it, so I settled on relaying to her the most important information. "There's been a breakthrough on the kidnappings."

Lyse still wasn't looking at me. She pinned up another cloth. "Oh?"

I winced at the distance in her voice but kept going. "I was right. There *is* at least one Dark mage kidnapping people in the city! Asher and I met a man whose daughter Emira was kidnapped two years ago by a mage with black magic. Asher and I tried to tell the Lieutenant of the city guard's northwest quarter, but he wouldn't listen."

"Asher," Lyse repeated, her voice so brittle it reminded me of the first time the streams near Thamir freeze at the end of the summer: the lightest blow would shatter the fragile ice into a dozen pieces. Lyse forced a smile across her face. "You seem to really like her."

I tried to keep defensiveness out of my voice. "She's very helpful. She was the one who found out about Emira."

Lyse nodded as though agreeing, then gave me a hollow smile. "I'll see you later, perhaps. I have some things to do in the infirmary. Timo will be returning tonight, and I want everything to be perfectly put away by the time he arrives."

"But Lyse—" I started to protest, grabbing for her hand. Whatever had gone wrong between us, I wanted to fix it. I didn't like this void yawning between us.

"You should get to class," Lyse said. "You don't want to be late."

She turned and walked into the infirmary without looking back. I rubbed my temples, squeezing my eyes shut. Why was Lyse treating me like a stranger? Why didn't she want to hear more about the kidnappings? Lyse cared deeply about the inhabitants of King's City; she would want the kidnappers stopped just as much as I did. So why wasn't she excited about the progress I'd made? I wanted to follow her, to demand she tell me what was wrong, but she was right. If I didn't hurry, I would be late to Raelan's class. I determined to find her later, after dinner, and discover what the matter was with her.

The problem with fighting Cayleth was that she was growing more powerful by the day. It was clear she would one day be a Great Mage, and that day wasn't too far off. From the moment Raelan had called start to our bout, I found myself in the middle of the Ice Crown. How Cayleth had perfected the glare of the sun off the ice and the shadows cast by the tall pine trees, I didn't know. As far as I knew, she'd never even seen snow. But had I not known that her affinity was illusion, I would have assumed that she had Gated me to some place in the Ice Crown similar to Thamir but not exactly like it.

Had it been any mage but Cayleth, the illusion of my homeland would have been a cheap trick, a taunting reminder that I'd been kidnapped and barred from returning to see my family. And had it been anyone but Cayleth, I might well have broken down and cried out of self-pity or set the room on fire with my rage, depending on the day. But since it was Cayleth, I knew she meant it as a supportive action: She was helping me keep the memory of my home alive, giving me hope that I'd see it again soon. As Pavo had written, I might be caged, but that didn't mean I had been tamed. My captors couldn't keep me away forever.

I cast a probing wave of magic into the room, trying to find Cayleth's shield behind the illusion. When my magic bounced against it, I sent a second wave to lift and throw her backward against the wall and daze her. Although her shield could protect her from the heat of my mage fire, it didn't totally stop her from being thrown by its force. I had discovered that if I could break her concentration, her illusions would start to shimmer, and I'd be able to see where she was. After that, I would have a very narrow window to begin blasting her shield with mage fire, trying to break through.

Although the trick didn't always work, this time it did, and when the illusion flickered, it revealed that Cayleth had started to try and flank me to the right. I began driving bright-blue magic bolts into her shield, trying to crack it before she was able to reset the illusion or create a new one. Cayleth was too quick for me, however. A giant brown bear began to roar to my left, so loud and so close that I instinctively flinched, even knowing that it couldn't hurt me. That was all the time she needed to spring into action. She dove through the magic shield that Raelan had made for me, wielding a rapier in front of her.

I barely had time to block her blade with mine as she swung it down on my head. To buy distance, I kicked her in the stomach, then stepped back and grabbed my mace with my left hand. Cayleth straightened back up and we began to circle, but I knew that the end of the fight was a foregone conclusion now; it was only a matter of time. Cayleth had been all but born with a weapon in her hand, *and* she was a naturally gifted fighter. How long we continued to fight depended on how playful she was feeling.

The tip of her rapier darted forward, and I parried it to the outside at the last minute. With my left hand, I swung the mace down toward her head, aware I'd have to halt the blow before it landed if Cayleth somehow failed to parry. I didn't really want to hurt her, after all. I wasn't like Faegan. Cayleth dodged easily, however, and kicked the outside of my left leg well above the knee where there was no armor. I grunted and slashed wildly at her with my sword, trying to keep her back. She parried and kicked my leg a second time in the same spot. I groaned. What had been an ache after the first kick turned to numbness. Fast as lightning, she dashed in and struck the same spot a third time, causing my leg to buckle.

"Halt!" Raelan's voice echoed in the small room.

Panting and staring at each other warily, our swords held between us, Cayleth and I separated. My left leg dragged behind me. It was unlike Raelan to separate fighters before one had submitted, but I was glad. I didn't need my leg to be numb for hours. Raelan snapped his fingers impatiently. He seemed restless and bored. He motioned with his long, thin hand to Faegan, who had watched the fight from a corner of the room.

"Faegan," he ordered, "take Cayleth's place."

This would be the first time I'd face Faegan since he had almost killed me. While I didn't exactly bear him a grudge, I didn't forgive him either. He should have been more careful. What if I'd died? Faegan nodded and changed positions with Cayleth. Feeling started to return to my leg as a tingling, aching pain. I winced and rubbed at the bruised spot with my knuckles, trying to dispel it. I didn't want to fight Faegan injured.

Raelan was watching me with his black, Dark Magic-stained eyes. "Aeryn, from now on I will no longer make you a shield; you must make one yourself."

I gritted my teeth. It wasn't as though I hadn't been trying. Both in class and outside of it, I'd done everything I could to try and raise a shield that wouldn't crumble into blue dust. But for some reason, my magic refused to bend itself into the shape necessary to keep me safe from other mages. It reminded me of how I'd struggled to tame my magic at the beginning. Why was my magic so willful and unruly compared to others'? Why did it have to be so hard for me when magic came so naturally to all my friends?

I took a breath to calm myself and began building a shield, determined to make it work this time. It was the same grim vow I made every time. The shield I created around me shimmered blue, weak, and insubstantial as the gossamer wings of a dragonfly, however. It didn't look like it would hold against a puff of air. I didn't have an alternative: It was the best I could do. It would have to work.

I nodded to indicate I was ready for Faegan to test it. Immediately, his pale-purple magic flashed out and blasted into my shield, creating a shower of sparks that rained down on the gray stone floor and dissolved. My shield twinkled, but held, and I released the breath that I'd unconsciously been holding. Faegan threw two more bolts of magic in quick succession. When lines of purple danced across the shield like cracks in the ice and then were absorbed, I experienced a whisper of hope. The shield was not only still holding, but now it even seemed stronger, pulsing with power. I was doing it!

Eyes narrow with concentration, Faegan began to try to drill through my shield the way I'd tried to drill through Cayleth's. This time, however, the shield didn't even last a minute before it crumbled around me like stale bread, melting away where it hit the ground. Faegan stopped his attack immediately lest I be hit unprotected by the full force of his mage fire. This was not a sparring match, and he didn't need to win.

"Better," Raelan pronounced coldly. "But not good enough. You'll have to do much better, Aeryn."

I briefly bowed my head, acknowledging the criticism. Yes, I would have to do better. Raelan began to make a point to Faegan about magic bolts, and as he raised his hands, I noticed a trickle of dried blood had run down the back of his hand. The blood was black and crusted. Then the sleeve of his black robe slipped down, revealing a row of neat lines cut into the outside of his arm as far up as I could see. It was from one of these cuts that he had bled. My heart stopped. There was only one reason for those cuts: He was practicing Dark Magic again.

Raelan abruptly stopped talking to Faegan and turned his black eyes upon me. For a bone-chilling moment, I worried he knew what I had just seen. I began to panic, sweat breaking out on my palms. But all he said was, "Take a seat and we'll discuss Therion mages, or what are called more simply 'animal mages.'"

That evening, Timo and Lyse joined me, Pavo, and Kaylara at dinner. Timo looked slightly thinner and paler than usual, but he was in good spirits, his blue eyes twinkling as he laughed and joked. He had his arm wrapped easily around Lyse, enveloping her familiarly with his long arm. It had taken him two weeks to stop the plague at Port Bluewater, working with the city's healers to contain the spread and treat the infected. Now he was back and acting as though he had never left and nothing at Windhall had changed. He *had* left, however, and Lyse had changed while he was gone, no matter how she tried to pretend that she hadn't. She didn't fit against him quite the way she had before, and when her eyes met mine, there was discomfort in them and guilt.

"How was Port Bluewater?" Kaylara asked Timo. "This time of year the merchant ships are mostly at anchor, right?"

Timo nodded. "Most of the smaller sailing ships are in the harbor now. In the high season, the white sails coming and going through the port look like hundreds of white birds in flight. In the winter months, however, the winds are too strong and only the biggest galleons can cross the seas."

"They say it's one of the most beautiful cities in Ilirya," Kaylara said.

"It's unmatched," Timo agreed. He smiled at Lyse. "But I prefer King's City. It's good to be back. I'm tired and looking forward to some rest at last. I could sleep for a week." He mock yawned.

"It will be easier to travel when you're not alone," Kaylara suggested, her gaze shifting to Lyse.

Timo kissed Lyse on the top of her head. "And easiest yet when there's a family of little ones at home waiting for me. How could I stay away from that?"

Lyse's eyes flickered to mine, full of quiet, desperate unhappiness. She dropped her gaze immediately, then untangled herself from Timo. She stood, picking up her plate of uneaten food. "I'm not hungry. I must be tired, too. I have a pounding headache. Please excuse me."

Timo looked surprised. White magic gathered automatically at his fingertips. A man who could heal an entire city of plague could easily heal his partner of a headache, but Lyse gently pushed his hand away and then squeezed his shoulder. "I have yellow lady's slipper in my room. I think a nice tea and some quiet is all I need. Nothing to worry about. Good evening, everyone." She didn't look at me as she left.

I waited for as long as I could stand it, until Timo was well into a lecture on plague containment methods in cities with no healers, then politely took my leave as well, citing reading work for Professor Kalmath's class. I went back to the dorm and slipped up the stairs to the second floor, waiting for a moment in front of the third door on the right, debating what to say. Would Lyse even want to see me? There was every chance she wouldn't. Still, I had to try. I knocked gently. After hearing no answer, I slowly opened the door, peering in as I did so. Lyse was lying on her bed, staring at the ceiling.

"Hey," I said quietly.

Lyse rolled her head to look at me but otherwise didn't move.

"Are you feeling any better?"

I couldn't help but notice there was no tea around her. She had lied about the headache. When she didn't answer, I took it as tacit approval to enter and perched at the foot of her bed, prepared to leave if she asked me to. Lyse sat up and drew her knees to her chest, wrapping her arms around her legs and hugging herself tightly. I touched her foot. "Talk to me, Lyse."

"I'm tired is all. Nothing to worry about." She was lying again. I knew because she wouldn't look at me when she said the words. This wasn't the Lyse I knew. Lyse never lied.

I sighed. "Lyse, I know you. I know something's wrong."

Lyse tried to be strong for a moment, to put up a brave front, but her expression cracked almost immediately. Her lip started to tremble, and a look of wild desperation crossed her face. "I'm falling apart," she gasped, clutching the blanket in balled fists. "I'm...breaking."

I waited patiently for her to continue, feeling my heart cry for her pain and wishing I could hold her to my chest and comfort her. She had been holding in a maelstrom of emotions, and they were eating her up inside.

Her hands flew to her mouth. "I can't see you with Asher and not be jealous. I can't be with Timo and pretend that I'm not thinking of you. I can't..." She buried her head in her hands. So softly I almost didn't hear it, she moaned, "I can't love you."

She looked up. "Everything is so broken, and I don't know how to fix any of it."

I didn't know what to say, so I said nothing. Lyse continued, "I'm *supposed* to be with Timo. Together, we will heal the sick. We will attend court functions. We will have beautiful children…" She trailed off, and I knew in her mind she was seeing one future crumble before her, to be replaced by another, unknown one. Could there be any positive in it? Was there a world in which a kidnapped hunter's daughter from the Ice Crown and a beautiful noble from Rath lived a happy ending? If there was, I was determined to find it.

"You two can still heal together," I suggested. "You don't have to be married to do that, right? You do it now already. Nothing about that would change. You could still stop plagues. You're still bonded."

Lyse looked miserable. We both knew how much it would cost her to give up her alliance with Timo, how it would weaken her family. Yet there was more to life than a socially advantageous marriage. She didn't have to pay for Nagyar's sins. I said softly, "Don't you deserve to follow your heart?"

"I love Timo! I—I'm just so lost." Her head was in her hands again.

I moved closer to her. When she didn't shy away, I reached out and stroked the side of her face. It was a bold move, but it felt right. She leaned into my palm, closing her eyes as she did so. When she opened them, there was longing in them mixed with guilt. She asked, "What's wrong with me? Why can't I stop thinking about you, Aeryn? Why do I want you when I should only want him?"

I stroked her hair. The pull between us was so strong now that I thought of the great whirlpool in the sea that Sir Idras had once described to me: a sucking hole in the ocean from which no ships could sail free. Lyse and I were both trapped now, come what may. I whispered, "It's okay, Lyse. It will be okay. I promise."

"What do I do?" Lyse was begging, looking for someone else to make the decision for which she didn't want responsibility. It was too heavy, too consequential.

"You don't owe anyone anything. Not me, not Timo, not even your family. But you owe yourself whatever will make you happy. You owe yourself the chance to be happy."

"I can't hurt Timo." Her voice was a whisper.

"Timo's strong. He knows it makes no sense to cling to something that's no longer the right fit. Wouldn't you let *him* go if you had to? He'll understand."

"He *won't* understand! Without me, he can't be a Great Mage! He needs me!"

"There's a difference between needing someone and loving someone," I said. "If he loves you, he'll want your happiness. As you would want his." I ran my hand along her hair, leaving my hand on her shoulder. Her body was quietly shaking.

"I don't know what I want," Lyse moaned. "I can't throw everything away for…"

She trailed off, unwilling to say the words that would irrevocably change her life. For me. But it didn't matter if she said it or not: Her heart had already chosen, and deep down, she knew it. I took her hand in mine and said with a wry smile, "I'm not *all* bad, am I?"

Lyse burst out crying, shaking her head, and I gathered her up in my arms, rocking her until the sobs stopped. My heart was beating furiously, and my body seemed to burn where she touched me. At last, she lay back down in her bed, curled into a tight, scared ball, and pulled my arm to wrap around her. She wasn't choosing me in that moment, but she was opening the door to the possibility of a choice other than Timo. I settled in behind her, enveloping her in my arms. I nestled my face into the base of her neck and matched my breathing to hers, trying to be the support she needed right then.

It took a long time—how long, I couldn't tell—but eventually her body relaxed, and her breathing evened out as she fell asleep. I stayed for a while, then carefully unwrapped myself from her, left the bed, and gently covered her with her blanket. I slipped out of her room and back down the stairs. I would have to tell her later about the cuts on Raelan's arm that proved he was using Dark Magic.

I didn't feel like going back to my room, so I walked out of the dorm and onto the green. For anyone not born in the Ice Crown, the air must have felt chilly, but for me, it was a happy reminder of my former life. This breath of cold was like a summer night in Thamir, when we all sat around the fire dressing foxes and squirrels and de-feathering birds, preparing for fall. The memory was bittersweet now but inspiring, too. I would get home. I would see my family again. *After* I figured things out with Lyse.

A dark figure resolved itself in the moonlight near the academic building, and I squinted to see better. Who was up at this hour? I caught sight of a familiar shape. Raelan. I'd have known those billowing black robes anywhere. Judging by the angle of the moon, it was late into the night. No lights burned in the dormitory, and even the kitchen's great ovens stood idle.

Raelan strode confidently across the green toward the training rooms. On instinct, I began to follow him, creeping behind him with all the stealth that a decade of hunting in the Ice Crown had taught me. With no trees to hide behind, all it would have taken to discover me was Raelan turning around, but he never once looked back over his shoulder. What was he up to?

He slipped into one of the training rooms, and I took the opportunity to run to catch up. When I reached the room, I peered carefully inside through the crack in the door to make sure he wasn't waiting on the other side. Silhouetted by the dim moonlight that entered through the high, thin windows, he walked to the end of the room and opened the door opposite the one at which I stood, using a key that he drew from his pocket. I remembered Lyse telling me that only a few Windhall administrators had access to that key. Surely Raelan, who was confined to the university grounds as punishment for using Dark Magic, wasn't one of them. Where had he gotten it?

Once Raelan was through the second door, I entered the training room and sprinted across it quiet as a snow hare, pausing again at the farther door to see what would happen next. Luckily for me, Raelan hadn't relocked it, so I carefully inched it open and looked through in time to watch Raelan walk through the Gate at the end of the short corridor. The Gate that led to the university's city office. A moment later, he was out of sight. I bit my knuckle to keep from screaming. Raelan the Dark Mage was now loose in King's City.

A hand locked down on my forearm, and I screamed, throwing myself away from the assailant and calling magic to my hands to defend myself from whoever it was. The blue light illuminated a familiar round face with narrow eyes and black hair pulled tightly into a ponytail. "Cayleth? What are you doing here?"

Cayleth shrugged. "Evidently the same thing you're doing. Following Raelan."

"He passed through the Gate! He went into King's City!" I was still shocked. *How* had he done it? What had happened to the spell that was supposed to prevent it?

"I know," Cayleth said, crossing her arms. "He's been doing it for months."

"You knew?" I gasped. Then I remembered that Cayleth didn't know about the spell that was supposed to keep him tied to Windhall's grounds. That was why she wasn't stunned by the discovery.

"He always manages to lose me right after he gets into the city," Cayleth explained. "I don't think he knows I'm following him; I think there's some sort of a secret hideout he goes to. It must be hidden by an illusion. Maybe it looks like a house or a store, I don't know. Whatever it is, it's too risky for me to follow into the illusion even if I found it; I don't know what's waiting on the other side."

"What does Raelan do in the city?"

"I don't know. That's what I'm trying to find out."

"But...why have you been following him?"

"The same reason you are, I imagine: there's something not right about him, and whatever it is he's doing, I want to know."

That was Cayleth: brave to a fault. I couldn't believe she'd been tracking him for months. She had no idea how dangerous he was! Before I could reply, we heard the training room door next to us open. Cayleth and I looked at each other in surprise for a second, then both of us silently jockeyed to see through the crack in the door. Who was there? A figure all in black, their face hidden by the hood of their robe, entered the hallway and then confidently strode through the Gate.

"Who was it?" I asked. "I couldn't see the face beneath the hood. Could you?"

Cayleth swallowed hard and clutched the doorframe. "I'd know that walk anywhere: it's Chancellor Vandys."

In a flash, I knew where Raelan had gotten the key to the Gate.

CHAPTER 5

"Evil is a choice."

— Everyn Stargazer, "The Five Pearls of Wisdom"

"King's City is built on gold and rot; a beautiful snake eating its own tail."

— Knight Commander Bronwen Lionheart

MY FATHER ONCE SAID, "BE careful whom you trust. The world is full of people who aren't worthy of it." I seemed to keep running into exactly the type of people my father had warned against: first Jale and Gamiel, now Chancellor Vandys. It was the chancellor's job to protect her students. She should have shielded us from dangers like Raelan. Instead, it turned out she was a fox in the henhouse. Whatever she was up to, it couldn't be good if Raelan was involved.

Grabbing my arm, Cayleth growled, "We need to get out of here in case she comes back. *Now.*" Her face was pale. She clearly hadn't expected to see Chancellor Vandys either. Together, we turned and fled out of the training room, walking as quickly back to the dorm as we could without breaking into a full run. Cayleth guided me to her room, which was on the ground floor like mine, and lit several candles to give us light. Then she began pacing back and forth.

"Maybe the chancellor was following Raelan, too," I suggested. I didn't believe it for a second, but I had to say it anyway. The alternative was that the two were working together for some evil purpose, and I didn't want to think about that.

Cayleth shook her head. "Whatever Raelan's up to, the chancellor must be part of it. What could they possibly be doing?"

The time had come to tell Cayleth what I knew. "I think I know some of it."

Cayleth stopped pacing immediately. She crossed her arms, waiting for me to continue.

I licked my lips. "I believe it has to do with something called Dark Magic. It was outlawed in Ilirya years ago and most of its practitioners were executed, but Raelan was spared so that he could teach Ilirya's war mages. He was tethered by a spell to Windhall's grounds so that he couldn't leave. For him to pass through the Gate into the city, someone must have undone that binding spell. I don't know what he's doing in King's City, but I think he's practicing Dark Magic again."

Cayleth gaped at me.

I grimaced. "It gets worse. I don't think he's the only Dark mage in the city, either. Remember the kidnappings I've been investigating? I've found one person for sure who was taken by a Dark mage, two years ago, and I think there have been many others."

"What do they do with the people they kidnap?" Cayleth asked slowly. Her face showed her reluctance to hear the answer.

"Bad things. Pain and suffering is what fuels their magic."

Cayleth rubbed her forehead and started pacing again. "So Raelan is sneaking into the city to kidnap people? Where does he hide them?"

"I hope that's not what he's doing!" I shivered, wrapping my arms around myself. "I can't imagine Raelan any stronger than he already is. The Dark mage I found wasn't a warg…but I don't know who it was."

"Where does Chancellor Vandys come into all this? Do you think she's a Dark mage, too?"

I shook my head. "She can't be. She doesn't have black eyes like Raelan. That's a tell-tale sign of a Dark mage."

Cayleth stopped pacing and stared at me, her face shocked. "Aeryn! Didn't you know? Chancellor Vandys's affinity is illusion, like mine." Cayleth blinked, and her eyes went black, exactly like Raelan's. She blinked again, and her eyes returned to their natural dark-brown color.

My stomach dropped and my skin prickled. Cayleth and I were silent for a minute as the awful realization that the head of our university might be a Dark mage sank in.

"But she wouldn't…would she? Why?" I asked. I rubbed my eyebrows with my fingertips, as though I could rub away everything we'd seen in the training room. Everything was turning upside down. How had kidnappings in King's City led right back to my own doorstep?

"We need to find out what they're doing," Cayleth said, nodding to herself. "Maybe then we'll understand."

"No, we should let the Mages' Council handle it," I replied.

"What?"

"Asher told the Knight Commander about the Dark Magic. By now, the commander will have told the Mages' Council. The Council will find the Dark mages and fix everything. Now that we know for sure Raelan and the chancellor are involved, all we have to do is find a way to let them know and they'll take care of it."

To my surprise, Cayleth's face filled with horror. "Aeryn, the chancellor is a member of the Mages' Council! She'll make sure no one will believe that there are Dark mages!"

"What? But…" I didn't know what else to say. I was at a loss. Could the chancellor really get away with it so easily?

Cayleth put her hands on her hips. "We need irrefutable proof that she can't deny. We need to know what they're doing in the city. It's the only way."

I shook my head. This was beyond me. It was beyond all of us. We were just students. "What can we do? You said yourself that you can't follow Raelan. And even if you could, you shouldn't! It's too dangerous!"

Cayleth thought for a moment, then snapped her fingers. "Kaylara. We can use Kaylara to listen in to their meetings."

"What if they catch her?"

Cayleth waved her hand. "She'll be careful. And besides, neither Raelan nor the chancellor can detect eavesdroppers. I know it's dangerous, but we need something we can take to the Mages' Council. I don't want either of them worming their way out of this."

Leave it to Cayleth to brush off the dangers of spying on Raelan and the chancellor. I chewed on my lip for a moment. I thought of all the people they might have kidnapped over the years. Those people deserved justice. If we didn't help stop the kidnappings, who would? I could one day see my family again, but the families who had lost members to Dark mages like

Raelan had no such hope. I nodded. I was willing to take some risks if it meant we might be able to save lives.

"Okay," I agreed. "And speaking of worming one's way out of things, there's someone who might know something about how Raelan got off campus."

After an early breakfast, I made my way to Father Merek's office, where he could normally be found before class. I knocked softly on the closed door, then, hearing nothing, inched it open carefully. The old man was asleep in his chair, his chin sunk against his chest. He'd fallen asleep while reading; the book was still open on the desk in front of him. All around him, the walls of his office were lined floor to ceiling with volumes of books. Parchments, too, lay everywhere, including on the floor and beneath his desk. His office was so disorganized I could see how he could have misplaced the book he'd claimed to have lost.

We needed to learn more about the Dark mages we were up against, and Father Merek was the only professor I could think of who might have answers to my questions. How had the Dark mage managed to avoid the warding spells in King's City? How had Raelan left the Windhall campus? Although normally I would have been expected to direct any magic-related questions to Raelan, given they concerned Raelan's illegal nocturnal activities, I hoped Father Merek wouldn't find it odd that I was asking him instead. "Father Merek?" I called quietly.

He let out a soft snore in response.

"Father Merek!" I repeated, more loudly.

He jerked awake, looking around wildly. When he saw me, he straightened his robes and wiped at his mouth. "Good morning, Aeryn. I haven't slept through the morning bell, have I? Class hasn't started?"

"No, Father," I said, moving closer so that I stood across the desk from him.

"Oh, good. How may I assist you? Are you eager to hear more about the age of mercantilism, perhaps?" His face lit up in anticipation of the chance to lecture.

I shook my head. "No. I hoped you would tell me more about the history of the warding spells on King's City. They act as a web-like net that detects any magic in the city, right?"

"Quite so. In fact, they're designed to mimic a spider's web. When magic is used within the net, it sets off alarms that alert the city guard to its presence and location. Queen Yrvin had the wards laid two hundred and twenty-one years ago. You see, the Walreds were considered to be usurpers of the Iliryan throne, and she was concerned that mages would be used in a coup against them. The wards were a means to ensure that she could monitor and control all use of magic in King's City. Only people she trusted could use magic, hence the introduction of the Imperial Codex."

I sat down in the chair in front of him. "Could someone trick the wards, even for a few hours?"

Father Merek raised his eyebrows. "Are you trying to find a way to use your magic in the city, Aeryn? I would advise against it. It is impossible to trick, suppress, or avoid the wards. You wouldn't want a run in with the city guard. They're not particularly forgiving of youthful indiscretions, I must say."

I blushed. That wasn't what I was thinking at all. If the wards couldn't be gotten around, why didn't the city guard respond when the Dark mage used magic while kidnapping Emira two years ago? Was it possible the spells had weakened or dissolved over the years? I said, "Two hundred years is a long time. What keeps the warding spells alive?"

"They're very powerful spells laid by some of Ilirya's greatest spellcasters. Occasionally, new power is added to them, too. They're meant to last forever. The safety of Ilirya's rulers and people depend on it."

I was running out of ideas. If the wards were definitely still active, was the problem with the city guard itself? Were they too lazy to respond to the wards' alarm? Had the Dark mages bribed some of them to look the other way? Or was the answer something much worse? The Dark mage who took Emira had obviously been a spellcaster himself, based on how Yorel had described his magic, and Dark Magic made a mage stronger. I asked, "Could a mage ever be powerful enough to unbind the spells?"

Father Merek's face lost all its color for a moment, then turned bright red. "It was you who took the book!" He jumped out of his chair. His fat finger trembled as it pointed at me.

I was so surprised I almost tumbled backward out of my own chair. "What? What book?"

"How did you know about it? What have you done with it?" He was starting to come around the desk, charging toward me.

I scrambled out of the chair and held up my hands. "I don't know what you mean. What book, Father?"

Father Merek stopped. His face fell, crumbling into a look of despair. He rubbed his fat stomach anxiously. When he spoke, his voice was small and hoarse. "It was a book of unbinding spells." He shook his head. "It's too much of a coincidence. Why would someone be asking now, after all these years?"

My heart began to pound. So that was how they had done it! Raelan or Chancellor Vandys must have stolen Father Merek's book some time in the past and used it to undo the spell laid on Raelan. Since neither of them were spellcasters, they had to be working with the spellcasting Dark mage who had taken Emira. They'd used the same book to release the city's warding spells. That was how they'd managed to use magic in King's City without the city guard finding out. I let out a shaky breath. Things were far worse than I'd imagined. We needed to get evidence against them soon; the Mages' Council had to put a stop to this immediately. And the city's defenders needed to know that the wards no longer existed!

If I hurried, I could tell Cayleth what I'd learned before Father Merek's class began. I thanked him for his time and then made a dash for the dining hall. Luckily, Cayleth was there with Kaylara, tucked away at a table in a corner. Kaylara's serious, worried expression told me Cayleth had already shared with her what we knew. I looked around to make sure no one was close enough to overhear us, then sat down. "I know how Raelan managed to leave Windhall, and how they're able to use magic in King's City."

"Of course Chancellor Vandys can use magic in the city," Kaylara said, puzzled. "She's on the Imperial Codex."

"But not Raelan and not the third Dark mage working with them," I said. "I talked to Father Merek this morning. Someone stole a book of unbinding spells from him. That's obviously how they managed to free Raelan and practice Dark Magic within the city."

Cayleth and Kaylara stared at me in open-mouthed amazement. "But... how?" Cayleth said. "The warding spells are much stronger than any one mage. They're some of the strongest magic in the kingdom. It would take several Great Mage spellcasters to lift them, and Raelan and the chancellor aren't spellcasters."

"But if Dark Magic is involved? Maybe it's enough to break those spells," I said. "Or maybe there are other mages working with them. What if it's more than just the three of them? Last time Dark Magic was used in the city, there were several mages involved."

Horror flashed across Kaylara's face. Cayleth turned a little green. "Are Professor Raelan and the chancellor really going into the city to torture people?" Kaylara asked.

"That's what we need to find out, and soon, so that we can put an end to it," I said. "So, can you listen in on Raelan when he leaves Windhall?"

Kaylara's face was troubled. "Yes, but if he meets with any mages who can detect eavesdropping..." She didn't have to finish her sentence. None of us wanted to think about what would happen if we were caught.

"You don't have to do it," I told her. "We know it's dangerous."

Kaylara looked at Cayleth, who nodded encouragingly. "I'll try. No promises."

Lyse entered the dining hall and our eyes met across the room. "I'll meet you in class," I told Kaylara. "There's something I have to do first."

I got up and walked as quickly across the hall as I could. I reached Lyse as she was sitting down at a table with a scone topped with clotted cream. "Hi," I said, smiling.

"Hi," she replied, blushing. She ducked her head, and her dark hair fell across her face like a curtain.

I sat down across from her, checking to make sure Timo wasn't in the hall first. Whatever was about to be said wasn't for his ears to hear. "How did you sleep?"

"Well, thank you," Lyse replied, blushing harder. She looked around furtively, then, unexpectedly, took my hand under the table. I could feel her long, gentle fingers brush against my palm as they closed around it. My hand tingled where she touched it. When her eyes looked into mine, my heart started hammering in my chest. I wondered if hers did, too. In a low voice, she said, "We should talk."

The pull toward her was overwhelming. I was drowning in it, lost in her soft brown eyes. I nodded. Then Timo walked into the dining hall.

Instantly, Lyse dropped my hand. Panic and guilt flushed her face. Not only was the moment between us lost, but my window to talk was closing, too. I had to tell her what I'd learned about Raelan. "Cayleth and I caught Raelan going through the Gate into the city last night."

"No!" Lyse gasped. "That's impossible! It can't be!" She shook her head. She started to massage her left hand with her right vigorously.

"Accompanied by Chancellor Vandys."

Lyse's face turned ashen as shock and revulsion played across it. She was speechless. Since Timo was coming closer, I finished, "Kaylara has agreed to listen and see what they're up to, but I was right: It's all tied to Dark Magic. Raelan is back to using it for sure, and maybe Chancellor Vandys, too."

Lyse covered her mouth with her hand. "No, no, no. This is awful. How can this be?"

I heard the warning bell ring and knew I had to go, or I'd risk being late to Father Merek's class. I stood to leave. Lyse grabbed my hand. "Be careful!"

Combatives practice for the day was called "War": a campus-wide game in which all of Windhall's combatives students were divided into three teams, each headed by one of the instructors. Teams were assigned one part of the campus to defend and one part to attack. My team was led by Derrin, the big former knight who now taught assorted weapons. We had been given the academic building to defend and the training rooms to attack. Cayleth had been detailed to the team headed by Trick, the former assassin and swordsmanship teacher. They'd been given the dining hall to defend and the academic building to attack, making us adversaries. War was supposed to teach strategy, tactics, and teamwork. To prevent serious injury, students were equipped with weapons that had been rendered safe—maces and arrows were tipped with cloth balls rather than iron, for example, and steel sword blades were exchanged for rounded wood—and given strict instructions to act as though hit by a real weapon. "Mortal" injuries were to be treated as mortal, which ensured that the game didn't drag on into the night hours. The first team to capture the flag housed in the safehouse of their opponent won.

War was one of my favorite games in combatives class. It reminded me of playing with my brothers growing up. How many times had we brandished sticks, pretending they were swords, and chased each other around the woods? How many times had we defended or stormed imaginary garrisons? At Windhall, War was a boisterous, raucous reminder that although we were no longer children, nor were we adults. We hadn't yet outgrown dressing up as soldiers and enacting imaginary battles. It was an exciting enough game that I was even able to momentarily forget Raelan, the chancellor, and whatever their nefarious activities.

Today, Derrin selected me to be the lookout on top of the academic building. From that vantage point, I could see the entirety of the campus. I would see when Trick's fighters approached to attack and could relay their location to our defenders positioned below or shoot them myself. When the horn announcing the start of the game was blown, Cayleth and seven of her teammates approached the academic building at a run, laughing, whooping, and calling as they swung their weapons and challenged my team's defenders to stop them. I notched an arrow and waited, a smile on my face. I was a daughter of the Ice Crown, and there wasn't an archer at Windhall who could match me. Trick's team didn't stand a chance.

When the first attacker drew his sword, I loosed my arrow, easily striking him in the center of the chest. He stopped immediately and looked at the arrow now lying on the ground, disappointed to have been taken out of the game so quickly. Next time, he would think to look for archers before he charged heedlessly into battle. His teammates flooded past him, and I pulled another arrow, searching for my next target. Cayleth looked up, found my position, and angled away so that I couldn't engage her. One of our defenders missed a parry and took a jab to the stomach with a wooden sword, ending his participation in the game. I rewarded his "killer" with an arrow to the chest. He threw down his sword, pouting.

A girl with chin-length hair sticking out from under her helmet and a rapier in each hand backed one of my teammates against a wall, so I sent an arrow into her back. She looked around furiously for the source but was roughly pushed out of the way by Cayleth, who finished off my beleaguered teammate with a feigned cut to the throat. I fired an arrow at her, but she swatted it away easily with her shield, sticking her tongue out at me as she did so.

Unexpectedly, horns began sounding throughout the campus. We all froze, thinking it was part of the game, then started to look around curiously. It wasn't the horn signaling the end of War; it was something else. What was happening?

There was a clattering of hooves, unintelligible yelling, and the creak of wood as four wagons, accompanied by several armed horsemen and knights, rumbled through the green, headed in the direction of the infirmary. The man in the lead, who rode a tall chestnut horse with a wide blaze, was yelling, "Call for the healer!"

The group was accompanied by a strong smell of smoke, as from a campfire, that reached me even up on the roof. A familiar face and horse appeared among the newcomers, and I knew something terrible must have happened. My heart pounding, I raced down the stairs. As I burst out the door, I grabbed Cayleth by the arm, dragging her behind me as I ran for the infirmary.

Cayleth squeaked, "What is it?"

"It's Asher!"

"Who?"

"A knight. She knows about the Dark Magic. Come on!"

When we arrived at the infirmary, Asher was helping to carry an unconscious man on a stretcher inside. Half of his body was burned black, and I wasn't certain that he was still alive, given how bad his injuries looked. What wasn't black was a raw, bright pink. Three other people were being carried into the infirmary on stretchers, moaning in pain, while a fourth walked in cradling his arm. Cayleth and I pressed ourselves against the infirmary walls to stay out of the way. Lyse had been tending to the unconscious man, but she looked up and saw me immediately. Then she saw Asher, too, and her jaw twitched. I grabbed Asher's arm as she walked past and pulled her over to us.

"Aeryn!" Asher's eyebrows raised. There was soot shot through her hair, and her hands were stained with ash and blood. She coughed.

"What happened?" I hissed.

"Fire at the city guard's northwest quarter garrison." As soon as she said it, I recognized the dirty-green uniforms of the injured guardsmen beneath the soot. I shivered. The fire must have been enormous to have caused so much damage.

"Are you hurt?" I looked her over. I didn't see any obvious injuries.

"No, but all the records were burned. *All* of them." Her voice was tired, but her meaning was clear.

I drew in a sharp breath. "Mage fire?"

"The city's magic wards would have gone off if it was." She shook her head in bewilderment. Now was not the time to explain to her that the Dark mages had found a way to unbind the wards. I would tell her later. "But Aeryn, the garrison's walls were stone a foot thick, and now they're a pile of cinders. Normal fire can't burn hot enough to do that. Nor can the timing be coincidence. I talked to Commander Bronwen about Emira's kidnapping, but she hadn't yet sent anyone to investigate the disappearances. Now there's no evidence of them."

My stomach knotted. No! Without those records, we had nothing left with which to go to the Mages' Council but Yorel. Who would believe us now? How had Raelan and the chancellor found out about the records? Did they know Lyse and I had gone there? Had I inadvertently put Lyse in danger? From across the room, I could feel Lyse's eyes on us, watching. I didn't dare meet her gaze. I couldn't bear the thought that I might have drawn their attention to her.

They couldn't get away with it! Someone would know that the burning of the garrison was unnatural. There would be evidence. "Surely there will be an investigation?"

"The city's security forces are stretched thin," Asher replied, trying to rub some of the soot off her hands. Her shoulders were slumped. "The other three city guard garrisons will have to make up for the loss and won't have any extra people to spare to investigate. In all likelihood, it will be written up as an accidental fire and they'll simply build a new garrison."

The man who had been carried in unconscious began screaming as Lyse tried to wrap a bandage around his leg. I had never heard a man scream like that. Timo rushed over from where he had been treating an injured guardswoman, yelling, "Keep him still!"

"I'm trying," Lyse replied tensely. Timo's hands glowed white as he placed them around the man's head, and the man slumped into unconsciousness again. Lyse resumed bandaging his leg, but she couldn't stop herself from looking up every few seconds to watch me and Asher.

"Why were you there?" I asked Asher.

"Cloud and I heard the fire bells sounding and we responded." There was a slight quiver in her voice. I noticed some of her hair, as she ran her hand over her head, was singed. "I ran inside, trying to pull people out. The entire building was collapsing with people still inside. It was awful." She shook her head, closing her eyes.

"Did everyone...?" Cayleth asked.

Asher bowed her head and said nothing. I didn't know what kind of bravery it took for a person to run into a burning building, but I wasn't sure that I had it. My head was spinning. Could Raelan and the chancellor really have burned down a building and killed people? Were these more of their victims? Asher said, "I should go. Commander Bronwen will need to be told what happened. She'll want a full report."

"What will you tell her?"

Asher rubbed her temples. "A fire burned down the northwest quarter garrison. That's all we know for now. I can tell her my suspicions, but..." She pressed her lips together, shaking her head.

"Before you go," I said, touching her arm. "I think Chancellor Vandys is involved in this somehow. Last night, we saw her and the war mage instructor Raelan Bloodmoon use Windhall's Gate to go into the city. I know Raelan is a Dark mage, and...I think they've found a way to use magic in the city. I think they've dismantled the wards."

Asher winced and coughed. "That's very bad news indeed. The chancellor is well respected by the city's leaders. I'll tell the commander. She'll know what to do. In the meantime, be careful. The knights will likely have to help patrol the northwest quarter while the other city guard garrisons adjust their patrols, but if you find out anything else, send word to me in the city. I'll make sure the commander hears it."

Asher started to walk away. Before she was out the door, I was distracted by Timo shouting. "Stop shutting me out, Lyse! Now is not the time! Can't you see he's critical?" His voice was loud in the small infirmary.

"I'm not!" Lyse cried, her voice shrill with emotion.

Timo was bent over the unconscious man, trying to heal the burns on his side, but his white magic was flickering and misfiring. Sweat beaded on his brow as he struggled to control it. "Lyse, you're blocking the channel! Open it!"

"I'm not doing anything!"

Cayleth tugged on my sleeve. "Aeryn, we need to leave," she whispered. "We shouldn't be here."

I looked around and realized she was right. Apart from Timo and Lyse, the only other people in the infirmary were members of the city guard. Their uniforms were soot-covered, and their faces were haggard. Who knew how many friends they had lost? We ducked out of the building and began walking back to the training field. Cayleth asked, "Do you think Raelan and the chancellor burned down the city guard garrison themselves? Is that what they were plotting last night?"

Abruptly, I felt very tired. Too tired to feel any emotion at all, in fact. I hadn't slept in over a day, and I didn't have the energy anymore to do anything but put one foot in front of the other. "I don't know."

Her voice full of concern, Cayleth said, "Do you think they'll come after you, too? If they find out you were asking about the disappearances…"

I didn't have an answer. I had no idea what Raelan and the chancellor would or wouldn't do, but there was every likelihood that they'd just burned down a building full of people to protect their secret. We were in a race against time: We had to stop them before they stopped us. Under any other circumstances, I would have been terrified. I would have been shivering in fear, looking over my shoulder at the slightest sound. In that moment, however, all I wanted to do was sleep. I would process everything else later.

The next day, Raelan was sour in class. As he berated Faegan for some perceived failing, Cayleth poked me gently in the arm to get my attention. She whispered, "Do you think his bad mood is related to the attack on the garrison? Is he worried he'll be discovered?"

I shrugged. I'd been avoiding thinking about the attack as much as possible, mostly so as not to go out of my mind with fear. If Raelan *had* found out about my investigation of the disappearances and *had* been involved in the garrison's burning, I was in terrible danger. But then again, if he knew about me, I didn't think I'd be sitting in the training room right now. So I was safe for now. But for how long? Were any of us really safe with the chancellor and Raelan around?

"I wish we could we set a ward on the Gate to alert us if someone passes through at night, but there are no spellcasters here at Windhall right now," Cayleth said.

"I'll keep watch tonight, and Kaylara can watch tomorrow night. Hopefully they'll go to the city again soon. The sooner we have evidence, the sooner they'll be locked away."

Raelan finished yelling at Faegan and turned his attention to me and Cayleth. Snapping his fingers, he said, "Aeryn, come!"

I jumped to my feet and walked to him, my palms starting to sweat. What if I was wrong and he knew? He could easily make something look like an accident in our class. No one would be any the wiser. I took a deep breath. I couldn't let my imagination run wild. I had to pretend nothing was wrong, even if *everything* was wrong and Raelan was almost certainly a murderer.

"Raise your shield, Aeryn," he said. "We will test it again."

He motioned to Faegan, who began building a ball of pale purple fire in his hands. I willed my wall of shimmering blue magic to be impenetrable, then I nodded to Faegan, bracing myself. The blaze he cast in response was strong enough to push me back a few feet. I could feel it trying to melt my shield. I leaned forward, trying to physically hold against the blaze even though I knew it wasn't my muscles keeping the shield from shattering.

"Maintain the shield!" Raelan was screaming behind me. "Maintain it!"

I was fighting with every inch of my body, but I could see it starting to crumble at the edges. Almost imperceptibly, it was shrinking, dissolving under the force of Faegan's fire. And Faegan was only a mediocre war mage. Under the blazing fire of a stronger pyromancer, the shield would collapse in seconds. Desperate, I allowed my consciousness to drift back into my body, looking for some last, overlooked remnant of power that would allow the shield to hold. Unexpectedly, I found a burning thread of magic deep inside and followed it back to the source. It was a vast reserve of power I didn't know I had.

This was it! A way to maintain the shield! I could think about where the power came from later and why I'd never noticed it before, but right now, it was exactly what I needed. I tapped into the reserve immediately, allowing the power to run freely through my body. My shield exploded outward, driving Faegan back, and pulsed with renewed energy.

"Yes! Wonderful!" Raelan's excited voice called behind me.

Faegan's mage fire seemed weak and impotent now as it battered against my shield. I wanted to laugh. It would have taken far hotter and stronger mage fire than he'd ever produced to even dent my shield. My chest swelled with pride. After months of effort, I'd finally done it. I had found my shield. A minute later, Raelan called halt and I reabsorbed the magic back into me. Faegan wiped his forehead, his red hair matted with sweat. Surprise was in his eyes, and admiration, too.

Raelan said, "That is sufficient for today. You are dismissed. Aeryn, continue to practice shielding in your room, but that was excellent. You have finally created a credible shield."

Raelan floated out of the training room in that wraith-like way he had, and Cayleth wrapped me up in a bear hug so tight that for a moment I couldn't breathe. She squealed, "I knew you'd be able to do it!"

"I don't know where it came from," I admitted when she released me, "but I'm glad I found it!"

We started to walk to the door. I was lighter than air, overcome with relief. Cayleth asked, "Do you want to continue two-against-one attacks in combatives practice today? Trick says—"

Before she could finish telling me what Trick had said, Lyse burst in. Without saying a word, she grabbed me by the collar and hauled me out of the room and into the empty one next to it. She was so forceful that it was all I could do to keep my feet under me and not be dragged.

"What's wrong? What is it?" I gasped as I struggled to keep up.

Lyse didn't answer. He face was red, and she was breathing heavily as though she'd been running. Her hair was windblown.

Once we were in the second room, she kicked the door closed and released me. Then she put her hands on her hips and glared at me. Her eyes burned with simmering fury. "What did you *do*, Aeryn?" Her voice vibrated like a plucked string.

"What?" I gaped at her.

"What. Did. You. *Do?*" Lyse repeated, her eyes narrowed.

"I—I don't understand," I stammered.

"Aeryn, how could you?"

She wasn't making any sense. "Lyse!" I stepped to her and grasped her by the shoulders. "What are you talking about? What's the matter?"

Wordlessly, she lifted her hand and gathered magic to it. But it wasn't Timo's white healer's magic that danced in her palm. It was blue magic. My magic. I frowned, confused, and unconsciously took a step back. "I don't understand. Lyse, what's going on? How are you able to do that?"

Someone cleared their throat in the darkness behind us. Oh no. Raelan. Lyse spun around, and Raelan materialized out of the shadows, a floating white skull nestled in black clouds. So the room hadn't been empty after all. Raelan's black eyes peered at us curiously. He rasped, "It would seem that the bond Lyse shared with Timo has failed and re-formed with you, Aeryn. Interesting. I knew that shield wasn't yours, but even so, this is unexpected. Does Timo know about this?"

"No! And this needs to be fixed immediately. This is a mistake," Lyse said. Her eyes were wide with desperation.

Raelan shook his head. "The bond with Timo cannot be restored. Once a bond has been formed, it cannot be broken."

"But you said the bond with Timo was broken! So a bond *can* be broken! We just have to break the new bond and restore the old one. The bond isn't supposed to be with—"

Raelan held up a long, thin, professorial finger. "I said your previous bond *failed*. Two threads in a rope unwinding; not a break. Your thread has now bound with Aeryn. It is impossible to break." A smile curved Raelan's thin mouth like the silhouette of a bow. He was enjoying this.

Lyse, however, looked nauseated, and for a moment I worried she might vomit. Her face was whiter than I'd ever seen. Whiter even than when she healed the boy Colen in King's City using Timo's magic, or when she thought I might die.

Raelan purred, "Timo will survive. There are many healers in the kingdom. But a bonded war mage... That is unique."

"Please, put it back," Lyse begged in a small voice. Tears were streaming down her face. Her hands balled and unballed themselves, trying to grab back what had been lost. "It has to be with Timo."

"Oh, come now, this can't come as a surprise," Raelan chided, relishing Lyse's despair. "Bonds don't fail overnight. This has been coming for weeks, at least. Surely you felt it? A heat spark of sorts as the magical bond re-established itself? Or did you think that was...something else?"

Lyse began to visibly shake, and I blushed crimson.

"It will be an adjustment for you," Raelan continued. "You've spent so much time helping Timo to heal. Well. There's no use crying over spilled milk. You are welcome in my class anytime. In fact, I will ask the chancellor to have you reassigned to it. There will be new skills for you to learn."

Lyse covered her mouth with both her hands and ran out of the room, leaving me alone with a murderous Dark mage whose echoing laughter filled the room like frantic bats in a cave.

CHAPTER 6

"Even the smallest person can make the greatest impact."

— Everyn Stargazer, "The Five Pearls of Wisdom"

"No love worth having is easy."

— Rath proverb

MY FATHER HAD TAUGHT ME as a child that if I ever became lost in the woods, I should stay calm, think back to how I got there, take stock of what I had with me, and create a plan to find my way home. I was lost now, and home sometimes felt like nothing more than a memory; a distantly remembered dream of a time when life was simpler. It was easy to remember how I'd gotten here: traveling with Jale and Gamiel from Thamir after they'd kidnapped me and erased my memory, the long days with Sir Idras riding to Windhall, and everything that had happened since I had set foot on Windhall's campus. Taking an inventory of my life at Windhall was equally easy: I had several sets of clothes, mostly borrowed from Lyse, a rudimentary training in reading, writing, and history, and a handful of friends. But what sort of plan could I create from it all that would bring me home? Like a snowflake falling from the sky, I was at the mercy of the winds carrying me, and every gust seemed to send me farther and farther away from Thamir.

I tried to find Lyse after she ran out of the training room, but if she was in her room, she didn't answer when I knocked. Nor was she in the infirmary, the academic building, or the dining hall. I finally gave up and retreated to my room, where I lay on my bed staring at the ceiling. When I was still, I could feel the thin magical connection that now connected the two of us. The throbbing, subtle thread couldn't tell me where Lyse was, but like the way a fisherman can feel when a fish is on the other end of his fishing line, our new magical bond told me that Lyse was out there somewhere. And like a fish, she didn't want to be hooked. This was a disaster.

How had this happened? Should I have known sooner? Thinking back, things that had seemed odd—like the flash of heat whenever we touched—now made sense, but who would have ever guessed it was a reforming of the magical bond? Who, other than Raelan, would have known that such a thing was even possible? I didn't want this new bond. I was already asking Lyse to give up so much, to choose me over Timo. I would never want her to have to give up healing, too. I had to talk to her, to let her know that this wasn't what I wanted at all.

The next day passed in a haze. I stared out the window with unseeing eyes during Father Merek's lecture and doodled aimlessly in Professor Kalmath's class. At lunch, I pushed my food around my plate listlessly and pretended to listen while Pavo and Kaylara argued some finer point of astrology. Until I could talk to Lyse, it would be impossible to concentrate on anything. Mercifully, Raelan didn't show up to class, so Cayleth and I took the opportunity to walk Windhall's perimeter. Between its orchards, outbuildings, and surrounding fields, the Windhall lands were quite extensive. We walked in silence for some time, each lost in our own thoughts.

"Are you planning on telling me what happened yesterday with Lyse?" Cayleth asked finally.

I winced. If we could find a way to reverse the new bond, no one needed to know what had happened. Although Raelan had said it was impossible to break, surely he wasn't Ilirya's expert on these types of bond. He was only a war mage, after all. I tried to look casual and unconcerned. "There was an accident. Lyse was upset."

"Mmhmm?" Cayleth responded, waiting for further information.

"My shield... The magic came from Lyse." I purposely provided as little detail as possible, hoping Cayleth wouldn't probe.

Her forehead wrinkled. "How?"

"Like I said, it was an accident. I felt magic that I thought was mine and I used it. Only, it turns out it was Lyse's magic."

"How is that possible?"

"I don't exactly know." I shrugged, looking away. It wasn't a total a lie. I really didn't know why Lyse's bond with Timo had failed and why it had re-formed with me.

"Huh," Cayleth said with a shake of her head. "But—"

"I don't want to talk about it," I interrupted. If Cayleth started to ask questions, I would have to admit what I knew. I wasn't good enough at lying to deflect her.

Cayleth let the matter drop and we continued on in silence again. As we rounded the last turn on our way back to the main part of campus, my heart sank. There, waiting on a small hill, the wind swirling his gray hair, stood Timo. Even from a distance, I could see his bright-blue eyes glaring at me. There was no question: He knew about the bond with Lyse breaking. Without meaning to speak aloud, I breathed, "Oh no." I didn't want to talk to him. Not when I hadn't figured out how to put everything right yet.

Cayleth said, "If you don't want to talk to him, we can say we have to get back to class, that Raelan will be waiting for us."

Cayleth was a loyal friend. It would be better if I talked to Lyse first. Together we could figure out what to do. We could find a way to explain to him what had happened. But looking at Timo's face, I didn't think he would accept Cayleth's excuse, and I didn't want him to cause a scene in front of her. "It will be fine." I smiled to reassure her. "You should get back. I don't want you to be late for combatives."

Cayleth looked uncertain but accepted my decision. She stayed with me until we reached Timo, then gracefully dismissed herself, looking over her shoulder several times as she walked away.

Timo paid her no attention, staring only at me the whole time. His face looked sour, as though he'd taken a sip of milk that had gone bad. His eyes were full of disgust. "Do you have any idea what you've done?" he hissed at me once Cayleth was out of earshot.

My stomach twisted itself in an unhappy knot. I held my hands up, trying to placate him. "It was an accident, Timo! We'll find a way to repair the bond." My heart was starting to beat faster. Timo was so angry. I'd never seen him like this before.

"An accident." Timo's words dripped with acid. "It will be an *accident* when hundreds die of a plague ravaging unchecked. It will be an *accident* when people who could have been healed won't be and die. Did you even think of that? Did you think of those people? The bond can't be re-formed! It's over, Aeryn."

"I didn't do anything!" Timo was wrong. I hadn't set out to break his bond with Lyse. I never would have wanted to do that. I wanted Lyse to love me, but not to lose her ability to heal. "It *was* an accident, I swear. I'm sorry. I'm so sorry. I'll fix it."

Like a bellows whose air has rushed out, he seemed to close in on himself and deflate. His eyes filled with sadness and hurt. "I'm a good man. My life has been dedicated to helping others. It's all I've ever wanted."

I nodded. "You're an honorable man, Timo. Everyone knows that. The bond… I don't know what happened. I was just as surprised as you are. I didn't mean for it to happen. No one did."

"She fell in love with you, didn't she? That's why the bond failed." Timo's voice was flat. Defeated. His shoulders slumped. He wouldn't look at me.

My fingers twitched and my heart began to pound so strongly it made me weak. What did he know? I tried to think of a way to deflect his question. I couldn't talk to him about this, too. It was too intimate, too personal. "I don't know how bonds work."

"She asked to break our engagement."

I blinked, unconsciously taking a step backward. "What? I didn't know. Why—"

"She told me about you. So now it's truly over. There is nothing left between us. Everything is ruined."

I froze. My breath caught in my lungs. This changed everything. While part of me thrilled with the knowledge that Lyse had chosen me, another wrestled with asphyxiating guilt. As jealous as I had been of Timo and as careless as I'd been of his feelings when I pressed Lyse on hers, I hadn't actually wanted him to be hurt. He really was a good man, after all. I hated that any happiness I felt came at his expense and that this was how he'd found out about the growing relationship between Lyse and me. I shivered miserably. None of this was how I'd wanted it. When had I become a tornado, tearing apart everything around me?

Timo sighed and ran his hand through his thick silver hair. "I won't deny that I'm disappointed and angry, but I see that what's done is done. Only, remember this: As your bondmate, Lyse will have to follow you onto the battlefield. The life she would have had with me was one of healing and public service. With you, it is war and death. I hope you keep in mind what you have cost her already and the price she will pay in the future. I hope it is worth it. For both of you."

Without saying anything more or awaiting a response, he turned and walked away. The wind had picked up, and now it tore at his shirt and thin coat, which flapped around him like the blue wings of a bird. I let out the breath I'd been holding. My legs were weak and unsteady. Things could have gone far worse. I had half expected him to lash out at me in his grief and anger, but he hadn't.

I crossed my arms and began to march the long way around the campus. I needed to find Lyse immediately. There was so much to discuss. I searched high and low for her, but she was nowhere to be found. When I stopped by her room, some of her clothing appeared to be missing. Lyse had disappeared.

No one knew where Lyse had gone, and I could hardly ask Timo, so I stewed the rest of the day in my thoughts. Had she left Windhall and returned to her family in Rath? Where else could she have gone? How long would she be away? I wanted to beat my fists against the wall of my room in frustration. Our new bond told me she was alive, but it couldn't tell me anything else.

In the meantime, I had Raelan and the chancellor to worry about, too. Although I hadn't seen Chancellor Vandys since we'd caught her Gating into King's City, I still had to face Raelan several times a week in class. Knowing that he had likely burned people to death and could be sneaking into the city to kidnap and murder people chilled me to the bone. How was I supposed to pretend everything was fine and normal around him when I knew his secret? Especially when he could find out at any time that I had been the one at the city guard garrison investigating the kidnappings. I was walking a tightrope, and the fall... I couldn't bear to think about it. I had to avoid looking down at all costs.

Two days later, a surprise awaited us in Raelan's class. Raelan met us outside the training room accompanied by two strangers. The woman wore light scale armor that had been polished to a gleaming shine. Her blonde hair reached almost to her waist and framed her dark, almond-shaped eyes. The man, who was tall and muscular, wore a matching set of armor and a hooded brown cloak that revealed only his dark-skinned face. Both were armed with long, wide swords that gleamed scabbard-less at their sides. Neither of them looked particularly friendly.

"Halver and Balrak are here today to help in our sparring session," Raelan announced. "They are former students of Windhall. As they are temporarily on leave from the army, I asked them to come so that you may spar against other war mage types. Aeryn, you will fight Halver. Faegan and Cayleth, you will fight Balrak."

Balrak's eyes were flat and unreadable. Halver looked bored. I wondered when they had been students at Windhall. Balrak was older than Halver, and I guessed that he was somewhere between thirty-five and forty-five years old while she was around twenty-five. This precluded Raelan, who was likely only forty himself, from having been the teacher for either. How did he know them? Did he know all Ilirya's war mages? What did they think of him and his black eyes?

We marched as a group to the training field, which was unoccupied. I wondered what Halver's affinity might be. Was she an illusionist like Cayleth? A warg like Raelan? I shuddered. I couldn't imagine a time when warging wouldn't make my skin crawl. I hoped she wasn't a warg.

Raelan took us to the center of the field and set us up as two simultaneous contests. He warned, "As we are not in a training room, there is nothing to contain stray magic. Aeryn and Faegan, control your fire."

We nodded. It wouldn't do to accidentally set the grass, the armory, or anything else on fire. At Raelan's command, Halver and I both created our shields. I was careful to use only my magic and to pull nothing from Lyse, wherever she was. I called my magic to my hands and waited, watching to see what Halver would do. When no magic collected around her, I began to worry anew that she was a warg. Could my mental shield keep her out if she was weaker than Raelan?

Out of the corner of my eye, I noticed that Balrak had created a shimmering shield of green and...a massive stone giant. It was so unexpected that I turned my head to gape. The giant was a humanoid *thing* ten feet tall, made of what looked like boulders. It had two arms, two legs, and a large rock where a head would otherwise have been. As tall and broad as Balrak was, the stone giant made him look like a child.

"An illusion!" Faegan said to Cayleth.

"No" Cayleth replied, shaking her head and backing up. "It's a klant."

My mind flashed back to Raelan's brief lesson on klants: "Klants have no consciousness; they are not living things. They are the virtually indestructible creations of their mages, controlled by them like puppets. The only way to stop a klant is to stop its mage creator." But this klant was massive. How would Faegan and Cayleth get to Balrak through it?

Raelan called a start to the fighting, and then all my attention was focused on Halver. I immediately began to launch a fusillade of fiery bolts against her, trying to smash through her shield while I advanced upon her. She fell back a step as her shield absorbed the blows. Her mouth started moving, and I realized immediately that her affinity was spellcasting. As soon as she finished speaking, my shield turned brittle and crumbled around me, leaving me completely exposed. She uttered a new spell, and a long, crackling whip appeared in her left hand that glowed a bright yellow. Halver flicked this whip at me, and I barely ducked it as it sailed past my shoulder. The air sizzled around me.

I turned my attention to rebuilding my shield. I finished it as the whip struck again, hissing against the new shield. I launched a searing fireball at Halver in response. Halver's lips moved, and my shield dissolved a second time. Without a moment's hesitation, her whip flicked out, but now it was a rope that looped over my head and fell to my ankles, where it tightened instantly. Halver yanked the rope hard, and I toppled over. She began to pull me toward her, dragging me in the grass. I drew my rapier and hacked at the magic rope with it, trying to free myself, but to no effect.

I switched to trying to burn the rope away using my magic instead and was able to loosen it just enough to kick my legs free and escape. I ran back several paces to regain distance from Halver. My heart was racing, and I was beginning to wheeze when I breathed. This was a harder fight than I'd ever had with Cayleth or Faegan. How could I keep my shield intact when Halver kept dissolving it?

My arms prickled from the magic I was drawing to create my shield and throw as fire. I was burning through my magic quickly. If I couldn't break her shield soon, I would become drained and totally defenseless. Halver started mouthing the words to a new spell, and all of a sudden I found myself as frozen as a stone statue, unable to move even a finger. I struggled as hard as I could, but it was useless. Halver allowed her whip to dissolve and walked up to me, so confident of the strength of her spell that she didn't even draw her sword. "This," she said in a low, cold voice into my ear, "is how mages die in battle."

She ran her finger along my throat, imitating the cut of a blade, and I shivered. Nausea clawed its way up my throat. Halver reminded me so much of Gamiel: They had the same emotionless approach to killing, the same utter absence of compassion. Had they been born that way, or had they become it? Was this what war did to people? Halver released the spell, and I was free again. The other fight had finished, too, although I didn't know who had won. I could see Balrak talking to Cayleth and Faegan, gesturing with his hands as though teaching them something.

Raelan approached me from where he had been watching both fights. "A talented spellcaster can defeat almost any other mage type," he said. "Halver was gentle with you today. Learn from the experience."

I wasn't sure how. If I couldn't break her shield, what hope did I have? For every bolt I threw, she had two spells at the ready. Raelan led me over to where the others were standing, and for the rest of the class, Balrak demonstrated what his klant could do. Mage fire and weapons were useless against it. Even Halver was unable to topple it with her magical rope. I had a vision of the klant in battle, smashing through the enemy army like an unstoppable wave. I imagined the terror of the soldiers seeing the living rock coming toward them, crushing bone and armor alike with its heavy arms and legs, and the vision made me shudder.

Later, when I asked Cayleth what had happened during her fight against the klant, however, she laughed. "Faegan spent all his time trying to burn down the hunk of rock chasing him all over the training field. I hid my location with an illusion, then walked right up behind Balrak. Actually, I'm surprised you didn't hear Faegan's scream when the klant picked him up." She giggled. "Everyone has a weakness, Aeryn. The more you worry about a big stone monster, the more you forget that a klant mage can only fight what he can see."

Cayleth's cleverness never failed to surprise me. I wondered how she would have fought Halver. Did Halver know spells to dispel illusions, too?

It seemed likely. According to Raelan, a spellcaster was only as good as the spells they had learned. I guessed that Halver knew hundreds or thousands of spells. It was how she'd survived so long as a war mage at the southern front.

While Cayleth was energized by the fight against Balrak, Faegan was sour. He hated to lose, and he particularly hated that it was Cayleth who figured out how to defeat the klant mage. To make him feel better, I said, "Be glad you didn't fight Halver! I didn't stand a chance against her!"

Faegan turned his chin up. "The Southerner mages are mostly spellcasters," he sneered. "Maybe she has Southerner blood."

"Don't be ridiculous! Ilirya has plenty of its own spellcasters!" Cayleth said. "What a thing to say."

"It was a spellcaster who helped the assassins kill my family," Faegan said coldly. "They're all mercenaries. All of them."

I quickly did the math. Eight years ago, Halver would probably have still been a student at Windhall. Surely Faegan didn't suspect her of being involved. His face was closed and unreadable.

Cayleth said, "It's wrong to vilify an entire class of mages! One bad mage doesn't mean they're all bad."

"Oh? Haven't I heard you suggest that wargs are all, by nature, evil?" Faegan challenged.

Cayleth squirmed. Faegan had a point. Cayleth had said on more than one occasion that honest and good people didn't go meddling in the minds of others, and we had all agreed with her. It was hard to imagine a decent and positive use for warging and all too easy to imagine the dark and nefarious uses. It didn't help that Cayleth and I both knew Raelan was a murdering Dark mage. And yet if all wargs were evil, then what did that say about the correlation between the personalities of mages and their affinities? We had been told that there was no relationship, but was that wrong? If so, what trait did Faegan and I share that led us to be pyromancers?

Looking at Faegan, I saw only his brooding anger and haughty sense of superiority. He and I were nothing alike. Then again, how might he have turned out differently if his entire family hadn't been killed in one horrible night, leaving him all alone to become the Baron of Ardeth? I tried to imagine a gentler, nicer Faegan, but failed.

"Who is *that*?" Faegan exclaimed, breaking my reverie.

I followed his gaze. Standing on the hill above the training field was a hulking giant, accompanied by a smaller, female companion. The man was so large he eclipsed the sun behind him, casting his face in shadow, but I would know him anywhere. "Sir Idras!" I squealed and took off running up the hill.

It was a short run, and soon I could make out the smile on Sir Idras's face stretching from ear to ear. His long gray beard tickled my face where I buried it against his cuirass. In his full armor, I could barely get my arms around his sides to hug him. He thumped me on the back affectionately as I clung to him.

"Hiya, lassie," he said when I let go. "Aren't you a sight for these old eyes!"

"Sir Idras, I'm so happy to see you!" I beamed, overjoyed to see him. I hadn't realized how much I had missed him until that moment.

"Idras arrived back in King's City yesterday. I knew you'd want to see him," Asher said, grinning.

"I've missed you, lass. Look at you, a right mage here at Windhall!" Sir Idras looked around, taking in the campus. Licking his lips, he said, "My lips are a bit parched. Might we find a drink somewhere and you can tell me everything I've missed?"

I waved good-bye to Cayleth and Faegan, who had stood a respectful distance away while I greeted my friends and led the two knights to the dining hall. I directed them to a table in a corner while I scrounged up a few mugs of ale. Trick would forgive me if I missed combatives practice. This was more important. Sir Idras drank his mug in one swig, then downed the one I had brought for Asher, too. He smacked his lips and wiped his mouth with the back of his hand. "Much better! Now tell me everything I've missed. What's Windhall like? Is it true there are mages who can fly? Spare no details."

As quickly as I could, I told him everything that had happened since he'd dropped me at Windhall, leaving out only the parts I wasn't ready to tell him yet, which in this case was my new bond with Lyse. I didn't feel comfortable sharing something that was so unsettled and raw. I also didn't mention my kidnapping and the discovery that my family was still alive. We would need a quiet place away from Windhall to plan my return to Thamir, some place where we wouldn't be overheard.

When I finished, Sir Idras beamed and patted me on the shoulder. "It sounds like you've made a fine go of it here, as I knew you would. I'm proud of you." He winked. "Although you know you've always got a place with me, if you want it. I can think of a few ways to make use of a good mage who's learned to hold a sword."

I laughed. If our two weeks together had been any indication, traveling with Sir Idras full-time would be one misadventure after another. Which wasn't altogether a bad thing. It just wasn't for me. The knight shared in my laughter, then leaned forward and dropped his voice. "Now, Asher tells me you've got a mage problem on your hands."

Looking around first to make sure none of the handful of other students in the dining hall were close enough to overhear, I gave him a rundown of everything that I had discovered about the Dark mages, ending with the burning of the city-guard garrison. When I finished, Sir Idras leaned back in his chair, arms folded and a frown on his face. "It's a bad business, this. I don't like you here so close to these villains, Aeryn. It's not safe."

I shrugged. "I don't have a choice. I can't leave Windhall."

"Do you have any idea how many mages might be using Dark Magic in addition to Professor Raelan and Chancellor Vandys?" Asher asked.

I shook my head. "Raelan hasn't gone back into the city yet, so Kaylara hasn't been able to eavesdrop. What did Commander Bronwen say when you told her about the garrison burning?"

"I haven't spoken to her yet. She left King's City for the front on the day it burned. She hasn't been back since."

My heart sank. We were the only ones who knew. The Knight Commander hadn't been warned, which meant the Mages' Council didn't know either, nor the Lady Marshal. Sir Idras tapped his finger against his mug. "Asher and I could arrest the scoundrels for unlawful use of magic in the city. A few nights in a dungeon are enough to get anyone talking. We could round up the lot of them and have done with it."

I shook my head. "You can't. Even if the chancellor wasn't the head of Windhall University and a member of the Mages' Council, Raelan is a warg. You wouldn't make it past Windhall's gate before he'd have you untying them yourself. And if you did make it back to the city, he'd warg their way out of wherever you took them." I shuddered. "Having Raelan in your mind and controlling your body is…beyond awful. I don't ever want you to experience it. Nor do I want them to know we're on to them before we're able to stop them for good."

"Then what's your plan, lass?" Sir Idras asked.

"We don't have a choice; we have to keep waiting and watching. Raelan and the chancellor will go back into the city eventually, and then we'll find out what they're up to. We need evidence that they can't refute."

"There may be no alternative, but that doesn't mean I like it," Sir Idras said. "It's very dangerous, for you and the city, too."

"Idras and I will do what we can to keep an eye out for Dark mages, but every day there are fewer and fewer knights and soldiers in the city," Asher said. She looked at Sir Idras, then continued, "There is one thing I haven't mentioned yet. It has to do with Northmen. I think I've seen some in the city."

I boggled at her. "What? But they can't be. The ambassador is the only Northman authorized to be in Ilirya. How—"

"I don't know anything more. A few times lately I've been riding my rounds in the city and caught sight of yellow eyes staring at me. A man walking alone here, a woman in the crowd there. They always turn away quickly, but…I don't think I'm wrong. Maybe they're spies. I don't know."

"Dark mages and Northmen," Sir Idras muttered, shaking his shaggy head. "This city is falling apart."

At that moment, I noticed Lyse making her way through the dining hall, coming toward us. The world and all the things in it stood still, even time itself. Lyse was back. I forgot to breathe. It took everything I had not to jump out of my chair and run to her. To hold her and refuse to let go.

When she reached our table, she nodded uncomfortably at the two knights in greeting. Her face was haggard, its usual luminescence gone. Even so, she was still beautiful to me. She rubbed her hands together anxiously and wouldn't meet my eyes. "I'm sorry to interrupt," she said. "Aeryn, may I speak to you?"

CHAPTER 7

*"Conspiracies only work when the conspirators know they
must all swim together or else they will sink together."*

- Speaker unknown

*"Spellcasting's reputation as an affinity has been tarnished
by high profile instances of its misuse."*

- A Kingdom and its People, 4th edition

THERE WAS NO QUESTION: WHATEVER Lyse wanted, I would give it.
Whatever the cost, whatever the effort, anything she asked—I would do.
I nodded at once and rose, so distracted I almost forgot my two knight
companions. Remembering them at the last moment, I said, "Please excuse
me. Sir Idras, it was wonderful to see you. I'll come find you soon at the
Boar's Tusk Tavern as soon as I can. We can discuss...everything. Asher,
please let me know if you find out anything else."

I joined Lyse, and we left the two knights to find their way off the
campus unescorted. Lyse marched out of the dining hall silently, her back
straight and stiff. My heart was beating harder than it ever had before as I
walked beside her. She had returned, but what now? She had broken her
engagement with Timo, but where did that leave us? And where had she
gone the last few days? Why hadn't she told me she was leaving?

She led me back to her room, then positioned herself in front of the
window, out of which she gazed with dull and listless eyes. Uncertain what
to do, I sat on her bed, plucking anxiously at its beautiful blue blanket. The
same blue as my magic.

"Timo is gone." Lyse's voice was so flat and tired that it was emotionless.

I bit my lip. Was this about him? "I know. I'm sorry." I meant it. I knew that losing Timo and what he represented must have been awful for her. Despite her best efforts, everything had come crashing down around her head at the same time. She hadn't had time to properly manage any of it.

Lyse continued in the same voice, "He's returned to Parvel, to his family. He has a younger sister there. She'll be overjoyed to see him. She used to say I shouldn't keep her brother from her, so far away in King's City. She made me promise to return him to her. I wasn't supposed to keep that promise."

She raised her hand and chewed on a fingernail. She murmured more to herself than to me, "Timo loves his sister, but he never loved his home in Parvel like he loved King's City."

"Then surely he won't be away from the city for long," I said, trying to be optimistic.

Lyse closed her eyes. "Before he left, he said there's nothing for him here. He will not return."

I could think of nothing to say to that. Given what Timo had told me, I wasn't altogether surprised. Nor could I fault him. He had lost more than anyone when the bond re-formed.

Lyse continued to stare out the window as though looking for words, then she turned her head to look at me. "We had such grand dreams, Timo and I. We were going to heal the sick, and through that bring peace and healing to our war-torn kingdom. No longer would babies die mere days out of the womb. No longer would pestilence run unchecked through cities. With our bond, we could do so much good."

Her lips twitched at the edges, wanting to smile. "His hair was light brown when I met him, can you believe it? He was so vain about his hair that it drove him crazy when it turned gray. But he looked so handsome, so dignified, when it did. It suited him."

Pain flashed across her face, the kind that has no easy salve. She stopped talking abruptly and looked away. "I ruined everything for him and now he's gone, never to return to King's City. Everything I touch turns to ash."

"It's not your fault." I rushed to defend her, even if only from herself. "Things—"

"But it is," Lyse interrupted, turning her entire body to face me. Her eyes were deep and full of sorrow and guilt. "It's my fault, all of it." I shook my head and stood, taking a step toward her without thinking. She held her hand out, keeping me back. "I've ruined your life, too, Aeryn."

"That's ridiculous! Of course you haven't!"

"Yes, I have!" she insisted. "You're not supposed to be here. You're from the Ice Crown. The King's Scryer would never have looked for a mage there; would never have seen you. You're not a Great Mage, and scrying has limits. Finding you was more than a needle in a haystack. You should be with your family, not here at Windhall!"

Her voice was rising as she became more agitated. I held my hands out, trying to calm her. "How could any of that possibly be your fault, Lyse?"

"It is! Everything that's happened to you, it's because of me! It's because I Called you, Aeryn." Lyse's voice was hoarse with emotion, and she was starting to tremble.

I shook my head. "You called me? I don't understand. What are you talking about?"

"It's a spell."

"Okay, what does it do?"

Lyse began to pace, striding restlessly across her small room from one end to the other. "It was supposed to be a silly game, nothing more. When my sister and I were children, we found a book of spells in the castle library and tried one. It was a Calling spell, exactly the sort of spell that two foolish young girls would choose. It shouldn't have worked. It wasn't even intended to work, really. We were *pretending* to be mages. We didn't even know if we had magic."

She glanced at me, then looked away. As she spoke, it was as if she was telling a story to herself rather than to me. "There was no reason for the spell to have worked. Even if my affinity had manifested impossibly early *and* been for spellcasting, my family's magic was already bound. And yet somehow the spell *did* work. I Called you."

I narrowed my eyes, trying to understand. So far, Lyse wasn't making any sense. From what I understood, once upon a time, she and her sister had pretended to cast a spell that she for some reason now believed, against all odds, had worked. That alone was unlikely enough, but what did that have to do with me? "Okay, what does a Calling spell do?"

Lyse wouldn't meet my eyes. Instead of answering, she said, "I forgot all about that day. Why would I remember it? I must have been to the library a thousand times and read half the books in it. What made that day different from any other? Nothing. Later, I was sent to Windhall and met Timo. It was a perfect match; everyone said so. And I did love him. We were building a future together.

"But then you came, Aeryn, and everything was turned upside down. All the sudden I didn't want only Timo. I couldn't stop thinking about you. And…and the bond with Timo broke. Everything broke." She stopped pacing and hung her head.

My heart ached for her, but she still wasn't making sense. I couldn't help ease the pain if I didn't understand its source. "Lyse, what is this spell?"

"Calling is a type of finding spell, only you're finding another person, not a thing." She loosed an unexpected bark of laugher filled with so much bitterness I was taken aback. The sound was choked with pain and regret. "A ten-year-old child Called for love and eight years later, you came. Aeryn, you're here because the magic compelled you: It took you out of the Ice Crown and brought you to Windhall because *I* was here. The Call would have carried you over mountains and seas if it had to. It's because of *me* you were kidnapped from Thamir. Everything you've gone through, all the pain, has been because of me."

I let out an involuntary guffaw of disbelief and crossed my arms. "You think I'm here because of a spell you cast as a child? Lyse—"

"Think about it, Aeryn: Why else would my magic have bonded with yours? Why else would the bond with Timo have failed?"

I threw up my hands. "Who knows how bonds work? Maybe it's not that unusual. You, yourself, said there's no way you could have cast that spell."

"Spellcasters are common in the House Pan. Nagyar was a spellcaster, one of the kingdom's best. Had my magic not been bound, my affinity probably would have been spellcasting, too."

"But it *was* bound," I pointed out, "and you were years away from your magic manifesting anyway. It's simply not possible, Lyse. You didn't Call me. You're blaming yourself for nothing."

I sat back down on the bed. Lyse's face looked wan, and I realized that she probably hadn't slept in days. The lack of sleep must be taking its toll. When she'd had some rest, she would realize that this whole idea was crazy and impossible. Trying to divert the subject a little, I asked, "Why did you think of the spell now, after all these years?"

"I went home after...after Timo. I needed to think. And be alone. I found the book again in the library and remembered what I'd done. Until that moment, I didn't remember it at all. It sounds impossible, but I'm not wrong, Aeryn."

She picked up a traveling bag from where she'd set it at the foot of the bed and reached inside. When she withdrew her hand, she held a sheaf of parchment papers, browned with age, which she thrust into my hands. She said, "Before I came to Windhall, I used to have vivid dreams. I took to drawing what I saw in them the next morning. I found these in my room at home. I haven't looked at them in years. Do you know these people, Aeryn?"

I looked down and my breath caught in my throat. Lyse was an excellent artist. With a fine, delicate hand, she'd captured my father's face perfectly: the heavy black brows, the chipped left front tooth, his piercing eyes, and his thick nose. Next was my mother, her long hair sweeping over her shoulders with wild abandon. In the drawing, I could barely make out the fur collar of her coat. She seemed to be looking into the distance, squinting to see something that the artist could not.

"It's my parents!"

Lyse nodded grimly. Maybe because I had my mother's hair and my father's eyes, she had guessed. I shook my head slowly, trying to force these new pieces of information together in a way that I could understand, but it was too hard. All of it seemed impossible. Lyse sat down next to me and hugged herself, wrapping her light brown arms around her knees, which she had drawn to her chest.

"*I'm* the reason you were stolen from your family and brought here to be trained as a war mage. *I'm* the reason you can't go back. And *I'm* the reason the bond with Timo failed. I've ruined everything."

I staggered to my feet, running my hands over the top of my head. "I...I need to think about this. This is a lot to take in."

Lyse nodded, staring at the floor. All the life had gone out of her. I lurched out the door, everything reeling around me. What did this all mean?

An impossible spell cast by a magic-less girl. Could Lyse have really Called me eight years ago, or was it all a coincidence? Until Lyse had shown me the drawings, I was sure she was wrong. Now I didn't know what to believe. What did it mean anyway, to Call someone? How could she Call someone she'd never met and wouldn't meet for another eight years?

I sat down on the grassy slope by the training field. The combatives class I'd skipped was still ongoing. I could see Cayleth's stocky, armored form as she exchanged mace blows with a short, thin boy. Cayleth had chosen to be here, but if Lyse was right, then I was doubly a prisoner: physically carried to Windhall by Gamiel and Jale and compelled to come by Lyse's Calling spell. I pondered the implication. Was anything I did my own choice, or was it all the spell? Did I have no choice in anything at all that had happened to me after the age of eight?

I tried to wrap my mind around the idea that a spell had been behind my kidnapping from Thamir. How could magic be so powerful that it manipulated dozens of other people, moving them like pieces in a game to the exact spots necessary? Was Lyse right that if not for the spell, I'd still be in Thamir? I'd now been away from home for so long that it was hard to imagine an alternative history in which I'd never left. Would I have gone to Namoreth, as my parents had originally planned? How would my life have been different?

For one thing, I would never have met Lyse. But now even my feelings for her were in question. Did I really have them, or was everything the effect of magic almost a decade old? There were too many questions and not enough answers. I needed to know more about the spell itself. I needed Lyse to explain it exactly to me. Then I could decide what to do.

My stomach grumbled. At the least, it would help to think on a full stomach. As I sat alone in the dining hall, however, trying to force down mouthfuls of perch, the need for answers nagged incessantly at me. So long as this hung over my head, I wouldn't be able to think about anything else. We needed to resolve this. Today. Giving up, I pushed my plate away and made my way back to Lyse's room, hoping she was still there.

I found Lyse staring empty-eyed out the window. She tried to smile when I entered her room, but like a spark that won't catch, she couldn't. All the light had gone out of her eyes, leaving them as dull and listless as when she'd told me about Timo leaving. I closed the door but stayed near it, crossing my arms and leaning against the wall. "Tell me exactly what the Calling spell did," I said.

Lyse grimaced. She was shrunk into herself, a shadow of who she normally was. She avoided my eyes, staring at the ground instead. She murmured, "Two halves, made whole. That's the spell. I Called...my other half."

I shook my head and rubbed my temples. "What does that *mean*, Lyse? Does that mean I'm under the spell? Is everything I feel magic?"

"No!" Lyse lurched forward, coming as close to me as she dared. Her eyes, showing signs of life again, were tentative, concerned, pleading. "All the spell did was bring you to me. It didn't change how you feel. Those feelings are all yours...*ours*. None of that is magic, Aeryn. They're real."

Could I trust her? Could I trust anything? Lyse was so close that I could almost feel her quick, nervous breaths. She said in a tiny voice, "I've never been so scared in my life. I don't know what I'm doing anymore. Everything that I was *supposed* to do, the future I was *supposed* to have is gone. I can't bear to lose you, too."

Her words—small, sad, and desperate—reached through the whirlwind of my own emotions and brought me back to what was important. Whatever ten-year old Lyse had done, it wasn't her fault. Eighteen-year old Lyse shouldn't have to suffer for it. I reached out and traced a lone finger over the back of her hand. This was Lyse. The same Lyse I met my first day at Windhall. My lodestar. In the midst of her fear and sadness, she was offering me the last thing she had to give: herself. She would no more want to hurt me than I would her. I closed my hand around hers, my decision made. "You won't lose me."

Her eyes, when they met mine, were wet with unshed tears. She murmured, "You're not mad?"

I shook my head. She tried to smile, a small wave of relief washing away some of the tension in her body. I reached out and gently caressed her cheek from her ear to her chin. She brought her hands up and caught my hand, then kissed my palm. The feeling of her lips on my skin made my heart race. I inched closer to her, then tentatively leaned in, catching her lips with mine. She kissed back, then with increased urgency. Her fingers wrapped behind my ears, tangling in my hair. She tasted like Rath's desert plains and warm cinnamon.

The magical bond between us hummed with a pulsing energy. I anchored my hands on Lyse's hips and smiled into her kiss, enjoying the giddiness welling up in me. Lyse stepped back shyly after a moment, pushing her hair back behind her ears, and there was a glowing light in her eyes that hadn't been in them for days. She smiled, a genuine expression that crinkled the corners of her eyes.

"Not everything about the Calling spell is a bad thing," I said. "It brought me to you."

"Promise me—" she started to say.

I never found out what promise she wanted to extract from me, however, because at that moment someone started pounding on her door, beating against the wood so forcefully that the door all but jumped on its hinges. Lyse automatically ducked past me to open the door. This kind of knock normally portended a hurt student. Even though Lyse was no longer bonded to Timo, she was still trained as a regular healer, capable of setting bones and stitching wounds. With Timo gone and his replacement not yet arrived, she was the only healer on campus, which meant that if someone was hurt, she would have to tend to them.

It wasn't a messenger or a student standing there, however, but Cayleth, her hand raised to knock again. "Is Aeryn here?" She asked, looking past Lyse into the room. "I've been searching all over for her."

"What's wrong?" I stepped to Lyse's side so that Cayleth could see me.

"It's Raelan. He's gone through the Gate again."

"With the chancellor?"

Cayleth nodded.

"But it's barely evening! Why now?"

"I don't know, but he was in a hurry. I'd guess there was some kind of an emergency. It had to be something serious enough for him to risk being caught. Come on, Kaylara is listening now."

I looked at Lyse. There was still so much more to be said between us. We needed more time together. Even though this might be our chance to collect the evidence that we needed to get the chancellor and Raelan locked away, I wanted to stay in Lyse's room, talking. Let someone else stop the Dark mages. Lyse's hand snaked into mine and she squeezed it. "Let's go," she said.

If Cayleth noticed Lyse's hand in mine as we raced down the hall to Kaylara's room, she didn't say anything. We burst in without knocking and found Kaylara sitting cross-legged on the bed, Pavo in the same position in front of her watching with his head cocked to the side. Kaylara's eyes were closed. I arched an eyebrow at Cayleth and dipped my head toward Pavo. Cayleth said under her breath, "You two weren't the only ones having a romantic evening tonight."

I blushed. I hadn't even known that Kaylara and Pavo were anything more than friends. I experienced a pang of guilt that I'd been so wrapped up in my own affairs that I hadn't noticed. I vowed to pay more attention to my friends going forward.

Cayleth announced for Kaylara's benefit, "Aeryn and Lyse are here. What are you seeing, Kaylara? Did you find them?"

"They're headed toward the northwest quarter using a back street," Kaylara said. "Chancellor Vandys has Raelan hidden under an illusion. I think it's the sort of invisibility illusion that you use, Cayleth. They're walking really fast, and the chancellor has her hood up. Not that anyone from that quarter would recognize the chancellor of Windhall by sight anyway."

"Have they spoken to anyone since entering the city?" Cayleth asked.

"No, although the chancellor has nodded at some guardsmen as she's moved through the quarters. I'm not sure what that means, if anything."

Kaylara fell silent and we waited for more to happen. Lyse and I pressed ourselves to the wall across from Kaylara's bed while Cayleth sat down on the floor, her back against the wall opposite the door. Lyse rubbed her thumb against mine as we held hands, and my skin prickled at her touch. Pavo still hadn't taken his eyes off Kaylara to look at us; he was too busy watching her, concern etched across his face. What had Kaylara told him about Raelan and the chancellor? Probably everything. I should have told him sooner. He deserved to know, too, just as much as we did.

Interminably long minutes later, Kaylara began to speak again. "They've stopped at a door. They're in a narrow, dark alley. The chancellor has dropped the illusion over Raelan. They're going in after checking to make sure they're not being followed."

Everyone in the room leaned forward, eager to hear what would happen next. Kaylara continued, "It's a small room. Everything is dim and I'm having trouble making things out. There are eight other people there. I don't think they're all mages. One is a soldier. Another looks like a courtier or a scholar. I don't know about the other six. Chancellor Vandys is speaking.

"She's called the meeting on short notice because the Knight Commander has requested an investigation into the garrison fire. Someone told her Dark Magic may have been involved, and she asked the Mages' Council to look into it. The meeting attendees are all trying to talk at once. The chancellor is ordering them to calm down. She says she can bribe the Council's investigator to deny the presence of Dark Magic, that he's lazy and greedy."

Lyse looked at me, concerned, and without her saying a word, I understood her perfectly. If it was so easy to subvert the Mages' Council, did we really have a chance to stop Raelan and the chancellor even with our evidence? I didn't have an answer, but I wanted to know more. If I was right that Raelan and the chancellor had been kidnapping people for years to fuel their Dark Magic, why? Power for the sake of power? Who were the other people in the room if not other mages?

Kaylara continued, "The chancellor thinks the commander is dangerous. She says Commander Bronwen must be 'dealt with.'"

"What does that mean?" Cayleth asked.

Kaylara gasped, her hand fluttering to her chest. "There's an assassin in the room! Her name is Meandra. She's been told to assassinate the commander and make it look like an accident."

"She must be acting outside the Assassins' Guild," Lyse whispered to me. "The Guild would have her killed if it found out she's taking a job off the books! Not that the Guild would turn down a contract for the Knight Commander—after all, business is business—but this doesn't sound official."

I whispered back, "Then they must be offering her a lot of money. I wonder where they got it from."

Kaylara said, "The chancellor is warning the others to be more careful and to keep an eye out for spies. She says they're 'close, very close' and that they must not make any mistakes now. I wish she'd say what they're planning!"

"We're so close to finding out!" Cayleth moaned in frustration.

"The meeting is already breaking up."

"We have to find a way to warn Commander Bronwen about the assassin!" Lyse said.

"No one can get to the Knight Commander, not even an assassin." Cayleth waved her hand dismissively. "She spends almost all her time in the knights' garrison beside the palace or in the palace itself. To get to her, Meandra would have to go through a dozen or more knights. Not to mention she'd then have to face the Knight Commander herself, and Commander Bronwen is known to be one of the best swordswomen in the kingdom."

"There are still a few people in the room who haven't left," Kaylara interrupted. "I think they're the Dark mages. In addition to Chancellor Vandys and Raelan, there are a man and a woman in dark robes. They're talking about a woman. The man says that she was too weak for what they needed, that she didn't last long enough. I don't think I want to listen to this."

Her face twitched as she heard things she chose not to relay. Pavo reached out and massaged her palm comfortingly. Cayleth said, "Maybe they'll say where they took her."

"The chancellor doesn't want to discuss it," Kaylara replied, shaking her head. "She's telling the two to choose better in the future. They'll need many more people soon. They need more power. She says there are two others who have recently come to the city who may join them. Maybe two other mages who may go Dark?"

"Wait…the female mage is looking around. I think she senses me. I don't think she's very good at detecting eavesdroppers."

Kaylara went silent, then her face turned pale. Pavo reached out and grasped her shoulders. "What is happening? Kaylara?"

Kaylara didn't answer. She had collapsed unconscious on her bed, and Pavo was beside her, screaming for her to wake up.

CHAPTER 8

"Violence only begets more violence."

— *Kjelborn the Traitor*

"The world of the gods and the world of humans should never meet."

— *Reddek the Wise, first Chancellor of Windhall University*

THERE IS A POPULAR GAME called "Kill the King." It is a game of strategy and cunning, in which two players battle using small wooden pieces that represent tiny armies: infantry, pikemen, knights, and mages. Whoever kills their opponent's king wins. I had never been good at it. Pavo, who sometimes played with me, would chastise: "Aeryn, you are not seeing what is coming, only what is being. You are not winning until you are seeing what your opponent is thinking."

Kill the King had rules and boundaries and predictable moves. It was nothing like real life. In real life, the game we'd started playing with Raelan and the chancellor meant we were facing an opponent with an unknown number of pieces, who didn't move in regulated spaces across a flat wooden board, and who didn't have any use for "taking turns." This was an opponent who was willing to kill to win.

"Kaylara!" Pavo screamed when Kaylara fell unconscious. His voice was shrill.

Cayleth was on her feet, and without realizing it, I, too, had lunged forward. Lyse reached Kaylara first. She grabbed Kaylara's shoulders and shook her gently. Kaylara's eyelids fluttered, then opened. Her eyes traveled from Lyse to Cayleth to Pavo, dazed. She blinked slowly.

"Are you okay?" Cayleth asked. "What happened?"

"Raelan," Kaylara groaned. "He tried to warg me."

"No!" I gasped, covering my mouth with my hands. My skin prickled.

"Is it possible to warg an eavesdropper?" Cayleth wondered aloud.

"You are being safe now?" Pavo's voice was full of worry. He took Kaylara's hands and held them.

Kaylara's voice was shaky. "I think so."

"If he had warged you, Raelan would have found out everything. Then…" Cayleth rubbed her arms. She didn't need to finish her sentence. The implication was clear: Then we would have all been exposed. We would all be in mortal danger.

"You're sure he didn't?" Lyse asked. "Could he have gotten through for the briefest moment? Does he know about us?"

All it would have taken was for Raelan to look through Kaylara's eyes for a second, and he would have known exactly who had been spying on him. Pavo looked around anxiously, as though Raelan and the chancellor would Gate into Kaylara's room any minute. Kaylara shook her head. "No, I'm sure. There was no time."

She shuddered and covered her face with her hands, digging the heel of her palm into her eyes. "I feel like someone hit me in the head with an axe."

"Raelan must have assumed you had a mental shield," I said. "He put too much power into his warging and it knocked you out. That's what saved us."

My stomach roiled. Eavesdropping on the meeting had been a huge risk, and it had almost cost us everything. If the group had been willing to burn down one of the four city guard garrisons, they wouldn't hesitate to stop us, too. We should never have asked Kaylara to eavesdrop. I let out a gust of air. At least we could stop now. Now that we knew what had been discussed at the meeting in King's City, we could get the information to the Knight Commander, who could act to stop them. She could track down Meandra and force her to reveal her fellow conspirators.

I put my hand on Lyse's shoulder. "At least it's over now. We have what we need: proof that Raelan and the chancellor are up to no good. I'll talk to Sir Idras and Asher as soon as I can. In a few days, this will all be over."

"But what are they doing, exactly?" Cayleth said. "We still don't know. Kaylara, you said there was a soldier and a courtier at the meeting, too. What do they have to do with Dark Magic? What were they doing there?"

"It is being like a snake: We are seeing the head, but we are not knowing how long the body is being," Pavo said.

"What if the Knight Commander is still away from King's City?" Lyse asked.

"I wish we could approach members of the Mages' Council individually and warn them," Cayleth said, balling her fists. "They could stop it. But why should they believe us?"

"Maybe they are believing the Baron of Ardeth," Pavo suggested.

"Faegan?" Cayleth said.

The room fell silent as we considered the idea. Faegan was haughty and prickly, but as a baron, he had a strong stake in Ilirya's stability, and that meant stopping Dark Magic. But would he listen, much less believe us?

Cayleth picked at the skin on her lip. "Young as he is, he has influence by virtue of his position," she said. "It would be hard for Council members to ignore the baron of one of the kingdom's richest baronies. And as a mage and Raelan's student, he would have particular credibility on the subject. They might not believe him outright, but they would at least listen. It could work."

"Would Faegan believe us if we told him?" Kaylara asked.

"Faegan *hates* Raelan," Cayleth replied. "He'd believe it."

"I don't trust Faegan," Lyse said. Her eyes met mine and her mouth set in a thin line. "He tried to kill you."

"It was an accident...mostly," I said. I squeezed her shoulder to calm her.

Lyse rubbed her hands together, frowning. "In all his time at Windhall, he hasn't made any friends. He broods. I see some of Raelan in him."

"He could speak to Marshal Heika," Cayleth suggested. "She would believe him, and it would be faster than tracking down all the members of the Mages' Council individually."

"Yes!" Kaylara smiled, color returning to her face. "It's the marshal's job to protect the city! Plus she already has a stake in finding out who burned down the garrison. Between her and the Knight Commander, they can convince the Mages' Council. Then everyone can work together to root out all the Dark mages and their helpers in King's City."

"I'll talk to Faegan tomorrow," Cayleth said. "If nothing else, he'll hear me out."

"It sounds like everything is settled then," Lyse said, standing. "Cayleth will talk to Faegan, who will talk to the Marshal. No more spying on the chancellor and Raelan. We're students. Let the city's full-time defenders do their jobs."

Everyone nodded. Lyse was right: Everything was out of our hands now. Cayleth left first, grumbling about reading to do for class, and Lyse and I followed. When Lyse caught my eye in the hallway, my heart fluttered. Her look pulled me back to the events immediately before our arrival in Kaylara's room and the feeling of her lips on mine and her fingers in my hair.

Rather than returning to her room, this time we went to mine. Lyse walked in and sat on my bed, watching me as I closed the door, her fingers wrapped around the thin mattress. She said, "Promise me you'll step back from trying to spy on Raelan and the chancellor. Let the Lady Marshal and the Knight Commander do their jobs."

I sat down next to her, our shoulders touching. She reached out and twined the fingers of one hand in mine, staring at them. I turned our hands and kissed the back of her wrist. "I know. I will. I promise."

"I know you want to stop them, but I need you here with me, safe. No more close calls." She nuzzled her head into my shoulder.

"I want this to be over. None of us are safe at Windhall so long as Raelan and the chancellor are here," I told her.

She shivered. "I don't want to think about that. I'm sure they'll be stopped soon."

I untangled my fingers from hers and loosed a thin stream of magic that floated to the ceiling and danced there as tiny blue flames swirling in a languid whirlpool. I lay back on the bed with my head on the pillow, and Lyse followed, lying against my side. We watched the flames quietly for a while, saying nothing. Her body was warm and soft. "Tell me a happy memory from your childhood," I said.

She thought for a moment, and I could feel her cheeks move as she smiled. "My oldest sister, Leandra, was fifteen years older than me. We had never been terribly close, but one day, when I was five and she was days away from her wedding, she came to my room and said, 'Put on your nicest dress, we're going to have a picnic!' She snuck us through the kitchen, and we stole whatever we could find. Then we went to the roof, where we sat in our best dresses eating the lunch that we stole.

"The roof was high, and we could see for miles around us. Rath is flat, you know, so it felt like we could see everything. I don't think I'd ever been up there before. The temperature was just right, and the sun kept us warm. I think Leandra wanted me to have something to remember her by once she was gone. She left a few weeks later, and I only saw her a few times after that."

"It sounds lovely."

"I haven't gone back home to Madrigal much since coming here four years ago. Timo and I were always so busy that I never had time. When I think about it, I can still see everyone as they were when I left: the cooks in the kitchen, the washerwomen with their tubs of water, the grooms in the stable, the dogs running everywhere. It's like a painting frozen in time, like it will never change. But I've changed so much."

Lyse paused, thinking. Her hand drew a gentle design on my chest. "In Rath, family is everything. There's a saying: 'All fingers on the same hand.' But coming to Windhall taught me that I could be more than just a member of my family. I could choose a future and a life for myself. None of my sisters had that choice. If they did, I wonder what they would have chosen. Would Leandra still have gone to Avgaras? What would she have chosen to become?"

Although it was still early in the evening, she yawned. "I didn't choose Timo, you know," she said. "He was chosen for me."

"What? But you—"

"I was lucky. Timo was very handsome and kind. Leandra wasn't so lucky."

She yawned again, and I remembered that she probably hadn't slept in days. Those sleepness nights were finally catching up to her. I pulled the rough brown woolen blanket up over us, and Lyse turned her body to snuggle tighter against me, her head resting on my shoulder. "It feels right to be here with you," she murmured. "Don't leave me."

I kissed her on the forehead, then caressed her hair to lull her to sleep. Once she was soundly asleep, I watched the magic above me, and wondered what the future would bring. What if Kaylara was wrong and Raelan knew we'd been tracking him? What if Marshal Heika and Commander Bronwen couldn't stop Raelan and the chancellor? How could I keep Lyse safe?

I might as well have been holding my breath for the next week, waiting for some sign that our spying on the chancellor and Raelan had been discovered, but nothing happened. Faegan agreed to tell Marshal Heika what we had learned, but we didn't know when. Meanwhile, when I tried to contact Asher and Sir Idras, I was told they had been sent on a temporary detail outside of King's City and would be back in a few weeks' time. With our limited avenues exhausted, all that was left to do was wait and hope that Raelan and the chancellor didn't find out about us. Although they were likely to assume that the mage eavesdropping on them worked for the king's spymaster, Zaphrys, who was rumored to have eyes all over the city, there was always the small chance the chancellor would remember Kaylara.

In the meantime, Raelan demanded that Lyse attend our war-mage training sessions and my combatives lessons. In his words, Lyse's place was no longer in an infirmary but on a battlefield. It was a cruel reminder that she'd had to give up the healing that she loved to learn the last magical affinity she would have ever wanted, all for me. Worse, it meant she would see Raelan every day. So far, I had been able to hide my fear and disgust, but could she?

The only person happy about the new arrangement was Raelan himself. "You two are a war mage bonded pair now, the like of which has never been seen in Ilirya," he rasped when Lyse came to class with me for the first time. "You have much learning to catch up on."

Lyse's jaw clenched, but she nodded. I grimaced, wishing I could take her hand in mine to comfort her. Lyse's life had been dedicated to saving lives, but now Raelan wanted to train her to take them. It wasn't fair. I remembered, too, what Timo had told me: "As your bondmate, Lyse will have to follow you onto the battlefield." It was expected that one day we would be sent to fight on the southern front. How could I possibly keep Lyse safe there? Cayleth was the Great Mage, not me. I would have to find a way to keep her from danger, but I didn't have time to think about it now.

Raelan motioned Cayleth forward, then me, indicating that we were to spar. We squared off with practiced ease and waited for Raelan to signal the start of our bout, but unexpectedly, he motioned for Lyse to join us, too. I immediately stood from my fighting crouch, surprised. "What? No! Lyse isn't equipped to spar! Nor does she have any training in how to defend herself!"

"Lyse will observe. That is all. She needs to learn quickly in order to catch up to you, and you must learn to fight with her beside you. Until she can make her own shield, you will make one for her."

My anxious eyes flickered to Cayleth, and she nodded so subtly that Raelan couldn't see it. She would protect Lyse. I breathed a small sigh of relief, glad that Raelan hadn't picked Faegan as my sparring partner. I looked at Lyse, and she nodded, too. Sharing our magic, I built a shield for myself, then one for her. Lyse examined it curiously, reaching out to feel the shimmering blue that swam before her. I returned to my fighting crouch, reassured.

Raelan called start, and Cayleth sprang into action immediately. The illusion that she created was one of emptiness: Raelan, Lyse, Faegan, and Cayleth herself all disappeared, leaving the impression that I was alone in the room. I drew magic to my left hand and unsheathed my sword with my right. I was really, *really* starting to hate fighting illusionists.

"I'm to your left! I won't move!" Lyse called out helpfully.

I wished I could see her. Knowing that she was now part of this game we played and could get hurt made my stomach tie itself in knots. Cayleth burst through my shield to my right, and I was barely able to get my rapier up in time to deflect hers. In my distraction over Lyse, I had almost been an easy victim. I needed to focus, but it was hard with Lyse so near. All my instincts told me to protect her first and foremost.

I used my magic to throw Cayleth backward away from me, then followed up with a bolt of magic that crackled against her shield. Immediately, the scenery around me changed. Now I was standing in a desert, wind tearing at my face and howling in my ears. My eyes started to water even though the wind was an illusion. I threw more fire at where I'd last seen Cayleth, but she could have been anywhere. A moment later, she pounced from behind. The point of her rapier tapped against the back of my neck, in the vulnerable area between my helmet and my armor. I capitulated immediately. It was our quickest bout yet. Cayleth dropped the illusion, and I understood that she had carefully maneuvered us as far away from Lyse as she could. A rush of gratitude swept over me.

Raelan looked bored. "Thoughts, War Mage Lyse?"

Lyse bristled at the title. In a clipped voice, she replied, "I don't see how Aeryn possibly could have won. It was impossible to either see or hear inside Cayleth's illusions. How could Aeryn be expected to prevail under those circumstances?"

Raelan made a non-committal sound. "Every opponent has both a strength and a weakness. If you assume victory is impossible, then it will become so. Aeryn, rather than pushing Cayleth *away* with your magic, hold her in place so she can't maneuver around you. So long as you know her location, her illusions are of no consequence. One must be strategic in battle and not influenced by emotion. Sometimes, the best way to defeat an enemy is to keep them within arm's reach."

My stomach dropped. Was he hinting that he knew we'd been spying on him? Telling us that he was keeping us close because he knew we were a threat? No. He couldn't be. If he knew about the eavesdropping, he wouldn't have let us go. After all, Raelan always said, "Never allow a threat to persist."

Then I remembered Halver's immobilizing spell. That was what Raelan wanted me to do! I considered the idea for a moment. If I could throw, lift, and move things without touching them, then there was no reason I couldn't also hold them in place using my magic. They would be like flies trapped in a spider's web.

Raelan waved Cayleth away and motioned to Faegan. Faegan automatically adjusted his helmet and checked his sword, then stepped forward, staring hard at Lyse as he passed her. Unlike Cayleth, he would make no effort to keep her safe. But at least for now, I doubted he would target her. He was cold and vindictive, but not vicious. Faegan's shield rose around him, painting him a light purple, and I raised shields around myself and Lyse in response. Faegan drew his sword and called magic to his free hand, and then we were two pyromancers facing off against each other.

The moment the bout began, however, things began to go awry. Lyse's presence had disrupted my usual routine, and so I had forgotten to establish a mental shield at the same time that I raised my magic shield. After I released my first volley of fire against Faegan, I found my attention split, battling against Raelan to prevent him from taking over my body while I was trying to crack Faegan's shield. Had Raelan wanted to warg me, he could easily have done it, but his intention had only been to divert my attention enough to allow Faegan to enter my shield, which he did.

The two of us began exchanging blows with our swords. Faegan was quickly gaining the advantage over me, using his height and bulk to beat me back. I whirled and parried, trying to make up for his power with my speed, but it was tiring, and I wouldn't be able to last indefinitely. After one particularly late parry, I misstepped and fell to my knee, bringing my sword up above my head in a feeble attempt to ward off the blow I knew would come next.

Instantly, my magic began to wick out of me through the bond I shared with Lyse. I blazed through our connection over to Lyse. Faegan's sword crashed against mine, and I grunted as I struggled to hold him off. A few heartbeats later, the air crackled as a massive fireball blasted into him. It was the largest ball of mage fire I'd ever seen. Faegan went flying into the wall, then crumpled in a heap. His tunic steamed, the way a fire does after water has been poured on it. Faegan was knocked out cold. There was complete silence as Cayleth, Lyse, and I stared at Faegan's motionless body. Then the room began to echo with laughter. Raelan's laughter.

"It seems the mouse can roar," he purred, a smile snaking across his face. His Dark eyes glistened.

Horrified, Lyse ran to Faegan and slipped his helmet off his head. His eyes were closed and he was breathing shallowly, but he didn't seem to be otherwise injured. Lyse laid him on the floor and began to undo the fastenings on his armor as quickly as her nimble fingers would allow, grunting when her skin touched his superheated tunic. Raelan stopped laughing and stepped closer, looking down at Faegan's limp body. "He will learn from this mistake and never again ignore a potential adversary," Raelan said.

"I shouldn't have attacked him!" Lyse cried, her eyes wide. "He was *supposed* to ignore me. It was wrong. I didn't think about what I was doing."

"Did I tell him to ignore you?" Raelan's sharp voice was cold and unfeeling. "This is the consequence of his inattention. Better he learn this lesson here, in the classroom, than when it is too late."

He crossed his arms and stared at me and Cayleth. "Let this be a lesson to both of you: Never ignore a potential opponent, nor underestimate them." Then he turned on his heel and was gone out the door without even having checked to be sure that Faegan wasn't seriously injured.

Lyse put Faegan's head in her lap and slapped gently at his cheeks, trying to revive him. His eyes flickered and opened, then immediately narrowed as he recognized her. "You!" he snarled.

"I'm sorry, Faegan! I didn't mean to, it just happened. Are you all right?"

Faegan pushed himself away from her and staggered to his feet, his face flushed. "You tricked me!" he hissed, looking from her to me. "You ambushed me!"

"No, we didn't." I tried to keep my voice low and steady. His seething fury and hurt pride worried me. This was the Faegan who had thrown a knife into my chest and not cared that I could have died. Would he try to hurt Lyse?

Faegan's eyes darted back and forth between me and Lyse, his face twitching with rage. Then he drew himself up to his full height, glaring at us with his chin held high. "I made a mistake this time, but I won't make the same mistake again. Watch yourselves." After grabbing his chain mail from the floor and throwing it over his shoulder, he stormed out of the room. The door slammed shut after him, echoing loudly in the room.

"Nobles are so temperamental! Oh well, he'll cool off once his bruised ego has healed," Cayleth said.

I grunted. "Faegan seems like the type to hold a grudge until he dies."

Cayleth shrugged. "He must be dying with jealousy that you're stronger than ever now that you have Lyse."

"I—I'm so sorry! I didn't mean to do it! I just wanted to do *something* to make him stop," Lyse said, staring at the door. She looked down at her hands, gazing at them as though they were the hands of a stranger.

Cayleth stuck out a hand to help her stand. "Don't worry about it. Faegan is bristly on a good day, and he hates losing more than anything. You're a natural; that fireball was enormous! I'm glad you hit Faegan and not me."

Lyse's mouth quirked into an unhappy frown. I stepped forward and folded her up in my arms to comfort her. Her breath was short and shallow. I murmured into her hair, "It's okay, Faegan wasn't hurt, just knocked out.

You didn't hurt him. These things happen in Raelan's class. How many times did you find me lying unconscious on the floor?"

"I don't like it," Lyse muttered into my shoulder, her words muffled. "I don't want to hurt people."

"I know. You'll get used to sparring, in time. It's not so bad, I promise. Think of it as a game. A game of skill and cunning." It was no use mentioning that the game was only a game so long as we were in Windhall's training rooms. Outside the university, these skills we were learning were meant to be deadly.

I let Lyse go. Cayleth, who had been waiting patiently for us, said, "Come on, I'll show you how to beat Aeryn with a rapier. But you're on your own when it comes to bows and arrows."

I took off my helmet and carried it under my arm as we stepped outside. Now that winter was near, the temperature had dropped much lower, and the air felt nice and cool against my cheek. The sun was setting sooner as well, making for dark nights. Lyse threaded her arm in mine, borrowing my warmth. To someone from the arid plains of Rath, the weather must have felt downright freezing. What would she think of the blistering cold of the Ice Crown? Would I ever have the chance to take her and find out? I turned to tell her about Pavo's latest battle with Professor Kalmath but was stopped by the sound of Windhall's great bell ringing.

Lyse's forehead wrinkled as her eyebrows drew together. "No, that's not right; it's too early."

We stopped and looked instinctively toward the spire that rose from the academic building, where the bell was housed. What was happening? Behind us, one of the training building doors flew open as a man burst through. He started running toward the academic building, his unbuttoned coat flying behind him. I guessed he must work at Windhall's city office and had come by way of the Gate because I didn't recognize him as a teacher. Cayleth lunged at him, grabbing his arm and dragging him to a stop as he careened past us.

"What's happening?" she demanded.

"Didn't you hear? There has been an attempt upon the life of the Knight Commander."

Cayleth was so surprised that she let go of him. He took off running immediately, his feet flying behind him.

"Wait!" she called at his retreating figure. "Is the commander all right?"

CHAPTER 9

"After the second Northern War, all Northmen but for a single representative were barred from Ilirya on pain of death. When the Northmen implemented reciprocal rules, commerce between the two sides effectively ceased."

— A Kingdom and its People, 4th edition

"There is no mercy for the wicked, only justice."

— Gamiel, member of the King's Regiment

LATER, WE CAME TO CALL it the Night of the Long Swords. The Lady Marshal, Garreth, the head of the Mages' Council, and several other Council members. A record keeper from the Assassins' Guild. All slain in their beds. Only the Knight Commander had survived, and even then, it was only barely. It was a devastating, crippling blow that had been executed so smoothly that no one had been the wiser until the next day, when alarms began to sound around the city.

In a hastily called assembly, Chancellor Vandys relayed the news as a wave of disbelief and fear wash over her students. "Malcontents," she spat, her mouth twisting as though the word was sour on her tongue. "This terrible attack was carried out by rogue troublemakers who blame the king for everything from a bad harvest to the death of a few sheep here and there. Deserters who failed their kingdom and fled home like dogs. This is the work of cowards. We will not be intimidated by these villains! Have no fear; they will be found and punished. Justice will be done."

What? What was she talking about? I thought back to all that I had seen during my journey to Windhall. It was true there was simmering unrest in the kingdom, but the idea that angry farmers could have planned and executed such an extraordinary coup against Ilirya's most powerful leaders was beyond belief. Who could possibly believe such an obvious lie? And yet somehow, incredibly, not only the teachers but the students, too, were nodding. I could hear their murmurs of anger around me. With eighty students all seeming to speak at once, the sound was like the angry buzzing of bees. I felt weak with horror. The chancellor and Raelan had killed again. And this time, the strike was to the very heart of King's City.

The chancellor continued. "We here at Windhall University take the safety of our students *very* seriously. For that reason, Professor Raelan Bloodmoon has asked several war mages to temporarily take up residence at the university for your protection. For the present, all student travel into the city is prohibited. We will not allow the actions of a few malcontents to threaten the excellent education that we provide at this revered institution. Ilirya will emerge stronger from this devastating loss!"

Lyse, Cayleth, and I stared at each other, mouths hanging open in shock, as Halver, Balrak, and a third man walked up to stand beside Raelan. The man was short and stocky, with a shock of gray hair that started at his left temple. All three of the mages wore armor and weapons, as though we might be attacked at any time.

"No!" Lyse whispered beside me, horrified.

Cayleth shook her head. "This is all wrong, all of it." Her face was stormy, a combination of shock, anger, and despair.

"Come on!" I grabbed Lyse and Cayleth's hands and dragged them to the edge of the crowd, where it was quieter and we wouldn't be overheard. Where were Kaylara and Pavo? I hadn't seen them in the crowd. It was too difficult now to push back through the throng of students looking for them. We would have to find them later.

"It was Raelan and the chancellor, wasn't it?" Lyse said. She looked queasy.

I rubbed my face. "I don't understand. Even though she failed, the assassin Meandra was told to make Commander Bronwen's death look like an accident. A wave of assassinations is as subtle as a hammer. Did they change their plans after they discovered Kaylara eavesdropping?"

Cayleth's face was grim. "I don't think so. The attacks must have taken weeks to plan. This must have been their design all along, but why?"

"They're eliminating anyone who could stop them," I said. "What I don't understand is why the chancellor would blame the assassinations on imaginary dissidents. Surely no one in the city believes it. It's preposterous! Wouldn't it have been easier to blame, I don't know, Southerner assassins?"

Lyse chewed on a fingernail. "With Garreth's death, Chancellor Vandys is now the head of the Mages' Council. And with the death of the Lady Marshal and the incapacitation of the Knight Commander, the chancellor will be one of the most powerful members of the King's Council, too. It's possible her story about 'malcontents' is meant to distract the King's Council. Rich city dwellers are always ready to believe that jealous peasants are on the verge of beating down the gates to steal their wealth. She's trying to keep the Council off their trail."

"They're going to get away with it!" Cayleth's eyes were wide with horror.

My heart started to beat faster. All this time, we had counted on other people to stop Raelan and the chancellor, but who was left? With the Lady Marshal gone and the Knight Commander gravely hurt, we were the only ones left who knew about the Dark Magic. Whatever their plan, the chancellor and Raelan seemed on the brink of getting away with it. I asked, "Will the Assassins' Guild investigate? They must see that the assassinations were carried out by their own members. They could tell the king that the chancellor is lying."

Lyse's brown eyes were troubled. "They could..."

My heart thudded. "You think they won't."

"No. It's in the Guild leaders' best interest to perpetuate the chancellor's lie. If they admit that multiple assassins acted without the Guild's knowledge, it will be a massive scandal. It's better for them to sweep all of this under the rug. For all they know, this is just infighting between the city elites. It wouldn't be the first time."

I crossed my arms and looked back at the chancellor, who was still speaking. "How could this have happened? How were they able to kill so many people in one night?"

"With help." Lyse's face was drawn. "No assassin, however good, could have gotten to the Lady Marshal or the Knight Commander without assistance from the inside. This isn't about Raelan and the chancellor anymore. This is bigger than them."

"I need to get a message to Sir Idras and Asher. They have to come back to King's City immediately! We need them! They're our only hope," I said.

"You can't leave Windhall," Cayleth pointed out. "The chancellor said travel to the city was prohibited."

I unconsciously straightened. I had spent a decade hunting in the forests of the Ice Crown. If there was one thing I knew, it was how to be stealthy. "I can sneak out of Windhall without being seen."

Lyse's hand tightened around mine. "I'm coming with you."

"No!" I shook my head emphatically. Even though I believed I could sneak out without getting caught, it was still risky. There was no way I was allowing her to put herself in danger, too.

She squeezed my hand and nodded, her face determined. "We're a bonded pair now, Aeryn. Where you go, I go. Besides, if we're caught, we can pretend that we were sneaking out to have fun. Certainly it makes more sense than one student spending time alone in the city."

We had to wait four days until we could venture into King's City. In the meantime, Pavo subtly shifted the weather in our favor, calling in heavy clouds from over the sea. On the appointed morning, we awoke to a thick white fog so dense that it was impossible to see more than a few feet in any direction. Pavo had promised to hold the fog for several hours to conceal our escape, but warned that any longer could potentially raise suspicions, so he would have to release it. I promised we'd do our best to be back before then.

Lyse and I met on the back side of the armory a little after sunrise. She smiled when she saw me and kissed me gently with a quick caress of my cheek, but her face was tense, and the smile quickly fell. My stomach was in knots. I had barely slept the night before. What would the chancellor do if she found out that we'd gone to send a message to Asher and Sir Idras? She and Raelan had made it clear they wouldn't hesitate to eliminate anyone standing in their way. But despite the risk, we had to do it. If we didn't send word to Sir Idras and Asher to come back immediately, there was no one to stop them.

"Ready?" Lyse asked.

I nodded. "Pavo did a good job. I can't even see my hands in front of my face. Are *you* ready?"

Lyse nodded. I took a deep breath, then took her hand and began to jog across the training field, relying on my memory rather than sight. Moving through the fog was like being caught in an Ice Crown blizzard. There was nothing but white everywhere. Although we were completely hidden from any potential observers who might have reported our escape to the chancellor, I kept checking behind us, searching for any sign that we were being followed. Finally, I relaxed, confident that we were safe, at least for now.

"What do you think the chancellor and Raelan want?" Lyse asked. It was the same question I had asked myself every day since the Night of the Long Swords. The same question we were all asking ourselves. She wrapped her arms around herself, chilled by the late-fall air.

I shrugged. "Power, I suppose. By killing the Lady Marshal and taking over the Mages' Council, it guarantees that no one will come looking for them and they can practice their Dark Magic without fear of being caught."

Lyse rubbed her arm. "That would make sense if only Dark mages were involved, but why are non-mages helping them? Who were the other people in the room that night Kaylara eavesdropped? Who helped the assassins? I've been thinking about it, and I think the killing of the King's Shadow is part of all this."

"What?" I blinked, confused. I had forgotten all about the Shadow. It seemed like forever ago that he had been killed in some sort of incident on the southern border. I tried to remember what I had learned about him. Father Merek had said the job of the Shadow was to prevent rebellion by the Barons by creating Gates the army could pass through to defend the king. Now that the Shadow was dead, the king was protected only by the soldiers already in the capital. Although this meant that theoretically, one of the local Barons could overwhelm this small defense and capture King's City using their own army, none of Ilirya's Barons had armies anymore. So why was Lyse bringing it up?

"The city's defenses have been depleted for months. All members of the King's Regiment were ordered to the front months ago, while the knight garrison has been drawn down to almost nothing. How many knights and city guard members are in King's City right now? One hundred? Two hundred?"

I shook my head. I didn't know anything about the city, unlike Lyse.

She continued, "A courtier. A soldier. Insiders on the Mages' Council, the Assassins' Guild, the city guard, and the knights' garrison. Whatever Raelan and the chancellor are involved in, it's…big."

I pursed my lips. "What do you think it is?"

Lyse sighed. "I don't know."

We continued the rest of our walk in silence, each of us deep in thought. When we arrived at the western gate, I noticed that it was sparsely defended, with only a handful of soldiers lounging around the gate. I'd never thought about how many soldiers were necessary to defend a city. Certainly a small army would be needed to fight off an adversary beating at the gates, but what if the enemy was already within the walls? What if the enemy had a Gate of their own…from Windhall?

Half an hour later, we arrived at the knights' garrison. I had forgotten that it was located next to the king's castle. Tall and rectangular, the palace could hardly be called pretty. It had been built of a brown stone, with smooth, high walls that were punctuated by narrow windows from which archers could shoot. All of Thamir could have fit inside it twice over. Lyse tugged on my arm, pulling my focus away from the castle and toward the door to knights' garrison. Two guards stood outside, wearing the blue livery of the knighthood, their ceremonial pikes at their sides.

"Excuse me," Lyse said politely as we approached. "We're looking to pass a message to two knights who are currently out of the city. To whom should we speak?"

One of the guards looked to the other, who shrugged, his plate armor creaking as it slid against his chainmail. "I suppose you could speak to the majordomo," he said, scratching his red beard.

"Is he available?"

The guard shrugged. "Might be. Come with me." He motioned for us to follow him.

"What's a majordomo?" I whispered to Lyse as we fell in behind him.

"He'll be the official in charge of the administration of the knighthood," Lyse replied. "Not a knight himself, but an administrator like Chancellor Vandys, in charge of things like provisioning."

The guard led us down a short hallway that ended in a small office lined with mahogany paneling. Sitting in its center was a massive wooden table at which sat a fat man in a black leather jerkin with puffy black cotton sleeves. Around his neck was a silver chain, from which hung a large key. His moustache was twirled up at each end, and a small, well-groomed beard sprouted from his chin. He looked up as we entered the room, squinting at us as his gaze shifted from a sheaf of papers on the desk to the doorway. The guard bowed respectfully to him.

"Well, what is it?" the majordomo barked.

"My lord, these women have a message they wish to be passed," the guard reported.

"I am not a messenger service!" the majordomo growled.

"No, of course not, my lord!" Lyse raised her hands placatingly, stepping into the room. "We meant to imply no such thing."

The majordomo glared at us. Although Lyse and I had practiced what to say, my mind went blank. I wasn't used to speaking to nobles. I was terrified he would see right through me. A red blush began to creep up my neck as my mouth refused to open. I broke out in a sweat.

Lyse noticed my panic and straightened beside me, her chin high. "The message that I had hoped to convey is that Lady Lyse of the House Pan will be leaving the city in the next few days to return to Rath for safety following the reprehensible events of this week. I would like to see Sir Idras and Lady Asher before I depart. Due to my deep sadness over the attack on the Knight Commander and my close *personal* connection with these two knights, I want to leave the knighthood a gift as a token of my respect before I depart."

This hadn't been the message that we'd practiced. Lyse was improvising. Although implying that she was a senior member of the House Pan was a gamble, it could work. After all, it was unlikely that the majordomo knew the family trees of Pan's Houses. For all he knew, Lyse could be a daughter of the Baron of Rath or a favored cousin. The Majordomo licked his lips. "I will see that your message is conveyed to those knights, my lady, but why wait for them to return to bestow your generous offering? Your contribution is safe in my hands. In fact, there are no better hands!"

Lyse rewarded him with a small smile. "I don't doubt that, but you see, it really must be given to them personally. They are *such* good friends to

Rath. The sooner Sir Idras and Lady Asher return to the city, the sooner I may deliver this gift and be gone to Madrigal. It is better I not carry a heavy purse on the road anyway. There are bandits about."

The mention of a heavy purse was irresistible to the majordomo. "The knights shall be recalled immediately, my lady," he said, rising from his seat and reaching for her hand. "You have my word on it."

"Thank you, my lord. Rath will not forget you either," Lyse said, extending her hand for him to kiss.

I marveled at her bearing. If I hadn't known she was bluffing, I, too, would have assumed she came from the highest levels of nobility. The majordomo kissed her hand, and then we followed the guard back to the door of the garrison, where we left him with his fellow. As we walked away, I let out a long breath. "You were brilliant, Lyse!"

She smiled, ducking her chin bashfully. "Timo and I met many men like the majordomo. They're all the same: pandering to rich nobles while trying to gain their own wealth any way they can. I wouldn't be surprised if he didn't record the offer of a gift from Rath and instead tried to keep it all himself."

"What will he do when he finds out there is no gift?"

Lyse shook her head. "That will be for Sir Idras and Lady Asher to handle. Now, what do you say to a hot pie from Ada's cookshop? I think we can sneak one in before we go back, don't you?"

Ada's small, open-faced shop was exactly as I remembered it: full of wonderful smells and steaming, round pastries. My mouth watered just looking at them. Ada waved when she saw Lyse, her apron covered with flour. "It's been a while, young mistress," she said. "We need those healing hands of yorn round here."

Lyse instantly looked like she'd been kicked in the stomach. Her shoulders slumped, and her eyes started to glisten. Her hands would never again be able to use Timo's magic to heal. I resisted the urge to glare at Ada, who didn't know any better, and pulled Lyse into my body, cradling her head against my chest. She was limp and lifeless as a child's doll.

"You can still heal," I murmured into her ear. "We'll come back with herbs from the medical garden like we did before. You can still help people. That hasn't changed. You're still a healer."

Lyse didn't move, and I didn't know what else to say. All I could do was continue to hold her close and let her mourn what she had lost. I rubbed her back and stroked her hair. After a few minutes of silently shaking in my arms, she sniffed and looked up. Her cheeks were wet with tears. "You'll come with me?" she asked.

"Of course. But you'll have to teach me what to do. I'll be a real healer's assistant this time."

I heard footsteps walking past us and looked over in time to meet a pair of yellow eyes. I stiffened, my breath catching, but the man kept walking as though nothing was amiss. With everything that had happened, I had completely forgotten Asher's news.

"Lyse," I whispered, my fingers reflexively digging into her back, "it's a Northman!"

"What?" She turned her head to look, still cradled in my arms. "But that's impossible! The Northman ambassador is the only Northman in the city."

The man kept walking, his back to us. If I hadn't seen his eyes, nothing else about him would have been remarkable: He was of an average build, wearing dirty pants and a dull gray tunic. He looked like any other denizen of the northwest quarter. I let go of Lyse. "We have to follow him!"

"What? Why?"

"To see what he's doing! Come on!" I started to walk quickly, trying to catch up.

Lyse lagged for a moment, then joined me. She grabbed my arm. "Stop! We have to get back to Windhall! We're not supposed to be in the city as it is. The others will be worried if we're not back soon. They'll think something has happened."

I shook my head, determined to continue following the Northman. I had to know why he was in King's City. Would he lead us to other Northmen? The Northmen might not have killed my family, but I couldn't shake the animosity that still I had for them. I had spent months hating them. Even though the story of their attack on Thamir had been a lie, it had felt real, and the emotions the lie created were real. I had another reason to be interested in the man, too: Since it was illegal for any Northman but the ambassador to be in Ilirya on pain of death, he had to be here for some nefarious purpose. He rounded a corner. We were the only people on the new street.

Lyse pleaded quietly at my side, "Aeryn, let's go. Please. We've already done enough today. We don't need to follow him."

"I have to know! This could be our only chance! Why are they here? What are they up to?"

"We can investigate later, once Chancellor Vandys and Raelan are stopped. This isn't the time."

The Northman turned again, and I tried to work out which direction we were going in the northwest quarter's maze of streets. North, I decided. Lyse and I turned the corner, too, then stopped abruptly. The road onto which we'd turned wasn't a road at all; it was an alley that dead-ended some twenty paces after the turn. Standing in the middle of it was the Northman, a dagger drawn and held ready in his left hand, waiting for us. I realized with horror that all the time I thought we had been surreptitiously following him from a distance, he had actually been luring us to this spot. I had walked us into a trap.

The Northman's blade was short, no longer than a hand's length. It drew my eyes irresistibly to it. I forced myself to look away, watching his yellow eyes in his broad, sallow face instead. They were like a cat's, and they shifted cautiously between me and Lyse, alert but without fear. The tense crouch of his body, knees bent slightly and hands raised, suggested he was trained to fight. He might even be a soldier or had been one once.

My body sang like the plucked string of a harp, vibrating to the danger in front of me. I started to breathe quickly, and my hands shook. I drew the knife at my waist, stepping in front of Lyse to protect her. Protecting her was what mattered most. "What are you doing, Aeryn?" Lyse hissed, putting her hand on my back. "We need to run, not fight!"

The Northman continued to stand motionless in the alley, ready to defend himself but not yet attacking. The hair on my arms was standing on end, my body tingling. I had never been in a real fight. The reality of the situation was quickly sinking in: This wasn't a training exercise with Cayleth in the training room. I wasn't wearing any armor. I could be hurt or even killed. And for what? There was no way now to find out what the

Northman was doing in the city. I spun and, grabbing Lyse's hand, began to run back the way we came, glancing over my shoulder several times to make sure the Northman wasn't following us. Luckily for us, he wasn't.

Windhall's architect had planned for the university to be surrounded by flat fields. This ensured that the campus couldn't be ambushed and also provided the students a source of fresh produce and a reminder of Ilirya's agricultural roots. It made sneaking back onto the grounds almost impossible, however, now that Pavo's fog had lifted. Lyse and I stood at the edge of the last stand of trees before the fields, watching for a chance to make a run back onto the campus without being seen.

"You shouldn't have followed that Northman," Lyse said, her voice tense and still full of emotion. "He could have killed you!"

I kicked at a patch of moss, uprooting it. "I—I thought it would be easy to follow him. I wasn't thinking."

"It could be nothing, you know. Maybe he's a refugee. We don't know what's happening in their country. It doesn't have to be something nefarious."

"Maybe," I said, unconvinced.

She was silent for a moment, then smiled despite herself. "You were very brave."

"What?"

"You were ready to fight that Northman to protect me."

"Well…yes! Of course I would have!"

She twined her fingers in mine and kissed my cheek. "Even so, you shouldn't go challenging strangers to a knife fights. You're going to get yourself killed."

I laughed, and the last of the tension from the confrontation in the alley that I hadn't realized I was still carrying dissipated. I brought our hands to my mouth and kissed her fingers. "Fine, I promise not to get in knife fights. Happy now?"

"Is the rest of your family as crazy as you are?" Lyse looked down at our hands, unexpectedly shy. "I'd like to meet them one day."

I laughed. "You would hate the Ice Crown! You would freeze in an instant. Have you even *seen* snow?"

Lyse rolled her eyes. "We could go in the summer, when it's warmer. There can't be snow all the time!"

"Yes," I agreed, smiling at her, "we could."

I tried to imagine introducing Lyse to my parents, and to Kyan and Kem. The two worlds in which I had lived seemed so far apart that I'd forgotten that they didn't always have to be. The two things I loved most could meet. No laws said they couldn't. I warned, "Ice Crowners aren't used to southerners. And my family isn't…refined, like you."

Lyse shrugged, stepped closer to me, and playfully picked at the collar of my tunic. She was so close that her breath danced across my cheek, making my stomach flutter. Her eyes sparkled. I could feel the warmth of her body so close to mine and resisted the temptation to pull her against me. Lyse said, "If they're anything like you, I know I'll like them."

She started to lean in to kiss me, but at the loud growl of a dog behind us, her body went rigid. We both turned toward the sound. Out of trees stepped the third war mage, the one with the streak of gray hair. At his left side stood a snarling black dog. Although the dog made no move to attack, all it would take was an instant for it to be upon us and then tear us to shreds. "What are you doing here?" the mage asked.

CHAPTER 10

"Sometimes the darkness wins, sometimes the light."

– Speaker unknown

"Death loves a good battle, no matter the victor."

– Speaker unknown

MY BODY SAGGED. WE WERE caught. All our efforts had been for nothing. The war mage would report us to Raelan and the chancellor, and they would know we were onto them. It was all over.

"You are not supposed to be outside of the campus," the mage said, stepping closer.

My mouth moved soundlessly. Lyse, however, wasn't ready to give up so easily. "It's *almost* on campus. We're hardly breaking the rules here, don't you think?" She smiled coyly, raising her voice so it sounded girlish.

The mage looked at her. His broad face was blank and unfriendly. I couldn't imagine him letting us go. He said flatly, "This is not part of the campus."

"But it's such a small difference!" Lyse wheedled, twirling her hair with her finger. "A matter of feet. Couldn't you overlook it?"

The walls were closing in on us. He would drag us before the chancellor. It wouldn't matter if Sir Idras and Asher returned. By then we would be gone. I struggled not to hyperventilate but sweat broke out on my forehead. Everything in my body was trembling.

I jumped as Lyse placed her hand on my shoulder. At the same time, she inched closer to me, her body molding itself against mine. "The campus is very small and…communal, don't you agree? We needed a bit more privacy, so we came here. Surely you can understand that. It's not worth telling anyone about. We promise not to do it again."

The man blinked, looking from Lyse to me, then Lyse's insinuation landed. His right nostril twitched. He snapped, "Get back to campus! I will report this to the chancellor to punish as she will. Don't come here again."

Lyse tossed her hair. "Fine." Her voice came out petulant as a child's. She took my hand and pulled me away from the mage, marching across the field in full view of anyone who might be looking from the campus. I followed her, looking once over my shoulder at the mage, who remained standing in the trees with his dog, his arms crossed as he watched us go. Had we gotten away with it? My legs were so weak they could barely carry me.

"Do you think he believed you?" I asked, my voice cracking.

"At the very least, he can't prove we're lying. Even if he guesses we went to the city, he doesn't know what we did there. I think...I think it will be okay." She put her arm around my shoulder. "Students break rules all the time. Don't worry. It will be fine."

I hoped she was right.

We found Cayleth, Kaylara, and Pavo in the dining hall eating lunch. Lyse and I had decided not to immediately tell them about getting caught. Better to save the bad news for last. Lyse quickly relayed our experience with the majordomo and our hope that Asher and Sir Idras would return to King's City soon. When she reached the part of our morning in which we faced off with the Northman in an alley, Cayleth broke in excitedly.

"Trick talked about the Northmen, too! She said that in the last week, assassins have seen Northmen all over the city. She doesn't know why. She figures there could be anywhere from tens to hundreds of them."

"What did she say about the Night of the Long Swords? Does she know what assassins did it?" I asked.

Cayleth shook her head. "No. She says it's possible the murders weren't all done by assassins. Garreth and Marshal Heika, for example, could have been killed by people they knew. Their doors were unlocked; maybe they unwittingly invited their killers in. Trick said she'd keep an ear out for any more information. Assassins know a lot because of how much they get around the city. She hadn't heard of Dark mages, though."

"Wait, you told Trick about that?" I asked.

Cayleth blushed. "Well, we needed more allies! I thought she could help! She's a member of the Assassins' Guild, after all."

I had to admit she was right. And maybe Trick would uncover something that would help us. I looked at Lyse. The time had come to deliver our bad news. I cleared my throat. "Something else happened, too."

Everyone looked at me.

"Lyse and I were caught coming back to Windhall."

"*What?*" Cayleth yelled.

Some of the students around us turned to look, and Cayleth clapped her hands over her mouth. I waited until they turned away, then hurried to finish. "Right before we made it back, that new war mage found us. He said he would report us to the chancellor for being off-campus."

"*No,*" Kaylara breathed. "Does he know you went into the city?"

Lyse covered my hand with hers. "No. We made up an excuse for being in the woods. But I imagine the chancellor and Raelan will be watching me and Aeryn. We'll have to keep a low profile from now on."

"If you are needing a good book," Pavo chirped brightly, "I am stealing many books from the library for my room."

Kaylara smacked him lightly on the arm. "Pavo!"

"You're sure he believed you?" Cayleth asked.

Lyse shrugged. "I think so, but there's no way to know for sure."

Cayleth drummed her fingers on the table. "Trick told Maerys and Derrin about the Dark Magic. They're all willing to help. They can keep an eye on whatever Raelan and the chancellor are doing around Windhall. If there's going to be trouble, they might be able to give us a heads up."

I chewed my lip. "Okay. But remember that we don't know who's helping them. The last thing that we need is to tell one of their accomplices that we know that about Dark Magic."

When nothing happened that day or the next as a result of our excursion to King's City, I breathed a sigh of relief. We had done it. We had managed to sneak out of Windhall and back without the chancellor or Raelan finding out what we were up to. Now all we had to do was wait. Asher and Sir Idras would surely find a way to stop them.

The day after, however, brought a nasty surprise: Lyse and I walked into Raelan's class to find Jale and Gamiel in the training room. My breath came fast and shallow. They had kidnapped me. Taken me from my home and told me my family was dead so I wouldn't try to go back. They were terrible people. How did Raelan know them? They should have been at the front. Why were they here?

Sensing my agitation, Lyse whispered, "What is it?"

"What *are they* doing here?" I managed to choke out, caught between feeling furious anger and debilitating horror. I couldn't swallow. My hands were numb.

"Who are they?"

"Gamiel and Jale." I didn't have to say anything more. Lyse knew the names from the story of my kidnapping. She stiffened, staring at them.

Jale was thinner than when I'd last seen him. He was running through swordplay exercises with a long broadsword while Gamiel watched, a bored expression on her face. Jale's black armor was scuffed and dented. I wondered what had happened to his rapier. Had it been broken while he was fighting with the King's Regiment at the border? He ran his black-gloved hand over his long, dark-brown hair, sweeping it back from his face. I could see the faintest sheen of perspiration on his face, and I wondered how long he'd been doing exercises in the room. How many minutes or hours ago had he invaded my world without me even knowing, a parasite on the life I'd tried to build despite him?

I wanted nothing more than for my two captors from the King's Regiment to leave. This was my home, at least until I could figure out how to go back to my real home. They had no right to be here! But if either of them noticed me, they gave no sign of it. I didn't know what to do. My hands flexed, wanting to take action, but what action was there? All the young mages they'd kidnapped deserved justice, but I had no way to give it. Before I could flee the room, Cayleth walked in, Faegan and Raelan on her heels. I was stuck with my mortal enemies.

Raelan nodded at Jale in greeting, ignoring Gamiel. I guessed that he didn't have patience for a non-mage, even one as deadly as Gamiel, but Gamiel didn't seem to mind. She ignored him, too, picking at her nails with the tip of a dagger. Neither Gamiel nor Jale had even acknowledged I was in the room, although surely they'd noticed.

"Students," Raelan announced, "today you will experience what it is like to fight a war mage with the power to confuse and disorient you if you are not able to maintain your mental shield."

"No problem," Cayleth said under her breath. "If I can keep Raelan out, I can keep *him* out."

Raelan heard her and looked at her sharply, his black eyes boring into her. Cayleth wilted a little beside me, her confidence deflating. "If you are so sure of yourself, then you may conduct this exercise *without* a shield," he declared.

"What?" Cayleth squawked. "That's not fair!"

Raelan smiled mirthlessly. "War is never fair. You may go first, Cayleth, to demonstrate for your fellow students."

No! I looked around for help. How could Raelan expose Cayleth to Jale like that? I tried to grab Cayleth, to beg her to refuse to fight. What if he wiped her memory, too? But it was too late. Cayleth walked to the center of the room and squared off with Jale to spar.

Lyse tugged on my arm, trying to coax me to sit down on the floor next to the wall. I obeyed, helpless, but shivered with anxiety. Lyse took my hands and held them in hers, massaging them to try and calm me. Cayleth drew her rapier and glanced at us nervously, worry in her eyes. Jale didn't bother drawing his weapon yet, smirking smugly at her from across the room. A sick sense of dread settled in my stomach. Cayleth didn't know who she was fighting. What would he do to her?

When Raelan called start to the bout, Cayleth immediately threw up the illusion of a violent sandstorm. Even though I knew it wasn't real, it still felt like millions of sand particles were sweeping into my eyes, my hair, and my clothing, and I resisted the urge to cover my face. Lyse, still new to Cayleth's illusions, held on to me as though we would be separated and lost from each other in the screaming wind. The feeling was so real that I could only imagine Jale taking cover, overwhelmed by the masterful illusion. In his place, I would have. The illusion began to shift almost immediately, however. The sand particles, which had initially swirled in a tight, spinning vortex, began to fall straight down like snow instead.

"What's happening?" Lyse whispered.

"I don't know."

Cayleth's illusion began to fade, revealing her standing in the middle of the training room, her hands outstretched as though she were catching falling snow. Her sword had fallen to the floor, forgotten, and her face was a mixture of surprise and pleasure as she watched something invisible fall from the ceiling. Jale's orange magic glowed faintly around her head. Whatever Cayleth saw, it was only in her mind. Jale walked up to her and drew his heavy sword, leveling it at her throat. When he recalled his magic, Cayleth came back to attention with a start. "Oh!" she squeaked. "What happened?"

Raelan was uninterested in explaining the intricacies of Jale's magic to her for now. "Next!" he barked gruffly. "Aeryn."

Jale withdrew his sword, and Cayleth shook her head, trying to understand what had happened. For someone used to creating illusions, it was hard for her to reconcile how a different kind of illusion had been used against her. I stood shakily, my knees weak. The last thing I wanted to do was fight Jale. As much as I hated him, if he could wipe my memories of being kidnapped from Thamir, he could wipe *everything* if he wanted to. He hadn't hurt Cayleth, but that didn't mean he would be gentle with me. What was to stop him from taking *all* my memories of home if he felt like it?

Lyse stood, too, in order to fight alongside me, but Raelan waved her off. I stopped her when she started to protest. It was better she not draw Jale's attention. She gave me a sympathetic look and squeezed my hand. "It will be okay," she whispered. "Raelan won't let him hurt you."

Although her words were meant to be comforting, they only made things worse. If I was relying on a murderer like Raelan to protect me, then I was really in trouble. Jale raised a magic shield around himself, so I did, too, drawing on my connection with Lyse's magic. With the addition of her power, my shield barely shimmered at all around me. Next I raised a mental shield, hoping that the same principles that applied to defending against a warg like Raelan would apply to Jale. Whatever else happened, I had to keep him out. He couldn't have any more of my memories than the ones he'd already taken.

Raelan called start, and I began to blast Jale with the biggest fire bolts that I could summon. They hit with burning splashes of fiery blue, the magic sizzling as it fizzled out against his shield. In response, Jale drew a dagger from his belt and threw it. I barely managed to dodge in time, and it clipped the edge of my cuirass as it passed. I was slower than I should have been; in contrast to Raelan's inquisitive, methodical mental probing, Jale was attacking with what felt like sharp spikes of pressure like hammer blows. It was hard to focus on both what Jale was doing in front of me and what he was trying to do in my mind. I threw another series of bolts, then winced as a second dagger took a small slice out of my leg. The wound stung, and I regretted my choice not to wear greaves.

Jale's next attempt to get through my shield rang my head like a bell, momentarily stunning me. I staggered as though physically struck. He used my imbalance and disorientation to attack again.

When Jale broke through my mental shield, the feeling was like falling through ice: The shield was there—perfect, whole, and unblemished—and then it was gone, collapsed into a thousand irreparable shards. In an instant, I was no longer standing in the training room at Windhall. Instead, I was seeing my entire life in Thamir flash before my eyes. I had fallen through the ice into a river of my own memories.

They flowed thick and fast before my eyes. I was a small child, gathering firewood with my mother to burn and keep us warm, the thin sticks bundled in my arms as my mother sang me songs she had learned from her mother, and her mother before her. Then in the blink of an eye I was older, setting snares for rabbits along snow-covered rabbit runs while my father laid traps in the branches above them for pine martens. The scene shifted, and I was with Kem and Kyan, their faces stretched with laughter as they raced through the forest, competing to see who could run the fastest. Then I was alone in the woods around Thamir, despairing of ever controlling my wild and reckless magic.

Finally, out of the churning swirl of memories and emotions, a single figure appeared. It was an old man. He was tall and thin, and leaned heavily on a staff to counter a pronounced limp on his right side. He didn't seem to belong to my other memories. He stood out like a black crow against a blanket of white snow. Although I didn't recognize him, he felt familiar. Who was he? I tried to grab onto the mysterious memory and examine it, but it was hard to do in the maelstrom of other memories clamoring to be recognized.

Then memories associated with him swam to the surface of my mind. He was teaching me about magic, showing me how to use it. He was patient, working diligently with me when I felt most alone. It was because of him that I had learned to use magic when all hope seemed lost. *He* had been the one who taught me how to harness my power. He had told me about war mages and warned me about King's City, but he had also given me hope that I could be more than a weapon. Why hadn't I remembered him until now? How could I possibly have forgotten someone so important to me? Feeling a sense of desperate need, I grasped for his name. From the darkest recesses of my mind, the answer came: Firdas.

As though his name had been a key that opened a locked door in my mind, now the rest of the memories of Firdas came flooding back to me. I staggered under their weight, finally remembering the last time that I had seen him: We had been alone in the forest, or so we'd thought, but the king's seekers had found us. Firdas—no! His real name was Kjelborn, and he had once been a Great Mage in the King's Regiment—had tried to fight to protect me. He had challenged Jale, trying to summon his magic, but it had been bound decades before in punishment for deserting the King's Regiment, and he had lost. And then...

Hot tears ran down my face—real tears, not memories. They broke the spell of Jale's magic. I blinked, and the fog of memories that had been crowding around me, trapping me in visions of the past, dispersed. Jale was watching me from across the training room, an expression of boredom on his face. He couldn't see the memories he'd unlocked. He didn't know what I'd seen. Unlike during his bout with Cayleth, he hadn't even bothered to level his sword at me, to show how easily he had defeated my defenses. To him, we were mere children playing at soldiers, the way I had once played with my brothers in the woods. He didn't know he'd just given back to me the last thing he'd taken.

Now I remembered everything.

I launched myself at him, screaming incoherently as I swung my sword down on his head, no plan in mind other than to smash and crush his smug face. "You stole my memories!" I screamed at him as he parried the blow.

The crashing of our two swords together echoed in my ears like the crack of lightning and jarred my muscles all the way to my jaw. I quickly disengaged my sword and drove at him again, raining wild blows down upon him as I yelled, "You kidnapped me and told me that my family was dead! The whole time, you lied to me! You lied to me even as you pretended to have saved me!"

Jale was quick and well-trained, but anger can be an all but unstoppable force. When he tried to counterattack, raising his sword to deliver a slash across my shoulder, I used mage fire from my left hand to blast him backward. He slammed into the wall, his face a mask of shock and disbelief. I was on him in an instant, beating again and again against his parries, ignoring the growing heaviness in my arm as I desperately tried to pummel him with my sword. "How could you?" I screamed, a sound almost more animal than human. "How could you lie to me every day when you knew how much I hurt?"

He didn't respond. He didn't have time to, busy as he was fending me off. His silence only fueled the fire of my anger. I stepped back from him and held up my left hand. In it burned a small but intensely hot ball of blue mage fire. I was within Jale's shield. If I released my magic now, it would burn through anything at which I directed it: armor, cloth, or skin. Jale knew it, too. He froze immediately, then slowly held his hands up in submission. I commanded, "Tell me what you did to Firdas! To Kjelborn!"

"Nothing," Jale replied gruffly. The beginnings of a snarl played on his lips. "We left him and did nothing to him. He's a broken old man who will die soon. Living in that icy hell is torture enough."

"You lie," I growled, stepping closer. "Tell me the truth!"

Jale's eyes followed the fire in my hand as it came closer to him, and he unconsciously pressed himself against the wall in an effort to put more distance between the boiling heat and his skin. Then in an instant, my world was turned upside down. The ceiling flew into view as I landed heavily on my back. My legs clattered against the floor a moment later. Gamiel's dark fingers grabbed the tunic around my neck and started to pull me a few feet off the floor. "Enough!" she commanded.

"No! Not until—"

"He spoke the truth." Gamiel's green eyes were cool and emotionless, the same way they'd looked after she'd killed the bandits in Ithaka. Did nothing rattle her?

"You weren't there! You don't know!" My voice was high and wild.

"Kjelborn lives," she repeated firmly. "On my honor."

I stopped struggling. The moment I did, Gamiel dropped me. My helmet rang like a bell when it struck the floor, and I stared at the ceiling, dazed. The sound of Gamiel's footsteps walking away told me she was leaving. A moment later, I heard the training room door open, then close. Raelan's wraith-like face appeared above me, a half-moon on a dark night. "You know Kjelborn, the Sword of Ilirya? The greatest war mage in the history of the kingdom?"

"Kjelborn is a traitor…" Jale started to say, but Raelan cut him off, waving his hand in Jale's direction to quiet him.

Raelan licked his lips. His coal black eyes danced with interest. "Where? Where does Kjelborn live?"

I didn't want to answer. What did Raelan want with Firdas? It couldn't be anything good. But I didn't have a choice. If I didn't tell him, Jale would. I gathered my rapier and stood so that I could face Raelan standing.

"He lived in my village. I didn't know he was Kjelborn until Jale called him by that name. He never used his magic or talked about being a mage."

"He has been living in disguise," Raelan murmured, nodding to himself.

"He's nothing like what he once was," Jale sneered, still standing close to the wall against which I'd thrown him. "He's a doddering old man. His magic is gone, bound forever by an unbreakable spell. He's an old dog gone into the forest to die."

Raelan looked thoughtful. "You fail to see the bigger picture, Jale. A retired hunting dog still knows all the trails in the forest, even if he can no longer run them with the vigor that he used to. Knowledge does not simply disappear with age, and there are things that Kjelborn knows that no other living man does."

Jale made a face like a reprimanded child but held his tongue. Raelan waved his hand at me, dismissing me, then called Faegan to face Jale. I scurried back to where Lyse and Cayleth were sitting against the wall of the training room. They clustered around me immediately.

"Wow!" Cayleth's voice was full of admiration. "You almost took his head off!"

"What happened?" Lyse asked with concern, reaching out to stroke the soft skin on the back of my neck as I took my helmet off and set it on the ground. My hair was matted with sweat.

"When Jale broke my mental shield, it released the memories of when he kidnapped me from Thamir. I remembered someone he specifically tried to wipe from my memory: Kjelborn."

"The Sword of Ilirya," Lyse said, her voice tinged with awe.

I nodded. "He helped me learn to control my magic. He was... He tried to save me. He didn't want me to be taken. He hated the King's Regiment, and he hated the war."

Lyse caressed my hand. Unwillingly, I remembered Firdas as he had looked right before Jale used his mind-spike affinity on me. He had been standing in the woods, bleeding purple magic as he tried to break the shackles that bound him in order to save me. Firdas, once Ilirya's greatest warrior, broken and beaten at the farthest corner of the kingdom, unable to save even a single girl. I choked back a sob, wiping away tears that started to fall. Firdas had deserved better. He was a good man. War had taken everything he had, even in his twilight years.

Sniffing, I turned my attention to watching the bout between Faegan and Jale. It was a brutal match. Infuriated by the beating he'd taken from me, Jale destroyed Faegan's mental shield in minutes, then unleashed a mind spike so vicious that Faegan collapsed to his knees, holding his head in his hands. Jale kicked Faegan in the chest, flipping him onto his back, then sheathed his sword and, without saying anything, stalked angrily out of the training room. Faegan took gasping breaths where he lay on the floor. His face was white as snow, making his freckles stand out. His eyes were dazed.

Looking at the door, Cayleth muttered under her breath, "He's almost as bad as Raelan is."

His lesson in tatters and his guests gone, Raelan pronounced, "Class is dismissed early today. I have matters to attend to. Aeryn and Lyse, come to my office after dinner."

My heart skipped a beat and my breath caught. Raelan had never asked to see any of us after class. What could it mean? Had our trip to King's City or Kaylara's eavesdropping finally caught up to us? Was this the moment everything came crashing down? Lyse squeezed my hand, trying to give me courage that I knew neither of us had. My hands were shaking. Should we run? There was nowhere to go where we couldn't be found. My stomach twisted on itself, bitter bile rising in my throat in terrified anticipation of what Raelan might want.

"We shouldn't rush to conclusions," Kaylara said at dinner, trying to remain positive. "He could have something else he wants to discuss. Something related to war magic?"

I pushed my food away, untouched. How could I possibly eat at a time like this? I felt like vomiting. My legs twitched beneath me as if itching to run away. Lyse was no better. She hadn't even bothered to take food. She sat next to me, her body shrunk into itself, her hands between her knees. I rubbed my temples. "What could he possibly want to discuss that he couldn't say in class?"

"Maybe he is thinking you are doing well and is wanting to tell you this where Cayleth is not hearing!" Pavo chirruped brightly. Pavo had never met a cloud that didn't have a silver lining. Cayleth boggled at him as if he had two heads.

Kaylara pursed her lips. "Maybe he wants to talk more about Lyse's training now that you're bonded. Haven't you said she needs to learn mental shielding? That's a specialty of Raelan's, isn't it?"

Cayleth nodded. "It could make sense. There's no reason to assume it has anything to do with…you know."

"By now he surely knows that we snuck off campus and got caught," I said. "What if he's going to interrogate us about why we left?"

"Stick to your story! He can't disprove it," Kaylara urged.

Lyse said shakily, "Even if—He can't do anything too awful to us. If we went missing, everyone at Windhall would notice."

"Unless he said you ran away. Who would doubt a teacher? Especially if the chancellor backed him up." Cayleth doubled over with a puff of air as Kaylara elbowed her in the stomach. She quickly croaked, "But it's probably mage stuff, like Kaylara said."

After a moment's silence, in which we all individually pondered the horrible potential outcomes of the meeting, Cayleth added, "Of course, we'll be ready to help if anything happens. And if he tries to warg you, run."

I looked into Lyse's eyes. They were the first thing I'd really seen at Windhall. They were the start of one journey, and potentially its end, too.

As far as we knew, Raelan had kidnapped and tortured citizens of King's City. He had burned down the city guard garrison in the northwest quarter and masterminded the assassination of many of the city's senior-most leaders. There was no telling what would happen in his office if he'd found out what we knew.

I held Lyse's hands in mine. They were trembling. "Lyse, there's still time for you to run. You can take a horse and ride as fast as you can toward Rath. They might not come after you."

"What about you? Why wouldn't you come?"

I grimaced. "I can buy you time. It might not be much, but it's something. You can make it. You have to at least try."

She shook her head. "I'm not leaving you." As scared as she was, her voice was firm. She leaned forward, resting her forehead against mine. "It's no use trying to convince me to go, Aeryn. Our fates are linked. Where you go, I go. I would never leave you. Not now."

"Please—" I begged.

She kissed me, stopping me from saying more. When she pulled away, she said, "If it comes to a fight, we fight together. But maybe Pavo's right, and Raelan's going to tell you what a good mage you are. It can't all be bad news."

By the time we arrived at the academic building, night had fallen. Lyse and I walked slowly down the long hall to Raelan's office, our bodies heavy with trepidation. Eerie shadows flickered against the walls like creeping ghosts, and the torchlight reflected in the black windows like floating fire. Lyse gripped my hand tightly. I wished we were back in my room, me studying for Professor Kalmath's class and Lyse reading about the medicinal properties of plants found in the Ice Crown—a normal night like any other.

Unbidden, Cayleth's suggestion that if Raelan tried to warg me I should run came to mind. I shuddered at the memory of Raelan poking around my mind. I never wanted Lyse, who had only heard me describe it, to be subjected to the experience. Could I stop Raelan if he tried? At least he couldn't warg both of us at once.

The overwhelming sense of dread only grew stronger the closer we got to Raelan's office. By the time we arrived, I wondered how I was even able to breathe with all the weight that was pressing down on my chest. I stopped at the door and looked at Lyse, who nodded back at me with all the bravery she could muster. Her brown eyes swirled with emotion. I put my hand on the knob. My hand was shaking so hard I wasn't sure I could turn it. I pushed.

Raelan was sitting at his desk, his head tilted back, his eyes closed. His black hood had fallen back, revealing a totally bald, bone-white head. I had never seen him unhooded. He looked inhuman, more skeleton than man. Was the Dark Magic stripping the last of his humanity from him? He heard us and looked down, his black eyes meeting mine. It was impossible to read any emotion in them. I was quivering like a leaf in a windstorm, and so was Lyse.

"Sit down," he commanded, although not impolitely.

Lyse and I obediently sat in the two heavy wooden chairs across from his desk. Panic was clawing at my throat, trying to choke me. I had to fight the urge to run.

Raelan pushed his seat back from his desk and stood, turning his back to us in order to stare out his window, which looked in the direction of King's City. "I have lived at Windhall University many, many years. There is nothing that goes on here that I do not know."

My breath died in my lungs, and all my hope with it. He knew. It was over for us. He turned and gazed at us. "I know that you and your friends have been sneaking around, spying. I imagine you even thought you got away with it."

I fought back a wave of nausea that made my mouth water. We had been foolish to think we wouldn't be caught. Were Cayleth, Kaylara, and Pavo even now being rounded up by Raelan's collaborators? What would happen to them? How had everything gone so wrong? This was all my fault. I never should have drawn anyone else into my investigation of Dark Magic. And Lyse... I didn't dare look at her.

Raelan waved a dismissive hand. "None of that matters now. We have reached a cataclysmic moment in the history of Ilirya. The corrupt decay of the old order will be replaced by a new order, one that will be far more powerful than any that has ever come before." He gave us a hard look. "There are no other bond pairs in the entire kingdom. Together, you are not quite the equivalent of a Great Mage, but you are nevertheless unique and, in your own way, powerful. I would hate to see that unexplored potential wasted."

He held out a hand. "Join us, and you can help build a better Ilirya."

He stopped talking and stared at us expectantly, waiting. His eyes sparkled with the unholy light of fanaticism. What did he mean? What new order? Was he really asking us to join whatever Dark conspiracy he was involved in?

"Why... Why us?" I asked.

He pursed his lips. "There will be turmoil, at first. We will need mages who can keep order. Pyromancers have a way of...awing a crowd. Non-mages have a tendency to fear mage fire. They will capitulate more quickly in the face of it."

"What have you done, Professor Raelan?" Lyse asked, her voice soft and hoarse.

Raelan smiled at her with his sharp, pointed teeth. It was a genuine smile, the first I'd ever seen him give. "I have done what was necessary to cleanse this kingdom of its impurities and pave the way for a glorious future. I have set in motion a revolution that will echo for all eternity. Ilirya will return to her former greatness!"

A chill ran down my spine. "Marshal Heika and Garreth—were they among the impure?"

"In war, there are always casualties." Raelan tossed his head, casually dismissing them and their deaths as insignificant. "We are all of us pieces in a greater game. To win the game, some pieces must be removed from the board."

I was stunned speechless. Was he so blinded by his fanatical ideology—whatever it was—that he believed we would even consider joining him? We weren't pawns in a giant game of Kill the King!

Kill the...

"You're going to kill the king!" I said.

It wasn't a question. I knew I was right. This was why they'd killed the Shadow. Why they'd killed the Lady Marshal and attacked the Knight Commander. Before Raelan could answer, there was a distant boom. A tremor shook the room, causing the quill in Raelan's inkstand to rattle. I looked past Raelan out the window and saw a large ball of fire rise into the night sky from King's City. Smoke began billowing skyward, gray against the black night sky. Raelan turned to watch it, his body half turned away from us.

"It has started!" His voice was high and giddy.

While he was distracted, I grabbed Lyse's hand and we ran.

CHAPTER 11

"What death takes, it never gives back."

– The Salyar "Book of the Dead"

"The moral code of the Salyar requires individuals to render aid to anyone who needs it. This explains how Ice Crown communities have survived for centuries, against all odds."

– A Kingdom and its People, 4th edition

LYSE AND I CLATTERED DOWN the hall, our feet flying. My only thought was to put as much distance as possible between us and Raelan. Once we were safe, we could regroup and consider what to do, but first we had to get far enough away that he couldn't warg one of us. Or do something worse.

If he tried to pursue us, we were too quick for him, slipping out of the academic building with no sign of him in tow. We were halfway across the green, running toward the dorm, when the one of the doors of the training building flew open. We skidded to a halt as adults streamed out in front of us like angry ants from an anthill. Some were injured, with dark, wet blood streaming down their faces and limbs. Others were screaming in unmitigated panic. I grabbed Lyse's arm to prevent us from being separated as the crowd began to stampede past us out onto the green, spilling out like blood poured into water.

Raising my voice to be heard over the sound of their pain, panic and fear, I shouted, "What's going on? Who are these people?

"I don't know!" Lyse's eyes were wide. Her head swiveled from side to side as she tried to take it all in. "They must be coming through the Gate to Windhall's city office. Some of them look like Windhall administrators."

One of those administrators was Lethera, the first woman I'd met at Windhall. As she ran past, Lyse managed to catch her hand and tether her to us before she could be lost in the crowd. Her simple brown dress was torn at the hem, as though it had gotten caught but she had not stopped to untangle it. Her black hair was half out of its bun, flowing wildly behind her. Blood stained her hands.

Lyse asked, "What's happening?"

"Northmen! In the city!" Lethera cried, her eyes wild and her voice shrill with fear. "They're attacking the city guard. There are hundreds of them! Some came to the Windhall office, too. We managed to escape while a few others held them off. I locked the door …"

She held up a large brass key in a hand that shook so hard it was all but waving. Tears started to fall from her blue eyes. "If only we'd had war mages," she moaned. "None of our affinities helped. It was terrible. There was so much blood."

Lyse's eyes met mine. A Northman attack? Now? It had to be related to Raelan. Were they working together? Was this the army that Raelan and the chancellor planned to use to take the city, the reason they killed the King's Shadow? It must be. Lyse put her hand on the small of Lethera's back, gently pushing her onward. "Go to the dining hall. You'll be safe there. Try and get the others there, too."

Lethera disappeared almost at once into the crowd, which had reached its end. Whoever had not made it through the Gate before the door was locked was now at the mercy of the Northmen on the other side. Lights began to appear throughout the campus as students, teachers, and administrators heard the clamor in the green and looked out to see what was happening. Lyse started to say something but was cut off by the sound of more explosions in the city. The ground trembled under our feet. Plumes of flame and smoke rose into the sky. Based on what Derrin had taught us about weapons of war, I guessed the Northmen were igniting barrels of oil, possibly to breach the thick stone walls of important buildings in the city.

"What now?" Lyse asked. She looked over her shoulder at the academic building, checking to see that Raelan still hadn't followed us.

"I…"

I wanted to run. This was my chance to break free of everything that bound me against my will to Windhall. Under the cover of the chaos in the city, I could slip away and set off for home. But Lethera's terrified eyes flashed through my mind, and those of the rest of the scared, hurt people who had come from King's City seeking protection and shelter. Lyse had said that there were only a few hundred soldiers and knights in the city; they might be outnumbered by the Northmen. Even now, the Northman might be cutting through them like a warm knife through butter. All of Ilirya's best fighters were at the southern front; who would protect the citizens of King's City from the invaders?

I was young and scared, but I was a war mage. Thousands of people in King's City had no magic. Right now, they were likely fighting off the Northman invaders with pots and pans, brooms and rolling pins. If I wasn't willing to fight for them with my fire, then I was dooming them to die undefended. An image of Colen and his brothers cowering in fear flashed through my mind. As an Ice Crowner, I owed King's City no allegiance. They were not my people. But as an Ice Crowner, I was duty bound to help. "We need to find the others, and then I'm going to the armory. I'm going to help."

Lyse grabbed my shoulders. "Aeryn, we could run! No one will stop us from leaving Windhall now, and everyone in the city will be too busy fighting the Northmen. This is our chance to get away from Raelan! Besides, if the city falls, the Northmen won't come to Rath. We'll be safe there."

I put my hands on Lyse's hips and looked into her beautiful brown eyes. The fear in them brimmed over like too much water in a pitcher. Even in her terror, she was radiantly beautiful. She was a healer, not a fighter. Moreover, she wasn't from the Ice Crown. She wouldn't understand.

I leaned in and kissed her fiercely, savoring everything about her. The bond between us prickled. She had Called me, and I had come. Now the people of King's City were calling me, too. Asher's words came back to me: "No one becomes a knight who's afraid of riding into danger head on." As a war mage, it was my duty to run into danger, too. I'd spent weeks worrying about Raelan and the chancellor, worrying that they might hurt me. Now I understood it wasn't just me in danger: It was everyone in the city. Everything was connected. I couldn't run and hide, no matter how scared I was.

"You go," I said, "but I have to help."

Lyse shook her head. "This isn't spying on Raelan; this is a coup! This is war! People will die! It's too dangerous."

"I know. And I'm a war mage. I can protect people, Lyse. I have to try. I promise I'll be careful."

Lyse dropped her hands from my shoulders. Her body rocked back and forth as she covered her mouth with her hands. Her shoulders rose and fell with deep, heaving breaths. She closed her eyes. Then she grimaced and nodded. "Okay, then we help."

"What? No, not you! Just me."

Lyse's face was determined. "I told you: Where you go, I go."

"No, Lyse! Go to Madrigal. I'll find you there. It's too dangerous for you here!"

"You're right. Someone has to protect the people of King's City. It will be a massacre otherwise. You need my magic, and besides, I'm not losing you. Not to Raelan, not to Northmen, not to anyone. If we have to fight, we do it together." Before I could protest, Lyse cut me off. "It's my choice, Aeryn. You can't stop me. Now let's go."

She took off running in the direction of the dorm, and I followed. Kaylara, Pavo, and Cayleth met us at the door, their faces grim. I started to explain, but Cayleth stopped me. "We know. Kaylara was eavesdropping."

"Why are you still here then?" I asked. "You should leave. Run for the fields south of Windhall and don't stop until you can't see the walls of King's City anymore."

"Don't be ridiculous," Kaylara snapped. "We don't all have to be war mages to have something to contribute."

"But—"

"My family lives in King's City, in the southeast quarter. I have to make sure they're all right."

"We are having magic, too, Aeryn," Pavo said. "We are being helpful." He snapped his fingers, and thunder rumbled in the sky. I jumped.

Despite my misgivings, I didn't have time to try to dissuade my friends. "Fine, let's go," I said.

Maz greeted us as we came through the armory door. "What's happening? I heard explosions. It sounded like they came from the city."

"It's a coup, Maz," Cayleth explained, "and Chancellor Vandys and Professor Raelan are part of it."

Maz's lips thinned into a disapproving frown. "King's City draws trouble to it like offal draws flies. Figures its evil would one day reach all the way to Windhall. What do you need?"

"Everything to fight a war. There are five of us here. I don't think anyone else will be coming. They're all hunkered down in the dorm and the dining hall, trying to understand what's happening. They don't know about Raelan and the chancellor yet."

"Take what you need and be safe. I'll try to find some teachers to protect the campus. We're not soldiers, but we'll do what we can. I suppose Raelan's war mages are on his side?"

I froze. Where *were* Halver and the others? There wasn't time to think about it.

Cayleth ran through the armory, tossing armor, swords, scabbards and knives to each of us. She added a battle axe for herself and a bow and arrows for me. Kaylara held her new weapons awkwardly, and I was reminded that unlike me and Cayleth, she hadn't been trained to fight. It was dangerous for her to come into the city with us. Pavo gently took the weapons from her and helped her sheathe them before he laid his own sword aside and opted for a spear instead. Whatever he'd learned about weapons and fighting before coming to Windhall, I hoped it would be enough to keep the two of them safe. However this night ended, I wanted all of us together, in one piece.

When everyone was suitably armored and equipped, we ran out together onto the training field. Trick, Derrin, and Maerys were standing there, as if waiting for us. Each was heavily armored, their weapons sticking out from them like the quills of a porcupine.

Cayleth skidded to a halt. "Trick!"

"What can we do to help?" Trick asked. As if from nowhere, two curved blades appeared in her hands. They reached from midway down her forearm to past her fist: deadly, close-quarters weapons that would do significant damage to anyone or anything that got within range.

"Northmen are attacking the city. We're going after the chancellor and Professor Raelan. We have to stop them before they kill the king. Chancellor Vandys has her own Gate to the palace, right? Where is it?" I said.

"It's in her office."

"Where will you go?" Cayleth asked.

"It sounds like we're needed in the city. We'll go through the city office Gate and join in any fighting we find. We'd come with you, but...as non-mages, there's not much we can do against mages."

"No! You can't go through the city office! The Northmen captured it!" Lyse's voice was alarmed.

"Then we'll have to take it back from them." Derrin's fingers played across the weapons hanging at his sides. He drew a massive battle axe with a head as large as my two hands put together.

"Be careful," Trick told us. "And good luck." She signaled to Derrin and Maerys, and the three took off in a sprint toward the training hall.

I surveyed my friends. At least Derrin, Trick, and Maerys were battle-hardened fighters. We were a motley, desperate army. But somehow, we might be Ilirya's best hope for stopping Raelan and the chancellor. Speaking quickly, I said, "Everyone stay behind me and Cayleth. If you see something dangerous, let us know. Don't get separated; we have to stick together."

My heart was pounding. Smoke from fires in the city was starting to drift over the campus, and it made my eyes burn. Were we too late? Had the city already fallen? We'd have to assume it hadn't. I set off in the direction of the academic building, pulling magic to my hands and raising a shield that I hoped was large enough to cover Lyse, Kaylara, and Pavo, too. I could feel Lyse helping build the shield, feeding her magic into it. Cayleth's shield interlocked with mine. Where they overlapped, the shields shimmered brown. I smiled grimly at her, glad that if I was to face mortal danger, it was with Windhall's best fighter—and my closest friend—beside me.

The green was deserted as we ran through it. Fearful faces, student and adult alike, stared out from every window of the dorm and the dining hall. Like animals, they were hiding in their burrows, hoping the danger would pass. Hoping someone would save them. The silence over the campus was eerie in contrast to the distant noise from the city. Another explosion rocked the night and I tripped, almost falling over. Cayleth caught me and helped me back on my feet. I nodded my gratitude as we pushed on.

When we arrived at the academic building, we found Faegan standing at the main door with his arms crossed, watching the campus. He wore his own personal plate armor and chain mail. His House crest was embossed on the red gold breastplate. He looked surprised to see us. Cayleth's hair had started to pull from its ponytail, and our faces were flushed.

Cayleth stopped and put her hands on her knees to catch her breath. Relief in her voice, she wheezed, "Faegan, thank the gods! I'm so glad you're here! Now we have three war mages. Listen, we know everything. It's the chancellor and Raelan; they're planning to overthrow the king. We have to stop them from going through the chancellor's Gate to the palace."

Faegan didn't so much as blink. "I know." He said the words simply, as though they were weightless. His face was blank.

My eyebrows knit together. What? I couldn't process his words, his calm. Half the city was on fire. Wounded refugees bleating with fear had surged into Windhall. Our teachers were planning to murder Ilirya's regent. How could he be so composed? Why didn't he care?

"You...know?" Cayleth repeated. Her eyebrows were drawn together as she tried to make sense of it.

I noticed for the first time that Faegan had positioned himself directly in front of the door. He wasn't defending the academic building from attack, as I'd initially assumed. He was blocking entry into it. The hairs on the back of my neck prickled. "Faegan, why are you here?"

Faegan lifted his chin and took a breath, his chest expanding. "As leader of my people, I must do what is best for them."

"What are you saying, Faegan?" Cayleth unconsciously took a step backward.

"Ardeth has suffered greatly in the last few years, taken advantage of by her unscrupulous neighbors. Now that civil war has come to Ilirya, we cannot afford to be on the losing side. When the new king is in place, he will reward Ardeth for standing with him."

"You're part of the coup!" Cayleth gasped. "You joined them! How could you?"

I thought of the Lady Marshal and everyone who had died in the Night of the Long Swords. They'd never had forewarning because Faegan had never told them. Their blood was on his hands. "We trusted you!" I shouted.

Faegan's mouth twitched. He didn't like to be challenged. "Professor Raelan made very persuasive arguments, whose merits anyone could see. Ardeth is a primary supplier of soldiers to the army. My people have been decimated by this endless, senseless war in the south. When the new king finally puts an end to it, we will be able to rebuild. Ardeth will be greater than it ever has."

Inky blackness lurked at the corners of his eyes. It wasn't the night shadows. My skin crawled. A cold wave washed over my body. How had I failed to notice before tonight? "Who did you hurt, Faegan?"

Faegan shifted uncomfortably, but his unease turned to self-righteous anger in a flash. "Raelan had one of the assassins who killed my family brought to me as a gesture of goodwill. His suffering will repay mine a hundredfold. Can you really argue that he deserved any better treatment? One life in return for the lives of dozens."

He looked between me and Cayleth, his lips quivering. He wanted understanding, approval even. We would never give it, not for this. He continued, "I did what I had to for my people! Ardeth will never again fall victim to another barony! We will be respected and feared! This is what a great leader must do. These are the sacrifices he must make."

Cayleth shook her head. "When did you betray us? Or were you always working with him?"

"I chose the victorious side!" Faegan's cry was high and desperate. "History will remember those who won, not those who lost."

Cayleth drew her sword. In the silence of the night, the sound of the metal scraping against the scabbard was shockingly loud. To me, she murmured, "Go. I'll catch up."

In response, Faegan, too, drew his sword, eyes narrowed. I couldn't believe what was happening. Were they really going to fight here, in front of the academic building? Cayleth stepped left, angling to push him away from the door so that the rest of us could run past. Her voice was tinged with sadness when she spoke. And contempt. "Oh Faegan, you're weaker than I thought. This was not the way. Your people deserve better."

Before he could answer, she launched an attack, driving hard against him with a flurry of blows from her sword. With his back to the building, he couldn't maneuver, so he had no choice but to step back and away from the door. Cayleth hastened the process through calculated feints and jabs, herding him toward the green. We waited until the two were completely clear, then Kaylara grabbed the door handle and yanked, pulling it open. The four of us rushed through, piling into the hall and looking around to make sure there were no traps awaiting us. Who else might the chancellor and Raelan have recruited to their side?

"Should we help her?" Kaylara's eyes were wide as she looked back at the door. She clutched a dagger in her shaking hand.

"She'll be fine," I replied. She had never yet lost to Faegan in class. Even so, I wished she was still with us. Having her beside me made me feel more confident. But we had to push forward. There was no time to waste. I turned and ran down the hall toward the chancellor's office, the heel of my boots clacking against the stone corridor. My heart pounded in my chest. What would I do if I found Raelan and the chancellor there? How could I possibly stop them without Cayleth?

I needn't have worried. We were too late. The door to the chancellor's office had carelessly been left open, revealing that it was empty inside. Parchment was strewn on the ground, knocked there by bodies walking past in a hurry. The Gate shimmered against the far wall, a disconcertingly abrupt transition between the warm oak furnishings of the office and the rough gray stone of what must be a corridor in the palace. My heart sank. Chancellor Vandys and Raelan already passed through. They were in the palace.

Kaylara put her hand over her mouth. "Oh no. What do we do now?"

"It... It may be too late." Lyse's face was pale. "It could all be over by now, if they..." She didn't finish the sentence. If they had already killed the king.

I bit my lip. "Maybe it's not too late. Maybe there's still time to stop them."

"You want to go through?" Kaylara asked.

"I..." I stopped, momentarily overwhelmed by the magnitude of what we were facing. It would be so easy to let events take their course. Who was I to try and stop a coup? Then I remembered the Northmen rampaging through King's City, the explosions and the smoke. There were still people in the city who were under siege and couldn't protect themselves. What I'd told Lyse was still true: It was my duty to run into danger. But only mine. "I'm going through, but you should stay here, where it's safe."

Kaylara crossed her arms. Her chin was raised. "I already told you: King's City is my home. I'm coming with you."

Pavo hefted his spear. "I am not being scared."

I looked at Lyse and swallowed. I didn't want the responsibility of leading them all into danger. It was too heavy. Who knew what we would find on the other side of the Gate? In the best case, the palace soldiers would have put down the rebellion. In the worst case... I nodded, trying to appear braver than I was. "I'll go first, to make sure it's safe."

I squeezed Lyse's hand one last time, then stepped through the Gate, hands up and magic at the ready. My hair stood on end. Fear pulsed through my veins. What if there was an ambush? The hallway into which the Gate opened was deserted, however, so I waved the others through.

On the palace side, the Gate was camouflaged against the wall: To an observer, the wall looked hard and unbroken the length of the hallway. Anyone using the Gate would look like they'd stepped out of solid stone. This meant that if we had to find it again, we would only be able to by feeling along the stone blocks until we reached the opening. The others piled through behind me. Pavo, seeing how the Gate was masked, took off the necklace he was wearing and laid it on the ground. I gave him credit for his foresight. Now we would be able to find it again.

Lyse looked around. "Which way do we go?"

The hall seemed to go on interminably in either direction around us. Since none of us had ever been in the palace before, we'd have to guess which way would take us to Raelan and the chancellor. I chose to go to the right. The four of us crept along the corridor warily, each brandishing a weapon. No one spoke. Somewhere in the city, there was another explosion, and we all jumped. Finally, we reached a spiral staircase. We started to ascend.

"Where is everyone?" Kaylara whispered.

"Fighting," I guessed.

Although Kaylara hadn't yet heard it, the whisper of metal on metal was echoing down the stairwell. As we continued to rise, the sound became clearer. Judging from its violence, a pitched and desperate battle was raging nearby. I swallowed, wishing Cayleth was still with us. If it came to a fight, how could I protect the others all by myself? When we reached the door at the top of the staircase, I held my hand out to stop them. "I'm going to take a look. If someone tries to attack you, run. Don't fight."

Lyse's fingertips briefly brushed mine—an expression of support even as her eyes were dark with fear on my behalf. I pulled the door at the top of the stairs open and immediately saw that we had gone the wrong direction. We'd taken an underground hallway that led *away* from the castle keep, not into it. The door at which we now stood opened onto the farthest corner of the castle gardens, where a beleaguered detachment of the palace guard was fighting two familiar faces. My breath caught. Balrak and Halver!

Balrak's stone klant was wreaking havoc on the guard, throwing the soldiers' bodies like rag dolls while they tried ineffectively to hack at it with their swords. Halver, her magic whip crackling, was cutting her own swath through the soldiers. A dozen or so bodies lay motionless on the ground around the two war mages, some of their limbs bent at impossible angles. In the moonlight, it was impossible to see who was still alive and who dead. "Oh no." The words slipped trembling out of my mouth in a short moan.

"Which side are they on?" Kaylara asked, her question encompassing both the soldiers and the mages.

I flinched, startled by her unexpected appearance at my side. "Those are friends of Raelan. They're definitely not on our side."

As we watched, Halver's whip-turned-rope caught one of the guards and threw her against a stone archway. The soldier's body bent in half the wrong way and flopped to the ground. I was watching a massacre. The palace guard was no match for the two experienced war mages.

"We should go back through the tunnel." Kaylara's voice was quiet and full of horror.

"If we do, they'll kill every one of those soldiers." The soldier lying nearest to us on the ground moaned softly, too hurt to move. I ground my teeth together, trying to block the sound out.

Kaylara pulled at my arm. "Come on. We don't have much time, if we even any left at all. If we don't find the chancellor and Raelan, it won't matter what happens here."

Kaylara was right: we needed to stay focused on Chancellor Vandys and Raelan. But it was hard to leave the soldiers to die. Pavo pushed his way through the door. "We are fixing this problem quickly then, yes? Then we are going after the chancellor."

It was more than risky. "I can't shield you, Pavo," I warned, "not if we're both fighting. Are you sure you want to do this?"

Pavo scanned the scene, calculating. "It is not being a problem. Pavo is needing no shield. Pavo is being fast like a gazelle."

I wasn't so sure. It was one thing to summon fog and rain. It was another entirely to fight a spellcaster. Halver would tear him apart in seconds. But maybe Balrak... I couldn't fight both mages alone. If we were going to fight, I needed Pavo.

"Pav—" Kaylara's voice was high and strained. She moved to touch him, perhaps even stop him, but let her hand fall before it reached him. "Be careful." Her hands wrapped themselves in her tunic.

I caught Pavo's attention. "Go for the mage controlling the monster. Stay far away from the woman."

He nodded. Rainbow magic began to pulse around him. He stepped out onto the garden grass, and immediately black clouds began to gather in the night sky as he called them to him. Although they eclipsed the moon, cloaking us in inky darkness, Pavo glowed like a beautiful flame of sunlight. Balrak and Halver couldn't miss seeing him. I stepped up beside him and raised a magic shield around me. It was the mage equivalent of a battle cry. Now they couldn't mistake our intentions. We had challenged them to fight.

Pavo took off at a run in the direction of the two war mages. It took me a moment to react, and then I ran after him, throwing blue bolts to distract and preoccupy them. Pavo oriented himself to Balrak as I'd told him, launching his spear at the mage and then ducking under the massive fist of Balrak's klant as it took a swing at his head. Balrak stepped left, keeping the klant between himself and Pavo. The klant swung again. Pavo danced away. Pavo tried to dive-roll past it but was stopped. It was like watching a man fight a mountain. The former was fast and nimble, but the latter was so massive as to be invincible and unstoppable.

I didn't have time to watch any more of their fight because Halver started mouthing the words to a spell. To preempt whatever she was planning to do, I used my magic to throw her away from me and into a large black garden statue behind her. She slid heavily down it to its base. I loosed a blast of mage fire, which crackled against her shield and then dissipated. Snatching a dagger from my belt, I threw it. Halver rolled to avoid it, but it still stuck in her shoulder, eliciting a tiny scream of pain and rage from her.

She finished whatever spell she'd started, and my body began to sink into the earth as if I had stepped in quicksand. Using my magic, I pulled the statue over onto her. Soon I was caught in the ground to my knees. Pavo, somehow seeing my predicament while in the midst of his own trouble, summoned a small whirlwind that lifted me up and set me gently back on solid ground. I looked over to thank him and saw that he was sporting several small gashes on his face where the klant had managed to tag him. How long could Pavo keep up? We needed to end this fight quickly.

Halver kicked the statue off herself with difficulty and rose to her feet. I drilled her shield with mage fire. The fabric of my tunic steamed under the heat I was producing. Halver unfurled her magic whip, snarling. She raised her arm to cast the whip but stopped when a second stream of mage fire began to assault her from the left.

Surprised by the unexpected appearance of another mage's magic, I followed the column of fire back to Lyse, who had stationed herself behind a line of square cut hedges. Now that I was paying attention, I could feel that she was sharing our magic in order to open a second front against Halver. The bond between us pulsed with electric energy. Lyse's face was a mask of determination. She stepped closer to Halver, increasing the intensity of the blue fire that streamed from her hands. Uncertain how to confront two pyromancers at once, Halver faltered, and in that moment of weakness our combined attack was enough to shatter her shield.

Halver immediately stopped fighting, as vulnerable as a turtle without its shell. She held her hands level with her shoulders in the universal sign of surrender. Lyse and I stopped our attack. We weren't murderers, no matter how wrong it was that Halver had joined the Raelan and the chancellor.

A moment later, however, a sword blade materialized from the middle of her chest and thrust forward. Halver looked down at it, surprised. I gasped. The blade withdrew, and she collapsed into a shapeless pile on the ground. One of the palace guard soldiers, his right arm hanging limply at his side, stood panting where she had stood a moment before, the bloody sword in his left hand. Lyse and I stared at him in shock. Halver had already surrendered! He had murdered her!

The soldier was unperturbed. He stepped over Halver's body and began checking on the bodies of his comrades to see if any were still alive. I couldn't keep watching him; with Halver gone, I turned my attention to Balrak. His klant was still chasing Pavo around, but lightening was beginning to flicker in the clouds above us. Pavo danced easily away from the klant, and I realized that he had been luring it and its master into the center of the garden, away from everyone else. Balrak, intent on the fight, either didn't notice or didn't care how he was being manipulated.

I guessed what was coming before it happened. The air crackled, then a bolt of lightning flashed out of the clouds, striking Balrak with a charge that ran from his head to his toes. The mage collapsed immediately, his klant dissolving in a shimmer of magic. I didn't have time to think about what had just happened, how I was indirectly responsible for the deaths of two people. I would have to process it later, when we were someplace safe, and this nightmare was over.

Pavo wiped his hands on his pants legs. "Now we are going and finding the chancellor and Professor Raelan." His voice was more serious than I'd ever heard it. Sweat glistened on his forehead. His face was ashen. I wasn't the only one shaken by what we'd just done.

"I think not," said a familiar voice.

Jale stepped out from behind one of the tall white columns that ringed the garden. In the dark night, wearing the black armor of the King's Regiment, it was difficult to see him, but I would have recognized his haughty voice anywhere. My face flushed with anger. If he was here at the palace, it could only mean one thing: He had thrown his lot in with Raelan. He was a conspirator, too. Jale's body started to glimmer orange as he summoned his magic to him, illuminating his pale face. In response, I reflexively called my magic to my hands, too. I didn't want to fight again, but I would do whatever I had to.

Then a separate voice, rasping and awful and familiar, commanded, "Enough." It was Raelan.

CHAPTER 12

"The gods stopped paying attention to the mortal world centuries ago. They have their own quarrels to attend to."

— Reddek the Wise, first Chancellor of Windhall University

"Life is the interplay of decisions and their consequences."

— Everyn Stargazer, "The Five Pearls of Wisdom"

RAELAN, HIS BALD HEAD GLEAMING in the moonlight, stepped out from behind another column. The two men had likely been there the entire time, watching the fight from the shadows. Waiting for the time to reveal themselves. My legs went weak. We weren't strong enough to face Jale and Raelan on our own, and Raelan was ten paces away; close enough to warg us. We were trapped.

Addressing our small group, Raelan said, "Under different circumstances, I would have been impressed. A weather mage acting as a war mage? It's quite extraordinary. It suggests more thought be given to how war mages are categorized and selected in the future. And you defeated two strong war mages! I never would have anticipated that outcome. I must admit that I consistently underestimated you at every turn. Your commitment to following me has been remarkable. But it stops now."

Run! Run! Run! every fiber of my body was screaming. We had to get away. But we couldn't. I was the only one of us who could shield. Jale would happily cripple the others in an instant with his mind spike if we tried to run. I had to find a way to get the others out safely. How?

I heard a strangled sound to my right, a choke mixed with a snort. When I looked, Lyse's body jerked. Her eyes were wide and scared before they rolled back in her head. I reached out to her, but before I could touch her, her body went rigid. Her chest heaved with her labored breathing. Then she turned her head slowly to look at me. It wasn't her face that looked at me, however. Icy fingers wrapped themselves around my heart. I couldn't breathe. I whispered, "*No.*"

"What's happening?" Kaylara asked. She was standing behind us, too far away to see what I was seeing.

I was too horrified, too frozen, to answer. Slowly, her whole body shaking, Lyse drew the dagger at her belt with her right hand. Her left arm jerked wildly. Her legs swayed. But even as the rest of her body was fighting, Lyse's hand, controlled by Raelan, was perfectly steady.

"Nonononono," I repeated under my breath. "Not this. Anything but this."

What could I do? I had to find a way to stop Raelan, to get him out of Lyse's body. My mind was racing, but so muddled with fear that it went in circles. I was drowning in panic, sinking under it. My worst fear was coming true. I didn't know what to do. The only thing that would stop a warg was… I had to kill Raelan. But to get to him, I'd first have to go through Jale. It was impossible. It didn't matter anyway; I couldn't look away from Lyse, couldn't take a single step apart from her.

"What are you doing?" Kaylara gasped, as Lyse held the dagger up for all to see.

"Raelan warged her," I replied in a low voice. "Stay back."

Kaylara made a sort of gasping moan as she realized how much trouble we were in. Lyse's eyes stared at me, uncontrolled by Raelan. He had left that part of her body free, undoubtedly so that I could see the fear in them. I had never seen her so scared. Her eyes pleaded for help, but I was helpless. Raelan spun the knife in her hand, sharp tip against her palm, almost playfully. My heart was pounding so hard it rang in my head. *Think, Aeryn!*

When I spoke, my voice was shaky. "Let her go, Raelan. Please. We'll go home. Or leave the city entirely. You'll never see us again. I'll do whatever you want, just let her go."

Raelan continued to spin the knife, unimpressed.

"Let her go and take me instead! Please, take me. I won't fight you." My voice was becoming desperate. There was another explosion, so close that the ground rolled beneath our feet. I didn't care anymore. I didn't care what happened to King's City, so long as I could have Lyse back.

"I gave you the chance to join me." Raelan was speaking to me through Lyse's mouth.

"Let her go home to Rath," I begged, my voice almost a whisper. "Let her rejoin her family. Please…"

Raelan looked at the prone bodies of Balrak and Halver. "And then you killed two of my mages. We are all pieces in a greater game, Aeryn. To win, some pieces must be removed from the game. You took two of my pieces, so it's only fair that I take one of yours."

Tears began to fall from Lyse's eyes, and then I started to cry, too, because Raelan had moved the dagger in Lyse's hand so that its point was directly against her chest, over her heart. Raelan hissed, "Tell me, Aeryn: Which piece should I take?"

Anyone but Lyse. He could have anyone in Ilirya but Lyse. Both Lyse and I were crying profusely now. The lump in my throat was so thick I couldn't swallow. I could barely breathe. Anyone but Lyse. I wanted to wake up from this nightmare and find that everything was all right, that there was no danger and it was all a bad dream.

Raelan said, "Time is ticking, Aeryn. Whose life is a fair trade for my two war mages? The choice is yours."

There was no choice. There would never be a choice. A thousand times over again, the answer would always be the same. "Me!" I yelled at him. "Me!"

The knife burned like fire where Lyse thrust it in. I felt it rather than saw it: pressure followed by the sear of fire and then the coolness of flowing blood as she pulled it out again. I let out a grunt of pain. My tears stopped instantly as Lyse's flowed even more profusely. Even knowing the choice that I'd made, I couldn't help being surprised. No one is ever really prepared to be stabbed. My fingers instinctively grabbed at the wound, as though they could hold the blood in. But there are two flows that nothing can stop: time and blood. I was quickly going to run out of both.

His goal accomplished, Raelan released his hold on Lyse. Her body shuddered as she regained control, then her mouth made an "O" of horror as she watched the bright-red blood spill out and stain my pants. Raelan had gotten the blade up under the cuirass I was wearing. It was the exact type of wound that Derrin had said would, without exception, lead to death in a few short minutes. There was no saving the victim. Lyse lunged forward, hugging me to her tightly as though she could keep me with her forever. According to the Ice Crown's *Book of the Dead*: "What death takes, it never gives back." Even if she didn't know it yet, Lyse had already lost me to death. It didn't matter how tightly she held on; death was stronger.

The pain was overwhelming. I was spiraling down into it, struggling to focus on anything else. Lyse screamed, "Call for a healer!" She meant a mage healer, the only person who could save me now. But who was going to find a mage healer, and where? We were in the middle of a coup. If there had been any mage healers around, Raelan's fellow conspirators may well have killed them. Lyse was delirious with panic and not thinking clearly.

Weakness overtook me, and my legs gave out. Lyse caught my weight and gently carried me the rest of the way to the ground, laying my body out flat along the ground. Already, a pool of blood was forming around me. I hated that Lyse had to kneel in it. It was an awful thing to have to do. Like when Faegan's knife hit me in the training room, I was starting to drift apart from my surroundings, my mind separating from my body. I fought to stay tethered to where I was, just for a few minutes longer. It was all that I had left.

"No, no, no! Aeryn, hold on! We'll find help!" Lyse was pressing with both hands on the wound, trying to stop the bleeding. I couldn't look at the blood or I would be mesmerized by the sheer amount of it. I coughed, and a trail of blood trickled out of my mouth. I could no longer feel my legs. The burning slash had turned to a dull, throbbing ache.

Raelan, Jale, the king, the coup—none of it mattered anymore. Not for me. This was it. I thought of old soldiers hanging up their shields for the last time. Their fight was over. My fight, too, was over. In some ways, it was a relief. I could let go of everything. Whatever else happened in King's City, it wasn't my responsibility. At least I had done my best.

I remembered my family. Lyse would have to find a way to tell them what had happened. They would lose me twice in the space of only a few months. Well, that was life. I was too far gone to worry about the pain it would cause them. I put my hand on Lyse's and tried to smile. At least I could tell her good-bye.

Lyse was babbling, apologizing, crying, ordering me to stay with her, but she was trying to hold back the ocean tide from returning to the sea. I was slipping away, and nothing could stop it this time. There was no Timo to save me. I batted weakly at her arm to get her attention. She finally looked away from the wound and at me. I whispered, "It doesn't matter anymore. You can't stop it."

"What are you saying, Aeryn? You're strong! Fight for me! Fight until we can get you help! Don't leave me!"

"There's no one to come help. It's okay, Lyse. I'm not scared. I just wish...we'd had more time."

Our time together hadn't been nearly enough. I had wanted decades, and we'd gotten months. It wasn't fair. Tears dripped off her face and landed on mine like rain. "No, Aeryn! It doesn't end like this! We're bonded. I have to be able to help you somehow. Otherwise what did the bond matter? It can't have been a waste!"

The numbness was traveling north. It was above my waist now. "It wasn't a waste. We found each other."

Lyse was gasping, trying to breathe, choked by tears. I was gasping, too, but it was because my lungs were spasming. I didn't have much time left. Already, my vision was edged with black. I fought to stay lucid, to say the last of what I needed to say. Then the darkness could swallow me whole for the last time.

"Lyse, you have to get away." I didn't know if Raelan and Jale were still there or if they'd left. Maybe it was all moot. I had to say it anyway, for Lyse's sake. "Go back through the Gate while you still can. Find a horse and ride away from King's City. Go back to your family in Madrigal. You have to save yourself. That's all that matters now."

I couldn't feel my arms anymore. All that was left was the beat of my heart, and it was weak and irregular. Death was calling me home.

"I won't leave you! Aeryn..." I could barely understand Lyse. She was trying to stroke my face, but her body was shaking so hard that her hand kept slipping. I closed my eyes.

I whispered, "I love you."

Then the darkness swallowed me whole.

CHAPTER 13

"Despite efforts by the Crown to eradicate the cult of the One God, it has persisted in secret for centuries, likely because of the belief among adherents that they will be rewarded handsomely by the god."

– Expunged entry in A Kingdom and its People, 2nd edition

"From darkness, light."

– The Salyar "Book of the Dead"

EVERYONE HAS A STORY; THE circle of their life that begins with their birth and ends with their death. A circle that is relentlessly carried out, no matter how large or small that circle. Every ending is just that: an ending. Death comes for us all. Only the gods and nature are forever.

The light that shone against my eyes was so bright I could see it even through my eyelids. What was it? I opened my eyes and found myself lying on my back. For a moment, I had the ludicrous notion that I'd awoken in a cloud; above me and below me there was only white. I had died, hadn't I? But surely this wasn't the Eternal Realms. Where were the other people? I climbed to my feet and looked around, but there was nothing, only the unbroken whiteness. Where was I?

Behind me, a deep, rough voice intoned, "Where there is Darkness, the wicked and good are judged alike and share their misery until such time as the good can be ransomed by the living."

I spun around and saw that Lymon, the black-winged servant of Death, was standing behind me watching me. As in my dream, he wore a long black coat that reached mid-way to his calves and seemed to shroud him in shadow. His hat, too, hid the features of his face, which appeared ursine.

My shoulders sagged with hopelessness and despair. If I had been met by Lymon, not Zakariya, it meant I would be taken not to the gardens of the Eternal Realms, but to their darkest, most miserable depths. It was a villain's fate.

"No!" The word slipped from my lips without my meaning to say it. My hand rose unconsciously to cover my mouth. "It can't be! What did I do wrong?"

"You did nothing wrong."

"Then why... Why are you here?"

"The presence of Dark Magic in the mortal realm creates an imbalance in the Eternal Realms. Dark Magic draws power from Death and weakens the veil between the world of the living and the dead. Until the Dark Magic is controlled in the mortal realm, those who die will be in limbo, unable to pass on fully to the Eternal Realms."

"Then why don't you stop it?"

"Death cannot interfere in the world of the living." His words were curt. Simple. Emotionless.

He said nothing more, and we stared at one another for a moment. I looked around at the white world again. There was no sound, no wind, nothing. Only white. "What happens now?"

Lymon tapped his long black claws together. They clicked as they met. "That is for you to decide."

"What do you mean?"

"You may choose to remain here, trapped between the living and the dead, in which case the Dark mages in your world will prevail and all the Eternal Realms will be plunged in disorder until such time as the Dark Magic is eradicated again, or you may choose to return to the mortal plane and try and stop them. Know that even if you return, however, the outcome of the conflict is by no means certain. The Dark mages may still achieve their designs, and you may find yourself here once more. That future is unusually opaque. Even Death cannot foresee how this struggle will end."

"I can go back?" It was hard to understand everything he was saying, but I heard one thing clearly: I could go back. There was no choice. I *had* to go back. I had to make sure Lyse had escaped. I had to know that she made it out of King's City. If not, I had to save her. Even now, she could be Raelan's prisoner or, worse, puppet. And Kaylara and Pavo, too. I had brought them with me through the Gate. I was responsible for them.

Then the rest of his words sank in. Did he really expect *me* to defeat Raelan and the chancellor? How could I possibly succeed when my very presence in this space proved I wasn't strong enough? "But what if I can't stop them? Raelan already killed me once. I can't stop him on my own."

Lymon nodded, his face still in shadow. "It is true that you alone cannot stop them, but there is one who can."

"Who?"

"The one you know as Kjelborn. He is god-touched. I can bring you to him, but I can help no more than that. Already, I have interceded too much. Once you leave the land of the dead, you will be on your own."

"I'll do it!" I cried. "Of course I'll do it!" My joy was so overwhelming it was making me dizzy. I could get back to Lyse. I could protect her. I would see her again. Our story wasn't finished yet.

"Before you choose," Lymon interjected, holding up a single claw, "you must know that returning to the land of the living will come at a price. No gift from Death, even one that may help return the Eternal Realms to their rightful order, is free."

"Okay," I agreed impatiently, not waiting to hear the terms. "Whatever the cost, I accept." What did the price matter to me? It was worth anything to see Lyse again. To know she was safe. I fidgeted, eager to go back to the land of the living. I didn't have any time to waste.

"Are you certain? You may later come to regret your decision if you choose too hastily."

"Yes!" There was no question. If Lyse was in danger, I had to go to her. That was all that mattered.

Lymon nodded. "As you wish. I bear witness that you have agreed to Death's terms."

He gestured with his arm, and a Gate opened beside him. Through it, I could see the snow-covered forest of Thamir. My home. Small white snowflakes fell gently through the steel-gray sky. I took an unconscious step forward. My heart ached with longing. I had missed my home so much, and now it was only a few feet away. Four steps and I would be there.

Lymon said, "When you pass through this Gate a second time, it will take you back to the place where you died. Little time will have elapsed.

The Dark mages have not yet succeeded, but they are close." He paused. "Although it is not my nature to care about the outcome of human conflicts, I wish you luck."

Without waiting any longer, I ran through the Gate. I had to get back to King's City. I had to find Lyse. I landed in snow that reached to my knees. The heavy armor I was wearing made it hard to walk, but it didn't matter; Lymon had placed the Gate close enough to Firdas' hut that I didn't have far to go. I waded through the snow, plowing a wide path that would be easy to follow back to the Gate once I'd gotten him.

I didn't bother knocking on Firdas' door. There was no time for niceties. We had a job to do in King's City. When I burst in, he was sitting cross-legged on the floor, his brown cloak wrapped loosely around him. He was stirring something in a small black pot over the hearth using a long wooden spoon. He looked even older than when I'd last seen him a few months ago, more brittle and frail, with more white in his hair and beard. He was so surprised when he saw me that he dropped the spoon into the pot.

"Aeryn?"

My clothing was saturated with wet blood, although I was no longer bleeding. "I'm sorry to come like this, but I need you to come with me. Right now." My words were fast. Insistent.

"How—"

I didn't have time to explain everything to him. We needed to leave immediately if we were to have a hope of stopping what was happening in King's City. To preempt his questions, I said, "I came by Gate. There's no time to explain, but Dark mages have launched an attack against King's City, assisted by Northmen. Anyone who could fight them is dead. We have to go *now*."

Did Firdas even know what Dark Magic was? It didn't matter. All that mattered was that he was Ilirya's last hope. It was not the thin old hermit Firdas but rather the noble Kjelborn, the once Sword of Ilirya, who rose and grabbed his twisted wooden staff. Kjelborn may have walked away from the King's Regiment long before I was born, but he couldn't resist answering the call to protect the kingdom. It was in his blood.

I drew my rapier and handed it to him. He needed some kind of weapon since his magic was bound. He took it, feeling its weight in his hands with the experience of a longtime soldier. Kjelborn's eyes, when they returned to me, were fierce and determined. He limped to a box beside the hearth and, sinking to his knees, removed from it two of the most finely made daggers I'd ever seen. Their blades flashed in the firelight as he tucked them into his belt. "Let us hurry then."

I led him from his hut, sending a longing look down the trail that led in the direction of the village. I was so close to my family. It was unfair to be this near to them and no closer to seeing them than I'd been at Windhall. But now was not the time to think about it. No matter how much I wanted to dash down the trail, to hold and see them again, I couldn't. I had to find Lyse. Only after she was safe could I think about anything else.

When Kjelborn and I arrived at the Gate, the scene on the other side had shifted to the palace garden. The garden was abandoned but for the still and lifeless forms of Halver, Balrak, and the palace guard soldiers they'd slain. Kjelborn didn't ask how a Gate had appeared in Thamir that led back to the king's palace, and I didn't tell him. We stepped through cautiously, Kjelborn with the sword raised and me with magic drawn to my hands. I looked to where I'd last been, the place where Raelan had warged Lyse into stabbing me, but apart from a sickening amount of blood that still sat pooled on the ground, there was nothing there. Where had Lyse and the others gone? Was it too late to help them? There were no clues to suggest an answer. I shivered. When had the night become so cold?

Kjelborn quickly took stock of our surroundings. The smell of brimstone was still in the air. Smoke wafted in clouds in front of the moon. The city was at war. He said, "If we're at the palace, then I imagine it's because the Dark mages are here already?"

I nodded.

He said, "They will have tried to go straight to the castle's inner recesses to get to the king. That's where we'll have to confront them. How many are there?"

"At least three Dark mages. I don't know how many more. They have allies, too, mage and non-mage alike...including from the King's Regiment." I winced. It pained me to tell him that members of his own former Regiment had betrayed Ilirya. "Do you know what Dark Magic is?"

His jaw twitched. "Yes." He didn't elaborate. He stepped around me to the spiral staircase from which Lyse, Pavo, Kaylara, and I had entered the garden. I hoped that they had used it again to escape from Raelan and Jale after I had been killed. At least whatever happened between when I died and now, there were no new bodies in the palace garden, and for that I said a prayer of gratitude to any god who was listening. Whatever awaited us ahead, there was still hope.

Kjelborn and I began to retrace the path to the Gate to Windhall. I hesitated as we passed it, seeing Pavo's necklace on the floor. If I only knew Lyse was safe, I could follow her through the Gate. I could send Kjelborn to fulfill Lymon's wish to have the Dark mages stopped and order restored to the Eternal Realms and while I broke off to find her. But I couldn't risk it. If she was with Raelan, wasting time looking for her at Windhall could get her killed. I had to keep searching for Raelan and hope that she'd found her way to safety.

When the hallway reached a cross-section, Kjelborn checked for danger in both directions, then took the corridor to the left. His steps were firm and decisive. It made sense that having served in the King's Regiment for so many years, he remembered the castle layout even after having been away for decades. Despite being so close to the castle keep, we still saw no one else. Worry squirmed in my stomach. Where was everyone?

The crypt-like silence of the palace wasn't the only thing worrying me. "Kjel—I mean, Firdas, how will you fight the Dark mages?" I had faith in Lymon, not to mention Kjelborn's former reputation, but Kjelborn's magic was still bound. What could he do with a sword and two daggers against their magic? With no ability to shield, he would be overpowered in seconds.

He grunted, not looking at me. "You may call me Kjelborn, if you prefer. And I will figure that out when the time comes. There's no use thinking about it now."

We turned right through a door in the corridor and found ourselves in a musty wine cellar. Enormous wooden casks lined both sides of the wall. Kjelborn led me through the door on the other side and into a massive kitchen, which had obviously been abandoned in the middle of cooking preparations. Although the fires had now burned out, pots still hung over them, waiting to be stirred. It was as if the kitchen workers had vanished into thin air. It set my teeth on edge.

"Aeryn!" a voice hissed.

I jumped half out of my skin. "Cayleth?"

I bent over and found Cayleth crouching below a table, upon which sat a knife and a pile of chopped carrots. She crawled out on her hands and knees. Blood stained her shirtsleeves and armor, but it didn't appear to be hers. Her round face was pale and drawn.

"What are you doing here?" I asked.

She made a face. "Hiding from Raelan. I came through the Gate as he was coming down the hall with Jale, so I ran as fast as I could in the other direction. Just my luck, they passed right through here. I—didn't want to fight them alone." She dropped her eyes. I didn't blame her. I would have done the same.

"When did they come through? Were they with anyone else?"

"A few minutes ago. They weren't alone, but I don't know who else was with them. Lots of boots walked past while I was hiding."

So Lyse could be with him. Or she could be long gone. I had no way to know.

"Where are the others? And who is this?" Cayleth indicated Kjelborn.

"It's a long story. This is Kjelborn."

Her eyebrows shot up. "*The* Kjelborn?"

"Yes. Now listen to me: You should leave. The route is clear. It's not hard to find the way back to the Gate. Pavo left a necklace there so you can find it. Hopefully, the others have already made it out." Hopefully Lyse was on her way to Rath by now.

"What about you?"

"We're going after Raelan and the chancellor." And maybe Lyse, if Raelan took her.

"I'll come with you."

"No, Cayleth! You should get away from here. In case... In case we fail." I couldn't worry about Cayleth, too.

Cayleth drew herself up, hand on the pommel of her rapier. "I know it's dangerous. I just killed Faegan, for gods' sake! We're in this together. If you're going after Chancellor Vandys and Raelan, I'm coming with you."

A wave of nausea hit me. "You killed Faegan?"

Cayleth looked away. Her face was grim. She clearly didn't want to talk about it. I looked questioningly to Kjelborn, who nodded. "Okay," I said. "But be careful."

We set off again, going up a set of servants' stairs into the dining room. Under different circumstances, I would have stopped to marvel at the grandeur of the room: large, ornate wooden chairs around a long table, a giant gold chandelier lit with dozens of candles, and plates made of porcelain. Now, however, I had to be alert for ambushes. I pulled magic to my hands while Cayleth and Kjelborn brandished their rapiers. We crept through the room, heading to the far end. The unnatural silence around us was heavy and oppressive. My skin prickled. I whispered, "Where is everyone? Shouldn't the palace guard be here at least?"

Neither Cayleth nor Kjelborn answered. Kjelborn led us to a door on the opposite side of the room and set his finger to his lips, indicating we should be quiet. Then he motioned for us to position ourselves on the either side of the door and readied his sword in front of him. He whispered, "Inside is a library with a concealed staircase that leads to the antechamber of the Great Hall. Because it is not well known, it is our best chance to reach the Great Hall without having to fight our way to it."

On the quiet count of three, he turned the knob and slowly pushed the door open. When it caught halfway, we had to abandon stealth and rush through, weapons brandished. Only to be met by a ragtag group of defenders who were pressed anxiously against the far wall, their own weapons drawn. Their faces were full of fear as they huddled together, their hands shaking so hard that their weapons seemed to dance in front of them. They had backed themselves against a bookshelf, preventing ambush but also limiting their ability to move. A single face jumped out at me.

"Lyse!" I'd found her! And with her were Pavo and Kaylara.

"Aeryn?" Lyse dropped her sword and ran to me, hugging me so tightly that it was hard to breathe. I clutched her in return, savoring the feel of her warm body—so much warmer than mine—against me. It struck me then that since returning from the land of the dead, cold seemed to have settled in every part of my body. Lyse pulled back and ran her hands over my face, brushing my skin lightly with her fingertips. A dozen emotions flickered across her face, most of all joy. In that moment, we were the only people in the room. Raelan, the chancellor—nothing else existed. Just us. The way things were meant to be.

"How is this possible?" Lyse asked. "You were dead! Aeryn, I held you while you died! I left—I left your body... I..." Her body shook with the force of her sobbing. "There was so much blood!"

"Shhhh, it wasn't as bad as it looked," I lied. "See? I'm fine now. Everything is okay."

Now wasn't the time to tell her the truth. Later, when we were alone I could. I pulled her close to me, stroking her hair, murmuring words to comfort her. I could barely believe that I was able to touch her again. I never wanted to let her go. I wanted to run away with her and let whatever was going to happen to King's City happen without us. Let Kjelborn fight for Ilirya. He was the soldier, not me.

"Aeryn, I think we must continue," Kjelborn said in a low voice.

I tightened my grip on Lyse. I didn't want to go! Not when I'd just found her! I'd achieved my goal: Lyse was safe and we were together again. But I had promised Lymon that I would try to stop the Dark Magic. This was why he had allowed me to return to the land of the living and no other reason. And what's more, if Raelan won, then Lyse would never be safe again. I took a deep breath. Loud enough so that the others could hear, I said, "Kjelborn, Cayleth, and I are going to stop Raelan and the chancellor."

Lyse gasped. "No! You can't! He almost killed you!" Her arms tightened around me, trying to keep me safe with her. "We should run, like you said. We can get away from the city! It's not too late!"

I closed my eyes. It took more strength than I knew I had to let go of her. "Someone has to stop them. We're all that's left."

"And how exactly do you intend to do that?" an unexpected voice asked pointedly. From among the huddle of my scared friends, Professor Kalmath stepped forward. Her lips pursed together, and she arched a skeptical eyebrow at me. It was the same expression she frequently wore in our classes.

I stared at her. "Professor Kalmath, what are you doing here?"

"I was here when the fighting broke out. I have been protecting these students." She peered at Kjelborn. "And who are you?"

Kjelborn stood straighter, raising his chin and puffing out his thin chest. "I am Kjelborn Warhammer, the Sword of Ilirya, deliverer of the Battle of Twelve."

Professor Kalmath sniffed, unimpressed. "I may be a mere herbomancer, but I can smell magic, Kjelborn Warhammer, and you have none."

Something tugged at my mind. Lymon wouldn't have sent Kjelborn to fight the chancellor and Raelan if he couldn't use his magic. It wouldn't make sense. Kjelborn was only the Sword of Ilirya when he was a full mage. There had to be a solution, a way to return the full use of his magic to him. Lymon said that Death could see some of the future. He must have seen Kjelborn using his magic again. But how? The answer came to me in a flash. "We can unbind it!"

Professor Kalmath snorted. "Nonsense. To undo a binding spell requires five mages with power greater than that of the original spellcasters, and none of us are spellcasters. It's impossible."

The words tumbled out of me. "We're six mages right here. You're a Great Mage, right, Professor Kalmath? And one day Cayleth and Pavo will be. That's three Great Mages, plus me, Lyse, and Kaylara. With our bond, Lyse and I are almost the equivalent of a Great Mage. So almost four Great Mages. It's not the five we need, but it's worth a try. Please, it can't hurt!"

Professor Kalmath pursed her lips again while Pavo, Kaylara, and Cayleth looked at each other uncomfortably. They must have thought I was crazy. Kjelborn spoke quietly. "I am no spellcaster, but I can recite the words to the spell that will remove the binding if you're willing to try."

Professor Kalmath threw up her hands, huffing like an angry badger. "Fine. But so you know, I don't think this will work."

"It *will*," I said with conviction.

At Kjelborn's direction, we gathered in a circle holding hands. As he began to recite the spell, a tendril of Professor Kalmath's dark-green magic snaked out of her left hand and twined itself around Pavo's right hand, gently swirling together with his rainbow magic. Then the rope of green and rainbow magic traveled to Pavo's left hand, where it interwove with Cayleth's pale-red magic. The three-stranded rope next floated to me, and my blue magic was added as a fourth strand. Kaylara was the fifth and Lyse the sixth before the rope returned to Professor Kalmath and bound with the end of the thread. The result was an unbroken, shimmering, six-stranded rope floating before us.

Next, Kjelborn taught us the words of the spell we would have to recite. We would have to chant them over and over again until the binding on his magic broke…or the pain became too much for him to bear. Uncomfortably, casting subtle glances at each other, we began to chant. Almost immediately,

Kjelborn doubled over, gasping. Purple magic oozed out of the scars on his arms like blood and slowly dripped to the floor, pooling under him in a thick puddle. His body convulsed, and he gritted his teeth to avoid screaming.

"It's hurting him!" Lyse cried.

"Keep. Going," Kjelborn grunted through his teeth.

"It's not enough," Professor Kalmath said. Her voice was tense and her face flushed.

Kjelborn dropped to his knee, shaking from the pain. The binding spell was a grappling hook that had sunk into his flesh; we were trying to rip it free through brute force, and it was rending and tearing as it went. I willed Kjelborn to fight, to help us lift off the yoke so that he could be free of the binding, but he was weakening fast, and so were we.

No! We had to succeed. Everything depended on it.

Somewhere deep inside me, a door opened. Magic flooded through it like a raging river. The shimmering rope we had created began to burn so brightly that we couldn't look at it anymore. It grew and expanded and then in an instant, the spell binding Kjelborn shattered with a sharp crack that echoed through the room. We were all thrown backward with the force of the spell's release, while Kjelborn fell to his hands and knees, gasping. The rope disintegrated.

"We did it!" I cried. "We broke the spell!"

My legs still shaky, I ran to Kjelborn's side, helping him to stand. When he had regained his footing, he called his magic to him, watching with awe as tiny purple flames danced on his hands. Kjelborn, the fabled Sword of Ilirya, was a pyromancer once more. He looked from me to the others, his face full of wonder and gratitude. When his eyes fell on Lyse, however, an indescribable emotion flickered across his face. He reabsorbed his magic and walked over to her, stronger and straighter than I'd ever seen him move.

He took Lyse's hand in his. "The unbinding spell was stronger than I imagined. I can feel that your magic, too, has been released by this spell. But I'm sorry: The bond you shared with Aeryn has also been unbound. It is broken."

What? No! I reached out for the pulsing thread that had tethered me to Lyse but was met by emptiness. Not even the tiniest spark remained. Hollowness and grief settled within me. Losing the connection was like losing a limb. How could this have happened? My eyes met Lyse's. She was just as devastated as I was.

Gently, Kjelborn said, "I am sorry for your loss. Your spellcasting affinity is what allowed the spell to work. Were you not here, it would have failed."

"My affinity is spellcasting?" Lyse asked.

"Yes, and healing."

"*And* healing?" For a moment, Lyse's sorrow was interrupted by hope and joy. I gave her a sad smile. Even though our bond was sundered, at least she had the affinity she loved best of all.

"You can feel affinities?" Cayleth asked, cocking her head. "I've never heard of that."

"Yes, it is one of my gifts. Now, I'm sorry to say we must move quickly, while there is still time." He looked at me meaningfully.

"Lyse, Kaylara, Pavo, you go with Professor Kalmath back to Windhall," I ordered. Having found them safe and sound, there was no way I was putting them in danger again. "If we fail, you'll have enough time to make it out of the area and to one of the far away baronies."

"But you are needing us, too," Pavo protested, looking hurt.

I thought quickly. "The people at Windhall need to know what's happened. You can tell them, and then help keep them safe." Where was Raelan's third mage, the one who had caught me and Lyse off-campus? Was he lurking around Windhall?

"I'm coming with you." Lyse's voice invited no disagreement.

"No—"

"I can make my own decisions, Aeryn. Where you go, I go."

I took a deep breath, preparing to argue, but Cayleth touched me on the shoulder. "It's her choice. Plus we might need a healer mage," she said quietly.

I rubbed my face. "Fine."

As the others said their good-byes and well wishes, Kjelborn drew me aside. "The power that broke the binding on my magic did not come from this room. It came from the divine plane. I can still taste Death's touch in this room, just as it touched the Gate from Thamir. What has happened to you, Aeryn? What have you done?"

"Now isn't the time to explain." I looked nervously over my shoulder to assure myself that Lyse hadn't overheard.

"Later then. Only tell me you did not make a deal with Death. Mortals are not meant to—"

I cut him off. "Let's go." What was done was done. I'd done what I had to, and finding Lyse alive and safe in the library, I didn't regret my choice. Kjelborn pressed his lips together, his face full of misgiving, but said no more.

Having finished our farewells, our two parties set off in different directions. Professor Kalmath led Pavo and Kaylara out the way we'd come, while Kjelborn, Cayleth, Lyse, and I went through a hidden door in the bookshelf to find the staircase there. Kjelborn was looking stronger and more youthful by the second as his magic returned. At the top of the staircase, he stopped, then slowly opened the door wide enough to put his head through and see into the room beyond. After a moment, he closed it and turned back to us. There was sadness in his eyes. "This is a battle I must fight alone. Do not follow me." He slipped through the door and was gone.

Cayleth pressed her body to the door, trying to see with one eye whatever was happening on the other side. I scooted close behind her, trying to see, too, but it was useless. Whatever was happening was beyond our view. "You stay here," I said to Cayleth and Lyse. "I have to see what's happening."

Ignoring Cayleth's protestations and Lyse's efforts to hold me back, I stole out as surreptitiously as I could and crouched behind a chair by the door. The antechamber was lined on three sides with identical wooden chairs in which petitioners could sit while waiting for an audience with the king. Only two people were in the room now, however: Kjelborn and Vardan Ironwill, captain of the King's Regiment. Vardan wore the full black armor of the Regiment, along with a long black cloak. He was looking into the Great Hall through a crack in the big double doors and hadn't yet noticed Kjelborn standing ten paces behind him. What was Vardan doing? Was the king holding some sort of meeting and he was waiting to go in?

"Hello, old friend," Kjelborn said softly.

Vardan jumped at the sound and a second time when he turned and saw that it was Kjelborn who had spoken. "You?" The word was both a question and an accusation in his mouth. "How can you be here?"

"The gods have always chosen their own path for me." Kjelborn sighed. "I wish I hadn't found you here. It can only mean you have thrown your lot in with Dark mages. How has it come to this, Vardan?"

I gasped under my breath. Was it true? Had Vardan joined Raelan and the chancellor?

Vardan snarled. "I made the difficult choice you were never strong enough to. We can't all run away. Some of us had to stay and fight."

"Yet here I find you fighting against the very kingdom you claim to defend. You invited invaders into the city and joined a coup against the king you are pledged to protect. Do these things seem the actions of an honorable man? Death before dishonor, or has the Regiment adopted a new oath?"

Vardan's mouth twitched. "The war had to be brought to end! Otherwise the cursed fool would have let it go on forever and you know it. How many of the Regiment have I buried over the years? How many sons and daughters more should be thrown into this bottomless chasm? Something had to be done to stop the mad king!"

"Once you had my magic stripped from me for giving voice to the same thoughts. How times change. But I would never have made allies of Dark mages."

Vardan shifted uncomfortably. "I'm not a demi-god like you. I did what I had to."

A demi-god? What did that mean?

Kjelborn took a step closer. "You were a good man once. You can be again. There is still time. Step aside and I will end this."

"It's too late!" Vardan snapped. Color had risen in his cheeks. "The king is dead."

"And who will rule in his place? You are no fool; you know Dark Magic is not to be trifled with. Those who would use it are, by their very natures, not fit to rule."

"I cannot allow you to enter." Vardan was rocking on the balls of his feet, agitated, but he hadn't pulled his sword yet. Perhaps Kjelborn could still convince him to abandon the rebels.

Kjelborn's eyes narrowed. "What's going on in there? What have you done?"

Vardan's face convulsed. In a high, desperate voice, he said, "They said it would be better to have a god as king than a mortal. They said it was the only way to end the war…"

Kjelborn shook his head emphatically. Confusion was on his face. "No, it's impossible! No god can pass into the mortal world."

Vardan licked his lips. "They found a way."

"If that's the case, then it's even more imperative that we stop them! You know the two planes must not be bridged."

Kjelborn drew one of his daggers and moved another step closer to the door. In response, Vardan called light-gray magic to his hands, his body moving into a defensive crouch in front of it. Kjelborn took a step back, surprised, and pulled magic to his free hand, too. Vardan's eyes widened. "How?" he said.

"The bindings you had set on me have been broken. There is no need for more blood to be shed today than necessary. We have known each other far too long for things to come to this. Step aside and allow me to end this."

"It's too late," Vardan replied. He laughed in a high-pitched giggle, and I knew then it *was* too late for him. He had dug himself in too deeply to be able to get out again. Kjelborn knew it, too.

The fight that followed lasted mere seconds. Even as Vardan unleashed his first volley of mage fire, Kjelborn had already struck. His dagger lodged deep in Vardan's throat. Gamiel's words from our second morning together in Ithaka came into my mind: "Never rely only on your magic. To do so will only get you dead." She had been presciently right. Vardan's magic shield could have stopped Kjelborn's mage fire, but it did nothing against a steel blade.

Vardan fell to the floor, gasping and clutching at the knife as blood spilled out around it. Every time he breathed in, there was a guttural choking sound. His eyes were wide with shock and fear. Kjelborn walked swiftly to him and kneeled over him, his lips moving silently. Vardan's eyes met Kjelborn's, and, to my surprise, he felt for Kjelborn's hand.

Kjelborn took it, then tenderly laid Vardan's shaking hand on his chest. "I'm sorry it came to this. For all the things that have happened between us, good and bad, I regret that this is how we part. Good-bye, Vardan. May you find peace in the Eternal Realms," Kjelborn whispered.

Then like that, Vardan Ironwill, renowned captain of the King's Regiment, was gone. His death had taken no more than ten breaths. Kjelborn continued to look at the body for a moment, and a single tear traced its way down his cheek. Then he looked up and saw me hiding behind a chair. He motioned for me to rise.

"You were friends?" I asked.

"Yes, when we were young men. War turns even the best of friends into enemies." He straightened his robe and wiped the tear from his face. Then without warning, he swept past me and knocked the door through which we'd come shut, propping a chair under it so that it couldn't be opened. There was a shout of surprise from Cayleth, followed by a barrage of pounding and kicking. Muffled shouts from both Cayleth and Lyse protested the move.

"What are you doing?" I asked, frozen.

"I do not know what lies ahead in the Great Hall, but the threads of destiny tell me that this is a journey for us two alone."

"You can see the future?" Was Vardan right that Kjelborn was a demi-god? How was that possible? Were there others?

"Not exactly. That is a conversation for another time. Here is what you must know: For centuries, a small cabal in King's City has sought to bring the One God into our world. They believe he will give them extraordinary powers as a reward. If he is able to cross over, he will have all his divine gifts in the mortal realm. Thus, if Vardan was right and these Dark mages found a way to bring the One God through, we must stop them at all costs. He must not be allowed to enter our world. Do you understand?"

I nodded, glancing at the door behind which Lyse stood yelling. She was furious that we had locked her out, but this way she would be safe. While it was wrong of me to take away her choice, her protection was my primary concern. Everything I had done would be for nothing if I lost her now. I was willing to die again. I wasn't willing for her to die. Still, it would have been helpful to have Cayleth with us.

Kjelborn handed me back my rapier. "You'll need this," he said. He knelt and took the sword from Vardan's body, not bothering with a scabbard. Then with no more delay, we slipped through the double doors of the Great Hall.

Inside was a scene of bloody carnage so awful that it took my breath away. It looked as though a tornado of knives had whipped through the Great Hall. Courtiers and soldiers alike lay dead on the ground or hanging from the balcony that ringed the hall. Dark-red blood was half-dried in pools around them. Upon the dais at the end of the Hall, the king sat on his throne. But it was a mockery of a royal audience: His throat was slit, and the blood had flowed down his fine royal robes, staining them a blotchy crimson. His head had tilted backward, and his golden crown was wedged between it and the high-backed gold throne. We were too late.

The air was tangy with the smell of blood, and the sight of the massacred royal court made my stomach twist in knots. I choked back a simultaneous retch and gasp. I forced myself to look away from all of it and focus on what remained. On the dais, beside the throne, Chancellor Vandys, Raelan, and two other mages in robes were chanting. Above them, an unnatural black cloud swirled, growing until it was the size of the entire dais. Flashes of colored light appeared intermittently in it like lightning.

"What—" I started to say.

"They're opening a Gate!" Kjelborn cried, his free hand balling into a fist. "That must be how they intend to bring the One God through! We have to stop them! Whatever happens, he can't pass through!"

No sooner had Kjelborn finished speaking than a huge white foot descended from the black cloud. From a distance, it looked as long as a human was tall. Was that...the One God?

CHAPTER 14

"If you knew how the journey would end, would you still have started it?"

– Speaker unknown

STUNNED, I WAS UNABLE TO comprehend what I was seeing. How could anyone create a Gate to the divine plane? I couldn't believe my eyes. It was like watching the birth of a double-headed deer—both unexpected and seemingly impossible. And wrong. The air was thick with a palpable sense of perversion. What was happening in the room was an affront to the order of the world. My legs twitched, wanting to run. This was beyond anything I'd imagined. This was more than a political coup; it was a seismic shift in the relationship between the divine and mortal planes.

"Shut the Gate! Shut the Gate, you fools! You don't know what you're doing!" Kjelborn yelled. He began charging down center aisle of the Great Hall.

The four mages on the dais turned, their totally black eyes fixing on him. The Gate crackled with a sound like thunder. Then in the blink of an eye, everything slowed down. A bolt of white light languidly traced its way across the black cloud, illuminating the inhumanly large pale foot stretching down from the vortex. Raelan shouted something, but his words were too slow and too long, as though they'd become caught in pine sap. They were impossible to understand.

For a moment, I was confused. What was happening? Then I realized it could only be one thing: One of the mages in the room was a chronomancer, a mage with the ability to manipulate the passage of time. Someone was slowing down time.

Kjelborn pulled his remaining dagger from his belt with his left hand and threw it at the female mage slowly drawing black magic to her hands. Although it flew sluggishly, it was still faster than she was. It struck her in the chest, and she began to gradually sink to the ground, an expression of surprise on her face. The tense feeling of slowed time broke, and everything resumed its normal speed. Kjelborn drew his sword. He was almost at the dais.

His progress jolted me out of my shock. I sprinted after him, releasing a bolt of mage fire at Raelan when I was close enough. My fireball missed as Raelan managed to duck at the last moment. It crashed against the wall behind him, taking out several chairs sitting on the dais on its way. I kept moving forward, throwing fire as I went, pressuring his shield. My usual fear of Raelan was completely subsumed by my immediate concern over the Gate above him. Kjelborn and I had to close it. We had to push the One God back. I was more sure of that than I'd ever been of anything in my life.

"How are you here?" Raelan hissed when I was a dozen paces away. His black-gray shield shimmered in front of him, still strong despite my barrage. "I killed you! I watched you die!"

I didn't bother answering. Instead, I sent another volley of fire at him. It crashed against his shield, crackling. I followed up the attack with a dagger from my belt. Raelan dodged it, surprising me with his spryness. He was slinking to the right, trying to draw me away from the Gate and the chancellor, who was still standing beneath it chanting. Was Kjelborn's opponent their Gate mage? If Kjelborn killed him, would the Gate close? How had they managed to hide a Gate mage for so long?

The god's progress through the Gate was slow. The passage between the mortal and divine planes must have been difficult. How much time did we have? I couldn't worry about it. I needed to focus. Raelan was poking around in my mind, looking for cracks in my mental shield. I ground my teeth. I would not let Raelan in. I would not let him win.

Time began to stretch again. I chanced a glance over my shoulder. Kjelborn was avoiding a blast of ice. So his opponent was a cryomancer. Could he be both a Gate mage *and* a cryomancer? Then who was the choronomancer? After dodging the spray of shimmering icicles, Kjelborn slipped inside the mage's shield. His sword slid through the mage's stomach.

Time resumed its normal speed again as Kjelborn withdrew his sword, its blade coated with blood. The mage fell to the ground.

Now only the chancellor and Raelan remained, but the Gate looked no weaker than when there had been four Dark mages feeding it. More importantly, neither of them were Gate mages; how was it still open? The massive white leg was through almost to the groin and a second foot had joined it. My stomach twisted. We had to find a way to close the Gate. But how? A sound like the crash of thunder reverberated through the hall.

"You're too late!" Raelan hissed excitedly. "There's no stopping him now."

An involuntary shiver ran through me. My mouth was dry. The room pressed down on me like a heavy weight. It was more than fear: It was the consequence of the spillover of the divine plane into the Great Hall. Tendrils of sickly green magic were trickling through the Gate, spreading across the ceiling.

Raelan's slithering probing in my brain redoubled its efforts, and what had been a twinge of doubt lurking in the corners of my mind became a distracting whisper. What if he broke my mental shield and warged me? My mage fire didn't seem to be having any effect on his shield, and I was out of weapons other than my sword. We were in a race to see whose shield would break first, and I wasn't sure I would win. Before I could launch another volley of fire against him, time began to dilate again. At the same moment, a massive illusion enveloped the Great Hall. That could only mean one thing: Chancellor Vandys and Kjelborn were now fighting.

The illusion was of a deep, dark cave, in which not even a sliver of light could be seen. Wind screamed through the cave, masking all other sound. I immediately unsheathed my sword, holding it out in front of me. The chancellor and Raelan could be anywhere.

The hair on my arms stood up. My legs trembled. Under the cover of the illusion, Raelan could attack at any moment. I would have no warning before he was already on me. I strained to hear the stealthy creep of footsteps around me that would signal his approach. How many times had Cayleth used illusions to blind and befuddle me? How many times had those bouts ended with her standing with the point of her sword against the back of my neck? Unlike Cayleth, however, Raelan would not be satisfied with surrender. He would kill me. Again.

I crept forward, my muscles trembling. I held my breath, afraid to breathe too loudly and miss the sound of Raelan's approach. I thought I heard a sound and spun in a circle, certain that Raelan was stealing up behind me, but there was only the blackest black around me. The anticipation was agonizing.

Minutes that felt like a lifetime later, there was a high-pitched shriek of pain. Somewhere in the Great Hall, against all odds, Kjelborn had found the chancellor. Raelan's efforts to warg me became more intense—frantic, even. The tide was turning against him. If Chancellor Vandys had been mortally wounded, he was the only mage left. But that wouldn't matter if we couldn't close the Gate.

The illusion dissolved, and to my surprise, Raelan disappeared from my mind. He was still where I'd last seen him, but he'd turned to watch the Gate, his face rapturous. The One God now had two legs, his torso, and his arms up to his biceps through the Gate. He was slowly sinking into our world as though drifting down through water. A new wave of horror washed over me, making me shiver. His body was too large, too bloated. It didn't belong here. Why didn't Raelan see that?

On the dais below the god, Chancellor Vandys was collapsed at Kjelborn's feet. The scene presented a macabre tableau: the descending god, the murdered king and his court, and the slain chancellor with the aged Sword of Ilirya standing over her. It was all so surreal. And awful. The One God was almost through. We were too late. Raelan and the chancellor had won. The Gate made a sound like two steel blades scraping together. The green magic above me pulsed with its sickly green.

"Yes!" Raelan shrieked. His voice was high and excited. He was half mad. He had to be. No sane person would welcome the monstrosity entering our world. "Finally, the One God will rule! After all these years, we have succeeded!"

The blood rushing to my head made my ears ring. My heart was hammering with fear. I called to Kjelborn, "How do we stop it?"

He was looking up at the swirling vortex above him. His voice, when he answered, was resigned. "We cannot."

"What?" My heart skipped a beat.

"This Gate was created by a spell, not a Gate mage. It cannot be reversed."

We couldn't stop it. It was all over. I lowered my rapier. There was no use fighting anymore. What would become of us? What would become of King's City and Ilirya? What havoc would a god unleash in the mortal plane?

A deep, rumbling voice roared, "What in the names of all the gods is *that*?"

I jumped, then spun to face the door. Sir Idras, wearing his full battle armor, was standing in the doorway to the antechamber, flanked by Asher, Gamiel, Cayleth, and Lyse. What were they doing here? I gawped at them while they stared variously at the One God, the bodies littering the Great Hall, and Raelan, crouched to the side of the hall like a caged animal. No! They needed to get away! Why had they come? Now we were all doomed.

Kjelborn threw his hand out, as if to stave them off. "Stay back!" I doubted they'd planned to come any closer anyway. With the exception of Gamiel, their faces were full of shock and fear.

"There is no stopping what is to come!" Raelan crowed. "Bow now before the One God!"

Only the god's head was still on the other side of the Gate. I couldn't breathe. My body was numb. The room crackled with divine power. The Gate had become a violent maelstrom that thundered and roared. We had failed. We had run out of time... Time! I had an idea. It was a desperate, likely foolish idea, but at least it couldn't make the situation worse. I ran to the dais and jumped onto it. "Kjelborn, *you're* the chronomancer, aren't you?"

He cocked his head, confused, and nodded.

"Can you selectively freeze time?"

His white eyebrows knit together. "What do you mean?"

"Could you slow time exactly at the Gate, but not in the rest of the room?"

"I could, yes. Why?"

In a terse voice low enough that Raelan couldn't hear, I said, "If you can stop time at the Gate, maybe the rest of the One God won't be able to come through."

He didn't think for long. "It is worth trying."

He called his purple magic to his hands and sent it up into the black vortex above him. It swirled like ink into water, spreading out until I could barely see glimmers of it in the black and green clouds. For a heartstopping moment, nothing happened. Was the Gate too powerful? Was Kjelborn's chronomancy weaker than his pyromancy? Or was it simply too late to stop what had been set in motion?

Then, almost imperceptibly, the spin of the clouds slowed. The violent whorl gradually decelerated to a crawling swirl. I held my breath, willing Kjelborn's magic to work. A minute later, the clouds ground to a halt, completely frozen in time. Had we done it? I was on the verge of cheering when I noticed that below the clouds, the One God's body was continuing to move silently, sliding out from beneath the Gate.

No! I resisted the urge to sink to my knees in defeat. Then I noticed something: The god's body was no longer taut with life. Kjelborn dove to the side, rolling away from the Gate. Like snow melting from a branch in the Spring, the massive, pallid body of the One God plopped down onto the dais. Headless. By freezing time at the Gate but not the rest of the Great Hall below it, Kjelborn had created a guillotine. Even the One God's divinity hadn't been enough to save him from beheading as he moved into the mortal realm.

The god's body lay motionless where it had fallen. It didn't bleed. It took up the majority of the dais, the king's throne crushed to splinters beneath it. Kjelborn released time around the Gate, and it immediately began to dissolve, the black clouds eddying away into nothingness, leaving no evidence that they'd ever been there. The oppressive weight of the breach between the two planes evaporated. The Gate was gone.

"Nooooo!" Raelan screamed, rushing toward the body.

He was stopped mid-stride by a knife, which lodged itself to the hilt right between his eyes. Raelan dropped wordlessly, his body crumpling into a black heap of robes. I swallowed a scream of surprise. Gamiel, the thrower of the knife, crossed her arms, looking pleased with herself. "That's one less villain in this world," she said.

I was dizzy from everything that had happened. Kjelborn dropped his sword—Vardan's sword—and rubbed his face. I sheathed my sword. I was dizzy from everything that had happened. My hands were shaking. Together, we stepped down from the dais and walked back toward the antechamber. Lyse rushed forward and wrapped herself around me. I clutched her to me, hot tears running down my face.

"Is it over?" Cayleth asked. Her voice was small and uncertain, as though she expected the One God to rise at any moment. If he did, I had nothing left to give. I was finished. Exhausted.

"Yes," Kjelborn said. "It is over now."

"What about the Northmen?" I asked, stepping back from Lyse. In all that had happened, I had almost forgotten the rebels' foreign shock troops. Had they been stopped by a ragtag combination of citizens with makeshift weapons, city-guard members, assassins, and soldiers? Or had we defeated the Dark mages only to turn the palace and our kingdom over to our northern enemies?

It was Sir Idras who answered. "Don't you worry about them, lassie. When Asher and I got your message, we brought as many knights as we could gather along the way. They'll be riding through the city now, putting the sword to those brigands. They don't stand a chance. It will be a matter of hours to mop them up."

"What about the other coup plotters? How will we find them?" I imagined Raelan and the chancellor's accomplices melting back into the population of King's City, biding their time until they could try again. I shivered. I hoped no one ever tried to open another Gate to the divine plane again.

"They will be hunted down, however long it takes," Gamiel answered. For once, her face showed emotion. Anger. Hatred. Determination. She must have seen Vardan's dead body in the antechamber. Did she know he'd been one of the coup leaders? "Once they learn the coup has failed, they'll flee the city. Their rebellion is over. The king may be dead, but his Regiment will ensure he is avenged and the new ruler protected."

"Then—What do we do now?" I looked once more at the carnage around me. I couldn't wrap my mind around it. The entire leadership of Ilirya had been slaughtered. Who was left to rule? How could the city possibly rebuild? My eyes were drawn to the headless god. My body began to shake, and I worried I might pass out. Sir Idras's large arm swept up under me and held me upright.

"Lass, I think we'll leave all this for someone else to clean up. You've done quite enough tonight."

Lyse put her hand in mine. The ghost of a smile played across her lips. "Let's go home."

I didn't have the strength left to find out what had happened to my friends once we parted ways in the palace, nor what had become of Trick, Maerys, and Derrin. After returning to Windhall through the chancellor's Gate, I dragged my body to the dorm and fell into a deep sleep the moment my head hit the pillow. I didn't wake up again until late afternoon the following day.

"Let me get this straight," I said when we were all together again. "Sir Idras and Asher, accompanied by Gamiel, happened to run up the same stairs where you and Lyse were stuck?"

I shook my head in amazement. Kaylara, Pavo, Cayleth, Lyse, and I were sitting in the dining hall. Classes had been indefinitely postponed while Windhall tried to piece itself back together again. It would take some time. Many students had fled home at first light, petrified that the Northmen were still in the city. And, of course, Windhall had lost not only its chancellor and one of its professors, but a student as well. It was beyond scandalous.

Cayleth nodded. "As she tells it, Gamiel was in the city when the Northman attack began. She knew she'd better get to the castle, and she happened to run into Sir Idras and Asher on the way. Gamiel knew our staircase was likely to be less defended, so…"

"Destiny," Kaylara murmured.

I ran my hand gently over Lyse's fingers on my thigh. Although she hadn't left my side since the Great Hall, I was still amazed every time I looked at her or touched her. "I'm glad it's over now," I said. I thought of everything that had brought us to this point: the people that Raelan and the chancellor had kidnapped to power their Dark Magic, the burning of the city guard garrison, the Night of the Long Swords. So much had happened I felt as though I'd lived multiple lifetimes. I wasn't the same person I'd been before. I had seen things I couldn't unsee, done things I would never have believed I could.

"Did you hear Father Merek will be the new chancellor, at least until a new one can be identified?" Kaylara said.

Cayleth spat on the ground, indicating her distaste for Chancellor Vandys's memory.

"One thing I still don't understand is how they opened the Gate," Lyse said. "Did they have a secret Gate mage? How did they hide them?"

"They had no Gate mage." Kjelborn's unexpected voice behind me caused me to half jump out of my chair. My heart raced wildly, as though I were in the Great Hall again. He placed a hand on my shoulder to steady me. "One of the Dark mages was a spellcaster. They were able to create a Gate using a spell she wove."

Cayleth gaped. "How is that possible?"

"Gates require an extraordinary amount of power. Through Dark Magic, the four were able to generate the power necessary to rip open a Gate. It has always been hypothesized that such a feat could be achieved, but it had never before been attempted, to my knowledge."

"So it turns out anyone can create a Gate?"

Kjelborn shook his head. "I doubt that anyone will ever be able to replicate the events of last night. Nor should they. It was only possible through Dark Magic. Many people were killed for them to amass the power necessary to open the Gate." He turned to me. "Aeryn, may I have a word?"

I disentangled myself from Lyse and followed him out of the dining hall. Outside, the sun was bright and the temperature crisp. The smell of burned wood was in the air, a lingering reminder of the night before. Kjelborn squinted at the outline of King's City in the distance. "I will be departing in a few hours."

"What? No! You can't! Stay longer!" I had planned to spend the next few days with him, talking about everything that had happened since I'd left Thamir. How could he leave so soon? We'd had no time at all together!

He sighed. "Queen Alea will need help finding the conspirators who snuck out of the city under the cover of darkness. And…there are too many painful memories for me here in King's City."

"But… Will you eventually return to Thamir?"

"Time will tell." He turned his eyes to me, and when they looked into mine, they had an intense light. "Now you must tell me what brought you to me in Thamir. You have reeked of Death's corrosive touch since you appeared on my doorstep."

I dropped my eyes. I had done the one thing he had explicitly told me not to do: I had made a deal with Death. But it had worked: Lyse was safe, as was the rest of Ilirya. Surely he couldn't blame me for that? "Lymon sent me. He said you were the only one who could stop the chancellor and Raelan."

His jaw twitched. An inscrutable expression flickered across his face, and he rubbed at his forehead. In a tight voice, he said, "Only the dead meet Lymon."

My skin felt too small for my body. I shifted uncomfortably, still not meeting his eyes. He grabbed my hand. His eyes hardened for a moment as he felt the cold in it, but then his expression softened. I pulled my hand back and wrapped my arms around myself. Kjelborn put his hands on my shoulders and forced me to look at him. His face was both serious and sad. "Aeryn, living mortals cannot leave the Eternal Realms."

"What?"

"There is only one way to meet Lymon, who cannot cross into the mortal plane. You died, didn't you?"

"Yes." My voice was a whisper. I still hadn't told Lyse. I couldn't bear for her to know. She would worry, and I didn't want her to worry.

"Although Death allowed you to leave the Eternal Realms…" Kjelborn trailed off, allowing me to reach the conclusion he intended.

Living mortals can't leave the Eternal Realms. "I'm…still dead?"

"In a manner of speaking, yes."

The heaviness that settled on my shoulders threatened to suffocate me. I grabbed his arm to steady myself. My breathing came fast and quick. "What does that mean?" Had I been sent back to the land of the living only to immediately be returned to the Eternal Realms once the One God and his allies had been stopped? If so, how much time did I have left?

"I don't know." He put his hand over mine where it clutched his arm. "But take heart: I sense you have much more time in the land of the living. Your destiny is not yet complete."

I didn't know how to respond. Was this good news? What did it mean that my destiny wasn't yet complete? He kissed the top of my head. "I must go now. Take care. Our paths will cross again. The future is clear on this."

A week later, Lyse found me in the small stand of trees outside the university. I was sitting under an elm tree, twirling a piece of grass between my fingers. I hadn't yet gone back to magic or combatives class. I was sick of anything that reminded me of killing. Whenever I closed my eyes, I still saw the carnage in the Great Hall and the awful body of the One God slowly descending. For now, I preferred the silence of the fields outside the campus.

Lyse sat down and curled into my chest comfortably. Winter had set in now in earnest, and I wrapped my arms around her to keep her warm. "What have you been up to?" I asked, knowing the answer.

"Healing again. There's so much work to be done. All the healers from the surrounding baronies have been called in to help." She drew her pale-indigo magic to her hands and gazed at it. She had used it so often in the last week that it was easy for me to forget that her affinity was still new, even if the broken bond between us still left a void in my life to remind me of the magical connection we'd once shared. She continued, "Lord Marshal Damren thinks they've finally rounded up all the conspirators. The trials should begin soon."

I nodded. Did that mean Kjelborn would return to Thamir soon? If so, would he stop by Windhall to say good-bye first? I could send another message to my family through him. I still hadn't received a response to my first letter, although I hadn't expected one yet. When we'd met the queen to be thanked for our role in stopping the Dark mages and protecting Ilirya, I had thought about asking if she would send a message for me, but I had been too shy. She was a queen, after all, and I was a mere commoner.

"They caught the member of the King's Regiment who'd been smuggling Northmen into the city," Lyse said.

"Oh?"

"His name was Panwel."

I closed my eyes. There was a name I knew. He was the first mage I'd ever met. The illusionist who had come to Thamir long before my magic had ever manifested. So that was why he'd been sneaking across the border so many years ago. It hurt my heart to know he had been yet another traitor.

"Aeryn, about Jale..."

I stiffened.

"He's dead."

"What?"

"He was found in his cell with a knife in his chest. None of the handful of other men and women in the cell with him would say what happened.

I was called to help, but it was too late. I…saw the knife. The handle bore the mark of the King's Regiment."

"Gamiel." Of course it would be her. I bowed my head. Would the killing ever stop?

"Officially, the murderer is a mystery. But Gamiel has been made Sergeant at Arms of the King's Regiment while a new captain is selected. She would have full access to the palace dungeon."

Our conversation lapsed, and we sat in silence for several minutes. Then Lyse turned, kissed my cheek, and leaned her head once more against my neck. "The queen claims she's going to tear down the old castle and build a new one."

"That's understandable. It would be hard to sit on a throne in a place where so many people died."

Queen Alea had inherited a capital city in chaos and a country on its fortieth year of war with its southern neighbor and in the midst of renewed hostilities with its northern neighbor. At least she seemed reasonable, as far as I could tell from our brief interaction. From what I'd been told, her brother King Hap had been extremely mercurial, tending to ignore the advice of his advisors. Vardan had told Kjelborn that he'd participated in the coup as a way to stop the war. Maybe Queen Alea would finally end it.

Lyse twined her fingers in mine, snuggling close. "I still can't believe I can touch you. I thought I lost you. I don't know what I would have done without you."

I grimaced, but I quickly kissed the top of her head, looking at Windhall's buildings in the distance. I still hadn't told her the truth about that night. Although I knew I would have to some day, for now she didn't have to know that she *had* lost me. There was a coldness in my body that now I knew even the hottest fire would never chase away. Let her believe at least for a little while that we had emerged from the trauma of that night unscathed and that the future was ours because it was almost true. She deserved happiness, and I would do everything I could to contribute to her happiness.

In the Ice Crown, we have a saying that the dead are lonely. But I had Lyse, my family, and my friends to keep me company. Whatever my future, I would always be surrounded by people who loved me.

And now I had Lymon, too, who had visited me hours before to tell me the price of my return to the land of the living. And now for the first time, I understood why he had warned me about choosing rashly and what I had agreed to do.

To be continued in book three.

ABOUT KAREN

Karen Frost is an armchair pop culture pundit and blogger whose articles have been spread internationally by actresses, production companies, directors, and news outlets. She loves YA high fantasy and wants to introduce more lady knights and mages in the literary world. Karen is particularly interested in writing LGBT characters. She lives just outside of Washington, D.C, but has an active imaginary life in which she lives in a cabana on a beach instead.

CONNECT WITH KAREN

Website: www.karenfrostbooks.com

OTHER BOOKS FROM YLVA PUBLISHING

www.ylva-publishing.com

DAUGHTER OF FIRE

Conspiracy of the Dark
(*Destiny and Darkness series – Book 1*)
Karen Frost

ISBN: 978-3-96324-267-0
Length: 195 pages (76,000 words)

I am the daughter of winter. My people are strong and unbending as ice. I was born with the frozen winds sweeping through my hair, with snow dusted across my skin. I am. I am. I am...

For Aeryn, a girl born to the remote, wintry Ice Crown region of Ilirya, the outside world is a fantasy: a series of wonderful stories told by occasional passing travellers. She never imagines anything for her life beyond following in her parents' footsteps.

But the discovery that she has the rare gift of magic shatters her isolated world. Aeryn can create and tame fire. It's an intoxicating, raw, and thrilling power, but it also sets her apart. And her gift attracts attention.

She is whisked from her home in the wilds to train at Windhall University and master her magic. There, Aeryn slowly learns the truth about the real world, with its strange mix of people and powers, and so many intertwining threads of shadows and light. She's drawn to unattainable Lyse, a beautiful healer in training who makes Aeryn's heart soar. But she also senses a creeping darkness all around that could threaten the future of the kingdom itself.

A compelling, original, evocative fantasy novel for young and old. Part one of the Destiny and Darkness series.

Daughter of Fire: The Darkness Rising
© 2019 by Karen Frost

ISBN: 978-3-96324-300-4

Also available as e-book.

Published by Ylva Publishing, legal entity of Ylva Verlag, e.Kfr.

Ylva Verlag, e.Kfr.
Owner: Astrid Ohletz
Am Kirschgarten 2
65830 Kriftel
Germany

www.ylva-publishing.com

First edition: 2019

Credits
Edited by Zee Ahmad and Amber Williams
Cover Design and Print Layout by Streetlight Graphics